P9-ELR-544

Murder in a Basket

AN INDIA HAYES MYSTERY

Murder in a Basket

Amanda Flower

FIVE STAR
A part of Gale, Cengage Learning

Detroit • New York • San Francisco • New Haven, Conn • Waterville, Maine • London

Set in 11 pt. Plantin.

LIBRARY OF CONGRESS CATALOGING-IN-PUBLICATION DATA

Flower, Amanda.
Murder in a basket : an India Hayes mystery / Amanda Flower.
— 1st ed.
p. cm.
ISBN-13: 978-1-4328-2567-6 (hardcover)
ISBN-10: 1-4328-2567-4 (hardcover)
1. Women librarians—Fiction. I. Title.
PS3606.L683M87 2012
813′.6—dc23 2011034924

First Edition. First Printing: January 2012.
Published in 2012 in conjunction with Tekno Books and Ed Gorman.

Printed in the United States of America
1 2 3 4 5 6 7 16 15 14 13 12

For the congregation of
Goodyear Heights Presbyterian Church
and
in loving memory of
my father, Thomas Flower

ACKNOWLEDGMENTS

Laughter to all the readers who embraced my first novel, *Maid of Murder*. I hope you find this mystery just as amusing.

Thank you to all the librarians who selected *Maid of Murder* for their collections. Knowing my mysteries reach readers through libraries means more to me than you will ever know.

Special thanks to Rosalind Greenberg of Tekno Books and Tiffany Schofield of Five Star for their continued support of India and me and to my editor Alice Duncan for her assistance on this manuscript.

Thanks to my first reader Mariellyn Dunlap for her keen eye and to my critique partner Melody Steiner for her insightful comments that made this a better book.

Gratitude to Sara Smith, web mistress and friend.

Hugs to PGF and RTF who are constant sources of inspiration.

Blessings to the members of Goodyear Heights Presbyterian Church for their love and support.

Love to my mother, Rev. Pamela Flower. God couldn't have given me a better mom or friend.

Finally, to my Heavenly Father, thank you.

Chapter One

Late autumn is the best time to be on a college campus. By October, the freshmen—for the most part—know which end is up and don't have the deer-in-the-headlights look that haunts them throughout September. The students still appear happy to be back in school, the clean smell of new textbooks still lingers in the air, and the promise of extended Thanksgiving and Christmas holidays is on the horizon.

However, that October I wasn't feeling quite as optimistic about being on a college campus as I adjusted my mobcap on the top of my head. I stood in front of the small wall mirror in the tiny third floor office I shared with Bobby McNally, my fellow Martin College reference librarian and best friend. Sometimes I wondered how he'd earned either title.

The door opened and Bobby stepped inside. He appraised me with a smirk on his handsome face. His irritatingly blue eyes slid down my body from the white mobcap on my head, across the pink gingham dress and apron, to the black granny boots on my feet. His grin was so large I feared he might dislocate his jaw.

"Don't say a word," I muttered through gritted teeth. I snapped a fanny pack, which I would use as a money belt, around my waist with an angry click.

"Your groupie is downstairs looking for you." Bobby walked over to his desk and turned on his laptop. Our nineteen-seventy issue metal desks stood face to face, creating one monster cube of beige metal and gray plastic laminate. I noticed his files were encroaching on my side . . . again.

"Didn't you tell him I was running a booth at the Founders' Festival? I'm already late, and Carmen is going to have my head." In a momentary lapse in judgment, I'd agreed to run the face-painting booth in the Stripling Founders' Festival, which celebrates the settling of our fair town. This year, for the first time, the festival would be held on the Martin College campus. It was quite a coup to have the festival on college grounds. My sister, Carmen, was the chair of the Founders' Festival Committee because Carmen viewed volunteering as a duty and a full-contact sport. Compared to my parents, however, who have volunteered and marched for every movement that would make flower children proud, Carmen was a minor leaguer. I, on the other hand, tried to avoid volunteering as much as possible.

"I thought you would want to tell him yourself," Bobby said.

I rolled my eyes as I opened the office door. I looked left and right. The hallway was deserted.

"Afraid of something?" Bobby's voice was in my ear, causing me to jump.

"No," I said a little too quickly.

"He's at the reference desk. You can go down the service elevator, and he'll never see you."

I gnawed on my lip. "Is that safe?" The service elevator was a glorified dumbwaiter and at least seventy years old, the same age as the library. It was tiny in comparison to the one the library installed in the 1980s to come up to code. We used it to send carts of books between the building's floors. It was just big enough for one book cart or one librarian.

"You can't weigh much more than a cart of law books. You'll be fine."

I wasn't sure how to take that. Law books were mighty heavy.

Bobby marched me down the hallway to the elevator. He

pressed the button and the tired machine creaked up from the basement. When the elevator at last reached the third floor, Bobby opened the wooden trifold door. The space was cramped. I would have to crouch during the ride.

My courage waned. "Didn't we forbid the students from doing this because it wasn't safe?"

"You are not a student. Martin doesn't see you as being that valuable."

"Gee, thanks."

He gave me a little shove. "Get in." He looked me in the eye. "Or you can go down the stairs and come face to face with your buddy."

I hopped into the elevator.

Bobby shut the door. "See you on the other side."

I wondered what other side he meant exactly. I hoped he wasn't referring to the afterlife.

The inside of the service elevator was dimly lit. The ceiling was only five feet high, so I had to stoop my five-nine frame to fit. The elevator smelled faintly of book mold and dust. Both smells I was accustomed to in my profession. At each floor, the ropes and pulleys jerked slightly as if they planned to stop, and I banged my mobcap on the ceiling with each pause in the descent. Through the slats in the door, I could see the passage of floors. At last, the elevator jerked to a complete stop. On the other side of the door was the library's workroom, the private domain of our cataloger, Jefferson Island.

Jefferson blinked when I popped out of the service elevator. I waved before escaping out of the staff-only exit.

Outside it was one of those rare blue-sky days, the kind that almost make me forget I live in northeastern Ohio, where there are only two seasons: winter and construction. A handful of puffy cumulus clouds bobbed in the periwinkle sky. It made me want to lie down on the grass and pick shapes out of the clouds like I did as a child. I allowed myself a quick peek and spotted a lion. The air was crisp; an icy reminder that Old Man Winter wasn't too far behind those lion-shaped clouds. I pulled my shawl more closely around my shoulders and put my head down.

I received strange looks from students as I scurried across campus, so I pulled my mobcap further down, hoping to hide my face. I scolded myself for stopping at the library before going to the practice football field where the festival would be held. As a consequence, I had to parade my pioneer self in front of the underclassmen, who probably thought this was how librarians dressed every day. Thank you very much, Hollywood, for that stereotype. I'd gone to the library because I'd felt obligated to stop by to check my work email—all junk and complaints, by the way—as the college was graciously giving me free release time to take part in the festival.

The practice field was on the opposite side of campus just beyond fraternity row. On the walkway, I had no cause to fear catcalls. No self-respecting frat boy would be up at that hour.

The field was a glorified patch of grass. Martin's sports program could not afford a real practice field and certainly not a stadium for home games. Although Martin was heavily endowed for a college of its size, roughly three thousand students, the board of trustees viewed the sports program as overindulged intramurals. They were probably annoyed cricket wasn't on the roster and withheld funds in protest. Much to the head football coach's humiliation, the college rented the Stripling High School stadium for home games.

I spotted Head Coach Lions in a heated conversation with a woman as I crested the slight rise surrounding the practice field. He was a medium-height muscular man with just a hint of softening around his middle. The woman was none other than my sister Carmen. Carmen gripped the double-stroller handlebar in front of her with a vengeance. My infant nieces, tethered inside the stroller, cooed to each other, seemingly unperturbed by their mother's angry tone.

Carmen and Coach Lions weren't the only ones on the outskirts of the field. The Stop Otter Exploitation Commission, or SOEC, stood about ten yards away. They were a group of animal rights activist students who felt the college's mascot objectified otters and exploited them for sport. Yes, the school mascot is an otter. Terrifying, I know. They found the cartoon mascot of Otis the Otter, who frolicked with the cheerleaders during games, especially disturbing and demanded the college choose a non-animal to represent its athletic teams. Lately, the group had fixated on Coach Lions as their avenue of otter equality. They followed him everywhere, sometimes taunting him or his players, but in most cases they stood near him in silent accusation. The group of six students watched the coach's exchange with my sister with smug looks on their scruffy faces. They appeared pleased someone else was on the coach's case.

Behind the coach and Carmen, food vendors put the final touches on their concession trailers and carts. My stomach growled as I read signs for caramel apples, apple cider, and strawberry shortcake. Beyond the food were the crafters and artisan booths.

Within twenty feet, I could hear Carmen clearly. "You will have this field back when I say so."

The coach crossed his arms across his broad chest, resting their weight on his belly as if it were a shelf. His forearms resembled Easter hams, and he looked down his short nose at Carmen even though he was at best an inch taller than her. Carmen was my height and looked enough like me with her dark brown hair, strong profile, and gray eyes to be mistaken as my twin, although she is five years my senior.

The coach was bald. The brown skin on his head looked as if it were polished to a high sheen on a daily basis. He wore his sunglasses on the back of his head, giving the illusion he had eyes back there as well. He wore them that way no matter what the setting: practice, games, or graduations. I'd never seen the sunglasses on his eyes even when he was in direct sunlight.

His voice was gravelly from years of yelling from the sidelines. "No one told us you all would be here last night. I had to cancel practice when the guys needed it."

They would need a lot more than that, I thought, if they planned to win a game.

"I'm sorry there was a misunderstanding. I was very clear in my request to the college that I needed the field for five days."

This certainly was not a discussion I wanted to join. I started to slink away in the direction of my booth, which I had constructed the evening before, but I was too slow.

"India!" Carmen's harried, mother-hen voice assaulted my ears.

Against my better judgment, I turned.

She crooked a finger at me. I shook my head left and right. Her eyes narrowed, and I walked over.

Chapter Two

"What's up, ladies?" I asked my nieces as I wiggled their tiny feet. They gurgled at me and flashed their beautiful gummy smiles.

"India, tell this colleague of yours I had permission from Martin to use the practice football field last night."

Coach eyed me. I couldn't decide if the perplexed look on his face was due to my outfit or because he couldn't figure out who I was. Probably both. We didn't exactly roll in the same collegiate circles.

"Well?" Carmen prompted when I didn't say anything.

"I'm sure you have the situation well in hand," I said.

Carmen's gray eyes, which at present were the color of gun-metal, narrowed. "Of course, I do." She glared at Coach once again. "This conversation is over. I suggest you talk to the provost before you approach me again."

He looked like he had a bad taste in his mouth. "Trust me, I will." He stomped away.

Carmen made a checkmark on her clipboard. "You're late."

I'd hoped she was so annoyed by the coach that she'd forget the time. Sadly, Carmen forgets nothing.

"The festival doesn't open for another hour."

"The reason I asked all the crafters and vendors to be here two hours before opening is so all the preparations will be complete before the first guest arrives. It's unprofessional to look like you're scrambling at the last minute."

As if setting up picture samples and face paint bottles would take two hours, I thought. But I knew better than to argue.

I started toward the crafter area and made it all of two steps before my sister stopped me again.

"Don't drag your skirt through the grass," Carmen said. "It's an antique."

I looked down at the pink gingham skirt and repressed a shudder. "Why in the world would you give me an antique to wear?"

"I wanted this festival to be authentic."

I rolled my eyes. Right. Just like the acrylic-based paints I would be applying to the children's faces were available in the 1800s, not to mention the synthetic brushes.

My eyes widened as a disturbing thought occurred to me. "Where's your pioneer garb?"

Carmen looked down at her polo shirt embroidered with STRIPLING FOUNDERS' FESTIVAL over the left side of her chest. She wore a turtleneck underneath it, her dark bobbed hair tucked behind her ears. I looked at the people around me and the vast majority of them were wearing shirts like Carmen's. There was a smattering of pioneer dresses and men in period breeches, but it was most definitely the exception. "Where is their pioneer garb?"

Carmen sniffed. "I gave each vendor the option to wear period dress."

I crossed my arms over my ruffled apron. "There was an option?" Oh, the humiliation.

"It was hard enough to convince these people to sell their merchandise at the festival. I couldn't very well tell them to wear a mobcap, now could I?"

"That's what you told me."

"You're different."

Oh, right, I thought, I was the baby sister. There was no

question I could be ordered around.

Carmen gripped the handles of the stroller and did a quick about-face. "Oh, the Indian taco guy is here. I need to talk to him." She thrust the stroller onward. I hoped the girls didn't have whiplash.

You'd better run, I mentally told the Indian taco guy.

I moved on to my booth, hoping the festival wouldn't flop as it had in past years. If it did, my baby pink gingham humiliation would be in vain. Stripling held the festival every year in honor of Jem Stripling and his wife, Adel, who, like many middle class folks from Connecticut in the early nineteenth century, left their comfortable homes to settle Connecticut's Western Reserve, which now comprised the land from the Ohio-Pennsylvania border to the rollercoaster-happy Sandusky and as far south as football-crazy Canton. Stripling is on the far eastern side of the Western Reserve, just north of the city of Akron in Summit County. The festival had been in a downward spiral over the last five years. The committee had trouble booking quality artisans and food vendors, and attendance was discouragingly low. The *Stripling Dispatch* even declared the festival dead, and it was, for all intents and purposes, until last spring when my sister got involved.

At the time, Carmen, was pregnant with the twins and, therefore, unstoppable. She announced she would be taking over the festival committee. Carmen, a high school biology teacher, decided at the end of last school year to take a break from teaching to be a stay-at-home mom. This didn't mean she would actually stay at home. The day after her decision, she was already offering the time and energy she'd reserved for teaching to the festival committee. The group knew better than to say no to a Hayes on a mission.

The committee might not have been pleased with Carmen's heavy-handed micromanager approach, but both they and I had to admit she produced results. The caliber of the vendors this year was something Stripling hadn't seen in my lifetime. For food options there was roasted corn on the cob, barbequed ribs, apple dumplings, fried cheesecake, Italian sausage, beer-battered fried veggies, and just about everything else that gives cardiologists the cold sweats. The aroma enticed me as the sweet smell of barbeque mingled with the scent of freshly made bagels. Even the Italian sausage smelled good to me, and I'm a strict vegetarian. Just because I won't eat it doesn't mean I don't like a whiff of meat now and again. Please don't tell my mother.

My stomach growled, but I knew better than to stop. If I didn't finish setting up my booth in record time, Carmen would be after me. I didn't want to be her main target for the day. Beyond the food vendors, I came upon the crafters' booths. These too were at a higher level than Stripling had seen before. There were beaders, broom makers, papermakers, weavers, milliners, quilters, and even a blacksmith. It was apparent all the artisans were old hands at the arts and crafts fair scene. Their booths were professional, custom-made, and situated to display their wares to the best advantage. Even though I was doing this festival as a favor to my sister, I couldn't help wallowing in a little bit of booth envy.

I assessed my booth as I approached. What a joke. It consisted of two cafeteria-length tables with green table cloths from my mother's church and four eight-foot rods of PVC pipe holding up a bright blue tarp, which only some island-bound reality TV contestant would consider a tent. The booth could certainly use a spruce up, but that, just like the fried cheesecake, would have to wait.

I pulled the face-painting supplies and other items out from under one of the tables. In addition to the face paints, I arranged a selection of my paintings in an attractive cluster. The cost of each piece was discretely marked on the back with what

I considered a reasonable price. Being an artist is a constant battle to sell yourself, and I wasn't going to let this opportunity pass me by.

"What do you think you're doing?" an irritated voice demanded, causing me to knock over my painting of the town square. Lately, I'd found townsfolk were more interested in buying simple landscapes than portraits of their family members, with the exception of beloved pets. There's a commentary of American life in there somewhere, if I had the patience to worm it out.

"Excuse me?" I asked.

A pear-shaped woman with a tight bun knotted at the nape of her neck glared at me over her reading glasses. She wore pioneer clothing: a white high-collared blouse, a straw bonnet, and a drab prairie skirt, which brushed the grass.

"What do you think you're doing?" Her tone told me she wouldn't approve of my answer, whatever it might be, but I gave it a shot anyway.

"I'm setting up my booth," I said in the most pleasant voice I could muster. I reset the painting on its wooden stand.

The woman put her hands on her ample hips, which made her look the Hollywood version of a stern schoolhouse marm. "What is this jumble?"

Jumble? I mentally snorted.

She gestured at my painting of the town square. "This is the face-painting booth for the children. What are these paintings doing here?"

My jaw clenched. I was no longer finding her irritation amusing.

A voice came from behind me. "Goodness sake. Drink some tea, Lynette. I can sense your chi is constrained by stress."

I spun around. The newcomer was also middle aged, round all over, and had long dishwater blond hair that hung loosely down her back. She wore purple-rimmed glasses perched on the tip of her nose, and jeans and a festival polo under a blue windbreaker. And her hands were red. Bright red. Crimson red. Vermillion red. Fake blood red.

I glanced down at my own hands; the nails were a strange olive green. Strange-colored hands were a painter's occupational hazard. Whoever this second woman was, I bet she was an artist of some sort, or a butcher. I hoped for the former. The second occupation could be a real problem if she ran into my animal activist parents.

She held a hand-thrown mug of soupy-looking tea in those red hands and offered it to Lynette.

"This is none of your concern, Tess." Lynette glared at the mug.

Tess's eyes widened. "Trust me. This tea will change your life. I picked the mint fresh this morning."

Lynette recoiled, acting as if lighter fluid would be a more appealing beverage. "No, thank you." She turned to me. "I'm a member of the Founders' Festival Committee, and I know this booth"—she gestured wildly at my setup—"is intended to benefit the children. It looks like you are selling your artistic jumble instead."

This conversation was going downhill fast. I really wished she'd stop referring to my life's work as "jumble." Art was subjective, but no creative person really wants a direct attack on the ego.

"These paintings aren't jumble. Look at this painting of the library. It's so real, it's like I'm standing right in front of it," Tess said.

I had no time to revel in Tess's praise as Lynette snorted. "Do you have a permit to sell here?"

I riffled through my fanny pack, pulled out my permit, and handed it to Lynette. She sniffed and made a big show of reading it over. Perhaps she thought I forged it. She wrinkled her nose. "India *Hayes?*"

I sighed, although I should be accustomed to this reaction to my name by now.

"Are you related to Lana and Alden Hayes?" she asked with a slight tremor in her voice.

No use denying it. "They're my parents," I said.

She thrust the paper back at me as if she was too disgusted to hold it. I took it, folded it, and slipped it back into my fanny pack. She sniffed and patted her fraying bun. "Well, then, I can see how you got a permit so easily. Seeing how your sister's running the event. Some of us had to fight for our slots even as decade-old members of the committee."

Tess sipped her rejected tea. "I'm sure India earned her place here. Her paintings really are lovely. True pieces of art."

I smiled my thanks and tried not to preen under her praise. It was a challenge, and I can't say I was completely successful.

Lynette prickled. "I'll have you know my tea cozies are pieces of art, too. They've sold very well on the Internet. There's nothing worse than a cold cup of tea."

"I didn't mean to imply you weren't an equally talented artist." Tess tested the temperature of her own brew with her finger. "Warm tea is very important. Perhaps we can make some type of agreement. I think my tea would sell well next to your cozies."

Lynette scowled at me. "Don't think you've heard the last from me about this blatant favoritism." She spun on her heels, skirt swaying with annoyance.

Chapter Three

Tess shook her head as she watched Lynette stomp back to her tea cozy booth just a few yards away. She held out her hand. "Hi, neighbor, I'm Tess."

I shook her hand, liking her immediately.

She crooked a thumb to the booth directly to my left. "That one is mine."

My eyes followed her gesture. Baskets everywhere. Dozens of them. Big baskets. Little baskets. Short baskets. Tall baskets.

Tess caught me staring at her red hands.

"I was dying maple slats this morning to be woven into baskets. I do all the dying myself and only use natural dyes." She held up her hands. "This vibrant red color comes from crushed cochineal beetles. I import the beetles from the southwest, mostly from Arizona and New Mexico. They live on cacti and other hot weather plants that could never survive here."

Ick. Tess's hands were covered in beetle guts. I discreetly wiped my shaking hand on my skirt.

"I make my baskets in the Shaker tradition." She rose and held up a heavy block of wood I recognized from art school as a basket mold. She screwed the mold onto a stand. I realized I was about to get a lesson in basket weaving. Not that I wasn't interested. I'm always on the lookout for another art form to dabble in. However, I drew the line at crushing my own beetles. My parents would kill me.

Tess patted the mold. "This is a messenger basket mold and makes this basket. You weave each basket upside down." She held up a medium sized basket with wooden handles. She touched a large mold on her table with four pointy corners on what would be the completed basket's bottom. "This is a cat's head mold. One of the most difficult to use because of the curved bottom. See the pointy corners. They resemble cat ears. It's one of my favorites." She patted the mold lovingly. "On the other side of me is my husband Jerry's booth. He's a blacksmith. Very well known in his field."

My booth inferiority complex reared its ugly head. Both the basket weaver and the blacksmith booths were custom-made. Tess's was a polished oak cart that look like it had jumped out of the pages of a German fairytale, and Jerry's was a twisted iron monstrosity, shaded by a large forest green awning. I looked up at my sad blue tarp, which was listing heavily to the left.

She waved her husband over. He was a tall loose-jointed man with long silver hair pulled back into a ponytail with a thin piece of leather. A large chocolate brown dog whose curly coat looked like it had recently received electroshock treatment followed him.

Tess squatted in front of the dog and gave him a big bear hug. The animal gave her sloppy doggie kisses up and down both sides of her face. Tess giggled.

"Hey, no loving for me?" Jerry said, his handlebar mustache tickling his nose.

She stood up and planted a kiss on him. "And this is Zacchaeus. We just call him Zach for short."

I immediately thought of the old Sunday school song about the small man named Zacchaeus who climbed up the sycamore tree for a better view of Jesus. I wondered if the dog's name was a pun. He certainly was not a wee little dog. I suspected he was at least one-quarter bear, but he was friendly enough. I offered my hand to sniff and patted his head. It felt like cured wool. "What kind of dog is he?"

"A labradoodle. He's a sweetie. He didn't get any of the poodle smarts, but he sure got the lab's temperament." She rubbed his cheeks. "Didn't you, boy?"

Zach's expression was pure adoration.

"I'm surprised the committee allows pets."

Tess blushed. "We didn't exactly get permission to bring Zach."

"My motto is never ask permission, just forgiveness," Jerry said.

"We couldn't leave him at home," Tess said, a little breathless. "There are some special circumstances."

Jerry squeezed her arm.

I wondered what that meant but quickly decided I didn't want to know. "You're secret's safe with me. But you'll have to excuse me if I make myself scarce when Carmen comes by."

Tess's grin was wide. "Understood."

Lynette glared at us from the safety of her tea cozy booth. My guess was it wouldn't be long before the entire festival knew about Zach's presence and my relation to Carmen.

Later that afternoon, I returned to my booth with a warm vegetarian Indian taco in one hand and a fresh-squeezed lemonade in the other. Who knew face painting was such hard work? I wondered. I'd had barely a moment to myself since the festival began. It seemed like every child, college student, and grandmother clambered for war paint.

I inhaled the intoxicating scents of my lunch. Despite the risk of cardiac arrest or diabetic coma, I love fair food of any kind. I was already contemplating my dessert options. Should I go for the strawberry shortcake or a fistful of the hand-dipped buckeyes? I mused. Buckeyes are a local Ohio delicacy. They are candies shaped like the buckeye nuts that fall from Ohio's state tree. If you ate a real buckeye, you'd break a tooth or die from the nut's toxic poison, but the candy ones are pure heaven. I decided to choose the buckeyes. In my horrendous outfit, I thought strawberry shortcake might be a little over-the-top.

As I approached my booth, a man in an expensive dark suit stood with his back to me, his feet squarely planted in front of Tess's booth. Tess appeared unperturbed by his presence as she wove a berry basket and nodded in response to whatever the man said. I was a little taken aback by the man's outfit. The festival was definitely a jeans and sweats affair. Well, at least for the visitors, I thought forlornly as I looked down at my pink gingham nightmare.

I noted the ribs of the basket were red. Another batch of cochineal beetles bit the dust. The closer I got to the booth, the further my stomach began to fall. I knew that suited back and its owner. It belonged to my boss, Samuel L. Lepcheck, provost of Martin College.

Should I run the other way? Should I ditch my lunch? I wondered. I looked down at the delicious Indian taco, fried bread leaden with veggies, melted cheese, and black beans. No way was I choosing option number two.

Lepcheck was of medium height, a sturdily built man who sported a trim Vandyke beard and rimless eyeglasses. He ran his hand through his lush silver hair. "I don't think you understand the position you've put me in."

Tess glanced up from her berry basket, spinning it on its tripod. "I didn't put you into any position, Sammy."

Sammy? I wondered. Bobby was going to love that.

"I've talked to my lawyers. They said we can contest Uncle Victor's will if you're willing . . ."

Tess looked up sharply. "Well, I'm not."

"Be reasonable. The college was promised—"

"There you are, India," Tess said.

I stood five feet from Lepcheck at that point, holding my lunch as if it were some type of high-caloric shield. I dropped my lemonade. The plastic lid popped off of the paper cup and lemonade splattered the hem of my skirt. So much for the spotless antique.

Tess left her booth and rushed over. "Let me help you with that." She bent over and picked up the half-empty paper cup.

Lepcheck spun around and gaped at me. I wasn't sure if he was more shocked by my presence or my appearance. Probably both.

"Have you met India, Sam?" Tess asked.

"We've met." I glanced down at my damp skirt. Carmen wouldn't be happy, I thought glumly.

"She's on my faculty," Lepcheck stammered.

"Oh?" Tess said with surprise. "Really? Small world, huh? India, Sammy's my older brother." She gave me a quizzical look.

"Your brother?"

"Sam just stopped by to talk about Uncle Victor's . . ."

"Tess," Lepcheck snapped. "Our conversation is none of Ms. Hayes's concern."

Tess frowned but, much to my relief, said nothing more. Truly, I didn't want to know what they were arguing about. The less contact I had with Lepcheck the better.

"Sorry to interrupt," I said and smiled at Tess. "And thanks for helping clean that up. I'm such a klutz."

"I have a cooler of pop under my table. You can grab a can if you like."

"Thanks." I scurried over to my booth, stashing my taco under the table. No way would I be able to eat in front of Lepcheck.

I pulled a paperback novel out of my backpack and pretended to read. As I was trying to become as small as possible, Jerry with Zach in tow approached the siblings. Zach wasn't leashed and ran ahead of Jerry. The dog stuck his nose into Lepcheck's backside.

The provost said something that would shock the faculty, and then, "Control that animal."

Jerry grabbed Zach's collar and glared at Lepcheck.

Lepcheck glowered at the dog with distaste. "That thing is the center of this entire mess."

Tess scowled. "His name is Zach, and I'd much rather spend my time with him than with you. Your aura is a mess, Sam. You should consider getting it realigned. There are some masters I can suggest. They'd be happy to help."

Lepcheck looked like he'd rather swim through a sea of lava. "We'll finish our conversation later."

Lepcheck spun on his designer loafers to leave. As he turned, he stumbled into a little girl, knocking her down in the process. The girl wailed. Lepcheck stammered an apology and fled. The young mother helped the little girl up, but the crying didn't stop. I got up and squatted down in front of her. "Sorry that man bumped you. I'm sure he's sorry, too," I said, knowing nothing of the kind.

She sniffled.

"Do you want your face painted?" I looked up at the mother, who nodded her thanks. "It's my treat. Whatever you want."

The sniffles stopped.

"How about a teddy bear or a butterfly?" I suggested.

The little girl looked at me, her face scrunched up with concentration. "I want a skull. A big one and make it black."

"One black skull coming up."

I caught Tess's eye, and she smiled her thanks. She and Jerry walked a few feet away. When I looked for them five minutes later, as the little girl with the black skull was leaving, they still stood off to the side, deep in conversation. Zach lay under Tess's booth, asleep with his head on his paws.

Chapter Four

Finally, it was six o'clock and time for the festival to close for the day. My left wrist felt cramped from all the tiny face-painting strokes it had made. Before the clock tower finished marking the hour, I was packed up and ready to head home. I unsnapped my fanny pack and tossed it into the blue rolling crate under my table.

Tess noted my frenzied activity. "In a rush to get home?" She scratched Zach behind ears. The dog closed his eyes in ecstasy.

"Is it that obvious?" I folded one of the plastic cloths and slapped it on top of the crate. As I straightened, I realized she wasn't alone.

She had her arm around a pudgy Asian undergrad with spiky black hair. He wore baggy jeans and a Martin Otters sweatshirt.

"I'm glad you haven't left yet," Tess said. "I would like you to meet my son, Derek."

Oh, I knew Derek. He was a freshman library worker who had latched on to me the first day of the semester. He was the student I'd been trying to avoid and had used the library service elevator to escape.

Derek's face was beet red, which was quite a feat considering his complexion.

"Your son?" I asked.

Tess smiled. "He's adopted."

Now it was my turn to blush with embarrassment. "Oh, I didn't mean that—it's just I already know him. He works at

Ryan Library. I'm one of the librarians here on campus."

"I thought Sammy said you were faculty."

"The librarians are faculty." I paused. "Technically, anyway."

Tess's face brightened. "You're *the* India."

I didn't like the sound of that. "The India?"

"Derek tells me you are his special friend."

Derek looked at the ground with a pleading expression, as if asking the earth to open up and swallow him. He was going to wish it had after I was finished with him.

"Really," I said in a deadly tone that Tess, probably because her excellent chi alignment, missed. "Tess, do you care if I talk to your son a minute? Library business. It's nothing major."

"Sure, go ahead. I'll start helping Jerry pack up his booth."

I crooked a finger at Derek. "Let's go."

We walked to the end of the concession row behind the apple dumpling booth. The vendor had already left and locked up for the day, but the scent of baked dough and cinnamon still hung heavy in the air.

Derek took in my appearance. "I like your outfit. It suits you."

"Okay, that comment illustrates our problem."

"Problem? What problem?"

"I work for the college, and you're a student."

"So?"

I cut to the chase because he certainly wasn't following the bread crumbs I dropped in front of him. "Are you out of your mind? Are you telling people I'm your special friend?"

His voice was small. "But you are my friend, aren't you?"

"Do you have any idea how much trouble I could get in if there is a rumor I'm having an unprofessional or inappropriate relationship with a student? Even though I'm completely innocent, I could lose my job. It could ruin my entire career."

Derek looked as if he might cry. "I just told my mom. She

was worried I wasn't making any friends, so I told her you were a special friend."

Some of my anger dissipated. I sighed. "I'm glad you've only said it to your mom, but don't say it again to anyone. Ever. I don't think you realize how it can be interpreted."

Derek face was back to beet red. "I didn't mean anything like *that.*"

"It doesn't matter what you meant." I straightened my spine. This was a discussion I had needed to have with Derek for several weeks. "Also, the little gifts you leave for me at the reference desk have to stop."

"What gifts?"

"The anonymous notes about having a nice day, the flowers plucked from the flowerbeds outside the library, and the candy."

His eyes widened a little. "How did you know they were from me?"

"People saw you placing those items on the desk and told me."

He turned bright purple-red. I instantly felt badly for scolding him, but it simply had to be done.

"I'm sorry. It won't happen again," Derek murmured.

"Good. Let's go back." I had taken a step in the direction of the crafter booths when I realized something. I froze. "Tess is your mom."

Derek pulled on one of his hair spikes. "I'm adopted."

"I know that. But if Tess is your mom, that makes Provost Lepcheck your uncle."

Derek made a face. "I didn't tell him you were my friend."

Thank goodness for small favors, I thought. I would have to watch what I said about Lepcheck with Derek around.

I smiled at him, hoping to put him at ease.

When we returned to the crafter area, Tess stood behind her booth pouring a green liquid from a battery-operated teapot into her hand-thrown mug. Derek saw Jerry, struggling with a rolling cart full of his wares, and hurried over.

"Everything okay in the library?" Tess asked.

"Huh?" I looked under my table to make sure I had everything. I knew the Martin students well; anything left behind was free game and would undoubtedly end up in the college's fountain.

"The library. You said you needed to talk to Derek about something to do with the library."

"Oh, right. Yes, everything's fine."

She smiled serenely. "Thanks for being so nice to my son. He doesn't have the easiest time making friends. He's terribly shy. When he was a little boy one of his teachers told me he had stranger anxiety." She frowned and just as quickly her face cleared. "He likes you though. He might even have a crush on you."

Terrific.

Looking for some way to change the subject, I noted Tess hadn't started packing up her booth. "You're not eager to get home?"

Tess looked out over the green lawn. "I'll start packing when Jerry's done. It takes him much longer to close up shop." She nodded in his direction, where Jerry and Derek fought with the iron contents of a wheelbarrow. "I should go over and help some more. It was really nice sharing space with you, India. I can tell your chi is well-centered." Tess rose.

I smiled. "Uh, thanks," I said, although I had doubts about the centeredness of my energy flow. I could've used a nap and maybe a piece of chocolate cake.

"Oh, I almost forgot," Tess said. "I have something for you." She bent down and reached into a large tote bag at her feet.

"You do?" I asked warily, hoping it wasn't something to realign my aura.

She pulled a blue festival polo shirt out of her tote bag. "It might be a little big on you, but I had an extra. You looked so miserable today in that get-up."

I caught the polo in the air. "Be still my heart! I love you."

Tess grinned.

"I was debating on spilling paint down my front earlier today, but this solution is so much cleaner. Plus Carmen would freak." To put it mildly, I mentally added.

"Anything I can do to help another artist in need." She smiled again with that faraway sweet smile. She definitely had her chi in the right spot.

I thanked Tess profusely for the shirt as I tipped the rolling crate back on its wheels, slung my backpack over my shoulder, and grabbed my painting portfolio. "I'll see you tomorrow."

Tess waved. "Tomorrow." She joined Jerry at his booth, Zach trailing in her wake.

As it turned out, we were both wrong about that.

Chapter Five

I lived in one half of a duplex a mile east of campus, close enough to walk, if I ever was so inclined, but too far away from campus for students to frequent my neighborhood.

As I pulled into the driveway, Ina Carroll, my landlady and next door neighbor, squared off with a police officer in our front yard. Ina gestured wildly as she spoke. The cop, whose back was to me, had his arms crossed in front of his chest. I wondered if this was to exude authority or provide protection. Theodore, an obese Maine coon cat and Ina's charge, sat at her feet, munching on fallen leaves. Theodore was my brother's cat, but when Mark hit the road, I turned the cat over to Ina. My feline roommate, Templeton, had a personality disagreement with Theo, and I didn't want to referee a feline version of professional wrestling until my wanderlust sibling found himself.

I approached the pair cautiously. Ina waved me over. "India, thank goodness you're home. Tell this boy playing cops and robbers I'm not a crazy old woman."

Isn't lying to a police officer a crime? I wondered.

"What's going on?" I asked. As I did, the officer turned to face me. Oh great, it was Officer Knute. Knute was one of the cops I'd had trouble with last summer when my brother was in a legal mess. He was a sun-bleached blond, tan-skinned fit guy, who looked better suited for the beaches of California than the mild streets of Stripling, Ohio.

Knute grimaced. "Mrs. Carroll here is trying to report a

crime," he said as if that was in question.

Ina sniffed. "That's Ms. Carroll to you. I never got married, thank you very much. Just because I'm old doesn't mean I've ever been hitched."

Knute looked heavenward.

"Don't roll your eyes at me. I can tell you don't believe me. It's true. A crime has been committed."

I collected my mail from the box next to my front door. I flipped through it quickly. Bill, bill, junk, bill, junk, postcard. The postcard's picture was of Delicate Arch in Utah. I flipped it over even though I already knew who sent it. It was from my brother Mark, who was off seeking himself in the wild, wild West. It read, "India, I saw a moose today up in the mountains near Park City, Utah. Did you know there were moose in Utah? I sure didn't. Having a great time. Hope Theodore is doing well."

I looked down at Theodore, who was polishing off the fallen oak leaf that had drifted onto Ina's half of the porch. His girth spread around him like a deflated balloon. He looked fine to me.

"What's that?" Knute asked in alarm as he stared at Theodore.

"It's a cat," Ina said.

"It's huge. I thought it was a rug."

Theo squinted at Knute as if sizing him up for dessert.

"Are you all right, Ina? What kind of crime was it?" I asked.

"Of course, I'm all right," she replied.

Knute gave me a sideways glance. "The crime is jaywalking."

"Jaywalking?" I tried to keep the disbelief out of my voice with little success.

Ina put her hands on her narrow hips. "I could've been killed this morning walking downtown. This crazy man almost ran me over as I was making my way down the sidewalk in front of the

Lutheran church, then he ran across the street onto the square, nearly getting hit by a car. You don't even want to know what the driver of the car called him."

She was right, I didn't. All I wanted to do was get a bite to eat and sit down on the couch to watch mind-numbing reality TV. Was that too much to ask after the day I'd had?

"If you don't believe me, you can ask Juliet Burla. She was few steps behind me and saw the whole thing."

Ina didn't mention that Juliet, her best friend and co-conspirator, as sweet as she was, was just shy of blind and verging on senile. Juliet's eyewitness account of anything would never hold up in the court of law.

"I called that detective of yours to tell him, and he sent this kid over in his place."

I knew whom she was referring to—Detective Richmond Mains, who assisted me last year with my brother's case. Knute knew, too, since Mains was the *only* detective on the Stripling police force. I felt myself blush. "He's not my detective."

Knute's eyes narrowed.

"I thought because of my friendship with you he would care enough to do something himself."

I didn't like where this was going at all. In truth, I hadn't even spoken to Mains in three months. Mentally, I counted to ten backward in French. "Officer Knute, do you have everything you need for now?"

Knute nodded. "Yep. I'd better be off so I can hunt down some jaywalkers."

"I don't like your lip, young man," Ina said.

Knute walked to his car but got in one final parting shot. "Nice dress."

I looked down at the pink nightmare I wore.

Ina watched Knute drive away with contempt. "I bet that Mains character didn't come because he's English. You know how the English feel about our people. I can just tell he plans to treat this like the potato famine and let the defenseless fend for themselves."

Not this again. Ina was on a genealogy kick, following her family's lineage all the way back to Ireland. During that research, she discovered her great grandfather immigrated to the United States during the potato famine of 1845. Obsessed with the horrors of that time, she talked about it nonstop, enjoying one gruesome detail after another. I thought the topic was sobering and interesting—at first. However, there came a point when the death and starvation of thousands of people lost its appeal. At least for me. Ina was another story.

"Detective Mains had nothing to do with the potato famine, Ina," I said, even though I knew it was useless to argue.

"That's what he wants you to think." She threw open her front door. "I'm going inside. I have work to do. I need to find the police chief's phone number and file a complaint. Do you think your parents have his number?"

She nudged Theodore to go inside with her. Slowly he lifted his body from the porch and lumbered into her apartment.

"Most likely." On that note, I excused myself and went into my apartment.

Thirty minutes later, Templeton and I sat on the couch watching a deliciously stupid episode of reality television and eating ice cream. It was just what the doctor ordered after a long day of painting faces under my sister's thumb. I sat Indian style on the couch in my I LOVE MY CAT pajamas with the ice cream pint in my lap so Templeton could get to the container more easily. I knew some people would be disturbed that I ate after my cat, but he's a finicky neat-nick and much cleaner than most people I know. More practically, he'd claw my eyes out if he didn't get his share.

In the past, I'd tried to give him his own bowl, but it never worked. He always polished it off before I could get my second bite in and then came after my serving.

On the TV, one of the women complained about the untidiness of the camp they were living in.

"You're in the jungle. What do you expect?" I said.

Templeton meowed and I interpreted his meow to say, "These people are morons." He twitched his tail for emphasis.

After swallowing a large spoonful of ice cream, I told him, "You're right."

I glanced at the cart of face paints and brushes sitting by my front door. I wasn't looking forward to tomorrow and round two. The fact I was both neighbors with Derek's mom and Lepcheck's sister didn't make it any easier, no matter how much I liked Tess. At that moment, my brain registered the cart was black. Not blue as it should be, but black.

"Oh crap! Templeton, I'm the one who's a moron." I jumped out my seat, sending cat and ice cream container flying. "I grabbed the wrong cart."

Templeton hissed and swatted at his right ear, trying to get off the bit of ice cream that somehow had landed there.

It was true. There had been two rolling carts under my table. The black one held the face-painting equipment, and the blue one held my paintings and, I realized, my fanny pack with all the money.

I had to go back for it. The paintings would be ruined if they got damp. Not to mention, my sister would have a conniption fit if I lost the face-painting money.

I grabbed my red trench coat and pulled dog-printed puddle boots onto my feet.

Templeton jumped on the kitchen table and started licking his long black tail, which was coated with strawberry swirl ice cream. He watched me between licks with disapproval in his eyes.

"It was an accident." I plucked the ice cream container off of the floor and tossed it into the kitchen wastebasket. I'd deal with the stain the spilt ice cream left on the rug later.

He bore his fangs, and I grabbed my keys and cell before leaving the apartment. The drive to campus took less than five minutes, but it felt like an eternity. I couldn't believe I'd forgotten something as important as my paintings and the fanny pack of money. I groaned. I'd been too eager to escape Derek, my alleged special friend. I prayed the money and paintings were still there.

The tacky Halloween decorations emitted an eerie orange glow as I drove by fraternity row. I pulled into the parking lot by the practice football field in my new-to-me small SUV. The parking lot had light posts, but the practice field was pitch black. The team sometimes practiced at night. Four giant dark floodlights loomed over the field, not that I knew where the switch was to turn them on. Instead, I reached into the backseat of my car for a flashlight.

My puddle boots skidded across the slick leaves that had blown across the field, and I stumbled over my own two feet. All the booths were closed up. The food vendors had padlocks on their carts. This was a good move; I could envision some of the male underclassmen breaking in and stealing all their frozen French fries. I neared the crafter booths and saw those booths were closed up tight as well. Apparently, the crafters trusted the Martin students as much the food people did. I hoped the underclassmen hadn't been to my booth, and if they had, that they took the money and not my paintings.

The weak light of the flash finally fell on the cheap blue awning of my so-called booth. I trained the light under the table and saw the wheels of the blue cart. I hurried over, relieved to find all the paintings and money present and accounted for. I snapped the fanny pack around my waist.

I swung the flashlight left and right before heading back to the car, and as I did, the light fell on Tess's booth. My light wobbled. Her display was still up. All the baskets were there as if waiting for morning. Tess seemed ditzy, but I couldn't believe she'd leave her precious baskets out all night. With my rudimentary knowledge of the effects of water on wood and wood's ability to expand and contract, I didn't think it could be good for the baskets to be exposed to the elements like that. Tess would have known this better than anyone.

Immediately, a knot developed in the pit of stomach. I inched toward the booth. The closer I got to the booth the more my stomach tightened.

The baskets hanging from the coat tree looked like withered pieces of fruit. I gave myself a mental headshake. I blamed my edginess on darkness and the closeness of Halloween. But deep down I knew it was more than that, much more. I stepped closer, although a part of me, a big part, wanted to get the heck out of there and fast.

Despite the cold night, sweat trickled down my neck and inside the collar of my pajamas. I looked over the edge of Tess's booth and made my gruesome discovery. My hand flew to my mouth.

Tess, still in the jeans, sweatshirt, and festival polo, lay sprawled face down in the grass. A huge sycamore leaf clung to her cheek. After a second, I realized it was held there with blood. A large dent dominated the back of her head, covered with blood-matted hair. If Tess had darker hair, perhaps the sight of the blood wouldn't be so dramatic, but up against her pale ash-blond mop, the blood was impossible to ignore. Dark cranberry red, a hue I doubted any pulverized beetle could duplicate.

I swallowed the bile rising in my throat. I shone my light

around the scene. A few feet away from Tess's body, the cat's head basket mold sat in a patch of blood-spattered grass.

Instinctively I stumbled back, knocking my hip into the side of the booth. Several baskets fell off the cart and bounced softly onto the field. Taking a deep breath, I dialed 911.

Chapter Six

The next call I made was to my sister's cell phone. I wrapped my coat tighter around me. I heard the twins screaming in the background. "Can you repeat that?" Carmen asked.

And so I did. I held the phone away from my ear as Carmen yelled at her husband, Chip, that she needed to go out. "India's found a dead body." She sounded almost nonchalant about it. I shivered to think what my nieces and nephew would consider alarming if that pronouncement could be said in their presence without a qualm. It wasn't that Carmen was callous or uncaring; she was in super-mom mode, which allowed no time for hysterics. It was better just to do as she ordered or get out of way.

Sirens interrupted our conversation. A minute later, the flood lights clicked on, washing the field and empty booths in a garish yellow light. If anything, the lighting made Tess's head wound look more gruesome. I clicked off my flash.

A small army of police jogged across the grassy field, with Officer Knute leading the charge. It would have to be Knute first on the scene, wouldn't it? He stumbled when we made eye contact, and his floppy blond hair fell over his eyes, but not before I saw the look of shock quickly followed by annoyance. The officer jogging behind Knute wasn't watching where he was going and ran into Knute's back. The pair tumbled into the damp grass. Despite the circumstances, I couldn't help but smile. Knute deserved a few grass stains on his pristine uniform.

The smile immediately died on my lips when I saw Detective Rick Mains maneuver around the officers, who fumbled about in an attempt to right themselves.

Mains saw me and closed his hazel-green eyes briefly, as if to wish away my appearance. When he opened them again, I did a finger wave. He muttered something to himself that I couldn't hear. Probably I didn't want to hear it.

He was just a foot away from me now. "You're the one who called nine-one-one?" He pushed his dark hair away from his forehead. He had great wavy black hair, which makes women insanely jealous. It was completely wasted on a man, as were his long dark eyelashes.

I nodded.

He looked down at Tess. "Did you check her vital signs?"

My eyes went wide. "No." I instantly felt horribly guilty. What if she was alive when I got there?

He put a hand on my shoulder. "Don't worry. Looks to me like she's been dead for a while."

His hand felt warm. I noticed he was looking at my legs. I gave an inward groan. My I LOVE MY CAT PJs were showing under my trench coat. "What exactly were you doing when you discovered the body?"

I was about to answer him, when I heard my sister call my name.

Mains took a deep breath and closed his eyes again. "Is that who I think it is?"

I nodded and watched my sister advance. She marched across the festival grounds with a clipboard firmly clutched in her hand. Everything about her demeanor said DAMAGE CONTROL. Her gait was the same Mom March she used on the playground when other kids teased my five-year-old nephew, Nicholas. The march was intended to make children cower. I felt a little shaky myself, but it could have been the dead body four feet away.

I shivered from the cold as much as from the presence of Tess's body. Winter was on the way; there was no doubt about it. I felt its icy fingers on my neck. I wondered if it would snow within the week. It had been known to snow on little witches and goblins on trick-or-treat night in Stripling. I glanced at Tess's feet. I couldn't bring myself to look at her head.

Carmen came to an abrupt halt in front of me and paled. She put her hand to her mouth. I suspected I looked much the same when I saw Tess's body laying there for the first time. "Oh my!" Carmen swallowed hard. She gaped at Tess's body. "I mean you told me, but . . . I . . . I thought you were joking."

"You think I would joke about this?"

"Well, I don't know. It's just so unbelievable." She swallowed again and ran her free hand along her fresh-pressed khaki pant leg. "Did you try to, you know, revive her?"

As if I didn't feel badly enough about that already? I thought. I bit my lower lip.

Carmen cocked her head. "Well," she said with her bossy persona firmly back into place. "Isn't that what you are supposed to do?"

Mains cleared his throat. "She's been dead for some time. There wasn't anything India could have done."

I smiled my thanks and, unheeded, I felt tears well up in the corner of my eyes. I tried to blink them away.

Carmen's face softened. "India, I'm so sorry."

I swallowed. "I just met her earlier today. I didn't know her very well, but she seemed like a cool lady. I wish—"

Carmen turned her attention to Mains. "Ricky, I want to talk to you—"

Mains held up a hand. "Not yet, Carmen. Trust me, you will have your turn." His eyes never left my face. "Are you okay?"

"I'm fine." I felt something catch in my throat and swallowed. "It's just so awful. Poor Tess." I pointed at the body partially obscured by Tess's cart.

Mains glanced down at her and grimaced. Knute and the rest of the officers walked the perimeter of the booth, peering intently at the grass, on the hunt for evidence. One of them held a huge camera with a telephoto lens. Mains waved her over. "Take a shot from every angle you can think of."

"You got it," Officer Habash said, another officer I'd met as a result of my brother's troubles last summer. She gave me a quick smile. At least she didn't hold a grudge like Knute did.

Mains turned his attention back to me. "Now, tell me why you came back to campus in what looks like your pajamas."

So I did.

"India, that money could have been stolen. I can't believe you were so irresponsible," Carmen said when I'd finished my story.

I gritted my teeth. "I came back for it, didn't I?"

"Still," she said. "Ricky, what about the festival?"

"The festival?"

Carmen made an exasperated sound. "Yes, the festival. That's why all of these booths are here. I'm the chair this year. I must know if we can open on time tomorrow."

I pulled my cell phone out of my pocket and checked the time. It was half past nine.

Mains put a finger to the corner of his eye as if to stop a twitch.

Carmen huffed. "I asked you a question."

"What time were you planning on opening?" he asked.

"Ten."

Officer Habash, who wore latex gloves, held up the cat's head basket mold for his inspection. "Here's your murder weapon, sir."

Mains nodded.

"What the heck is that?" asked Knute, who had to move

away from the patch of grass he searched.

I inched closer to the scene, but I refused to look down at Tess. "It's a cat's head basket mold."

Knute gave me a black look. Gee, and I thought someday the two of us could be friends.

"Tess was a basket weaver. She used it to make a basket. The corners kind of look like cat ears, don't they? That's where the basket gets its name."

Knute's eyes seemed to glaze over with my explanation. I knew the look well. It was the same look freshmen gave me during library orientation.

"Bag it," Mains ordered Habash.

"You seem to know a lot about it," Knute said suggestively.

"If you're implying I had anything to do with this . . ." I gestured at my haphazard booth. "I was face painting in the next booth all day. I learned a lot about basket weaving in the amount of time. It was part of her spiel."

"Her spiel?" Mains asked.

"You know, her sales pitch. Every artist knows you have to talk to make a sale, and most of us do it so often we repeat the same pitch over and over until we could say it in our sleep. Ask any of the crafters here, they'll tell you the same thing."

Knute didn't look convinced. He'd love to find an excuse to toss me into the pokey.

Carmen snapped her fingers, an annoying habit she picked up in the classroom to grab teenagers' attention. It worked like a charm on Mains. "Ricky, you are ignoring me. What about the festival?" She hugged her clipboard to her chest and ground her foot on the grass, turning the fallen leaves into mulch.

Mains winced as my sister called him Ricky for a third time. It was times like this that I was uncomfortably reminded that Mains was once Carmen's Ricky, her high school sweetheart. A fact she apparently planned to hold over him for the rest of his life.

"Carmen," Mains said in a pacifying voice.

Uh-oh! He'd spoken condescendingly to her. I'd think, after dating her, he'd remember that was not the best approach. "This is a crime scene. The festival will have to be closed for the time being. No one can come near this booth."

"Closed? Closed?" Carmen's voice was shrill. "The Stripling Founders' Festival has never been closed. In nineteen hundred, there was a tornado and the festival went on. In nineteen fifty-six, the mayor fell and broke his leg the morning of the festival but was still there in the afternoon for his obligatory appearance. In nineteen eighty-seven, there was an outbreak of chicken pox in the elementary school, but there was a fair."

Mains ran his hand through his lush dark hair, and a vein on the side of his neck began to throb.

"Let me tell you something, *Detective* Richmond Mains. You are going to do whatever it takes to get this festival up and running by ten o'clock tomorrow morning, so that we can open on time." She consulted her watch. "That gives you exactly twelve hours and fifteen minutes to do whatever it is that you do." Carmen's eyes blazed. I knew Carmen was nervous about the festival going off without a hitch. It was all she'd talked about for the last few months. A dead body was not a good start, but I thought she was being a little harsh on Mains. It wasn't like he killed Tess. He was just doing his job.

Mains clenched his jaw, holding back whatever remark he'd like to fire back at my sister.

The officers and EMTs stopped working to watch the show. Knute gaped back and forth between Carmen and Mains, his mouth hanging open like a bass.

Slowly, Mains's jaw relaxed. "We'll do our best to clear the scene before the festival opens, but you're yammering at us and prolonging the process."

Carmen's mouth fell open, and she started to speak. Mains was faster. "Now, please give us the space to work." His head snapped around at Knute. "Officer Knute, don't you have some ground to comb?"

Wordlessly, Knute turned on his heels and bent his head as if his life depended on staring at the grass.

Carmen got in one parting shot. "Jem and Adel Stripling survived countless hardships to settle here, and we have an obligation to honor them. They battled heat, disease, snowstorms, torrential downpours, and the death of their infant son, Matthew, all in that first year. If they hadn't survived, where would we be?"

We'd probably be here anyway, I thought to myself. I mean, if the Striplings hadn't settled here, someone else would have. Manifest Destiny and all that, and as far as I knew, none of the parties standing around Tess's body were direct descendants of the Striplings. I thought better of mentioning any of these musings to my sister.

Carmen ground her sneakers deeper into the earth as if setting permanent fence posts. She wasn't going anywhere. Mains and Carmen squared off. This could get ugly, I thought.

"Could we move the festival?" I asked.

Carmen stared at me. "Move it? Move it where? Do you know how hard it was for me to convince Martin to hold the festival on its grounds? Now, with this"—she paused—"situation, they'll never agree to it again." Her brow furrowed. "Does Martin know?"

"We called the president. She's getting her VPs together."

It was my turn to shiver. I hoped Mains hadn't mentioned my name when talking to the college president. I had enough notoriety on campus as it was. "You could move to the other end of the field. Closer to the parking lot on the other side of the food vendors."

Carmen sniffed. "That area's reserved for the corn hole tournament."

I looked heavenward. "I'm sure the college could move the corn hole somewhere else." I knew nothing of the kind. I almost suggested the library's quad but stopped myself. My director, Lasha Lint, would not look kindly on a bunch of children throwing bean bags back and forth in front of the library's entrance.

A slight man in a rumpled suit and carrying a large medical bag hurried across the field. Mains waved him over. "Thanks for coming, Doc."

Doc was Dr. Frank Maynor, the county medical examiner. He was a member of my mother's church.

Doc panted hard. "I came as quick as I could." He glanced at Carmen and me. "Girls, is your mother here?"

We shook our heads.

He smiled and looked relieved.

"Let me show you the scene," Mains said. He walked around the booth, and together the cop and medical examiner knelt beside Tess's body. Doc slid a penlight out of his jacket pocket and shone its light on Tess's wound. I looked away. Mains glanced up at Carmen and me, who were still standing there like gap-mouthed statues. He shot me an exasperated look. "Give your statement to Officer Habash and go home. I'll see you in the morning."

At home, my phone rang a few minutes after I walked through the door. It was Mains. "Tell your sister the festival can start at ten as planned."

"It can?" I was surprised.

"Yes, the college president thinks it will draw more attention to the murder if the festival was to be canceled." He didn't sound very happy with the decision.

I thought the crime scene tape around Tess's booth would do

the trick, but who was I to know?

"The crafters will have to move to the other side of the field as you suggested."

"What about the corn hole game?"

"Not my problem."

"Why don't you call Carmen yourself?"

There was silence, then he sighed. "Can you just tell her?"

"Sure," I agreed.

"We have a lot to talk about tomorrow, India, so get some rest." He hung up.

I held the phone in my hand, wondering if he meant there was more to talk about than just the murder.

Chapter Seven

The next morning, I parked in the practice field lot a little before eight. Carmen wanted me there early to help the other crafters move their booths.

As I approached my sister, Carmen looked at me in dismay. "Where's your pioneer dress?"

I wore jeans, the polo shirt Tess had given me, a warm hoodie, and a scarf. I opened my jacket to show her the polo. "See, I'm in uniform."

Her eyes narrowed. "You're lucky I don't have time for this."

I smiled. "Where do we start?"

Most of the crafters were gathered at the edge of the parking lot. Knute hovered close by to make sure the crafters didn't bother the crime scene. Carmen clapped her hands for their attention. "As I told you all on the phone, there was an accident in the crafter area last evening. We need to move all the crafter booths to this side of the field before we can open."

"What kind of accident?" someone called. "Was anybody hurt?" asked another, and everyone started talking at once.

The fifteen or so crafters formed a makeshift circle around Carmen and me. Knute, who was supposed to be controlling them, watched us with just a hint of a smile on his face. Carmen put two fingers in her mouth and whistled at painfully close range. When everyone quieted down, her teacher persona was firmly in place. "Listen up!"

I wondered if I'd ever be able to hear out my right ear again.

"One of our fellow crafters was attacked," Carmen said. Her announcement silenced them.

I inwardly groaned.

Knute awakened from his comatose state. "Ma'am, the detective didn't say you could tell the public."

Carmen looked down at Knute as if she was inspecting the expiration date on a gallon of milk. "Nor did he say I couldn't tell them. These people here are crafters and vendors who paid good money to be a part of this festival."

"But ma'am—"

"What happened? Tell us," Lynette said with a crochet hook clenched in her small fist.

The crowd agreed.

"I'm sorry to report that Tess Ross is dead."

There was collective intake of horrified breath.

One woman with red-blond hair standing away from the crowd burst into tears. She covered her mouth, and before I could ask who she was she ran off. I wondered if she was going to be sick.

A beader interrupted my thoughts. She was a small woman wearing a white puff-sleeved blouse and brown sprig-patterned skirt that fell all the way to her shoes, which I assumed were twins of my wretched granny boots. She gasped. "Dead?"

"She died here at the festival?" someone called out.

"How could that happen?" the weaver asked.

Carmen clapped her hands. "We don't know anything yet. The police are just beginning their investigation. But"—she paused—"It looks like she was murdered."

Knute moaned softly and shot me a look of loathing. Like it was my fault, I thought. Please, I never claimed any semblance of control over any of my family members.

"Murdered!" the crowd responded aghast.

"I know this is a shock, but the festival must go on. Detective

Mains promised the festival will open on time. The scheduled activities will continue as planned. Being a crafter and annual participant of the Stripling Founders' Festival, I believe that Tess would have wanted us to keep the festival going.

"The food vendors are free to set up their booths and stations at their present locations. However, the crafters and artists will have to move their booths to this side of the field. I suggest you all get to work now. We don't have much time. I'm sure if you have any questions, Officer Knute will be happy to assist you."

Knute glared at my sister. I think she just overthrew my throne on his loathsome list.

"Now if you will excuse me, I have some calls to make." Carmen walked away. I hurried after her, but not before I saw the crowd gathered around Knute. I didn't feel a bit sorry for him.

I caught up with Carmen at the concessions area. Still walking at a fast pace, she plucked her cell phone from her purse pocket and speed-dialed. "Chip. Call a babysitter. I need all hands at the festival to move everything on time."

Knowing my brother-in-law would be there soon, I left my sister to her damage control.

The food booths were already cooking. I inhaled the artery-clogging but simply delicious smells of fair food, and I realized that I was hungry. Unfortunately, most of the concession booths were empty as their owners tried to sneak a peek at the crime scene.

While I knew I should move my booth, the subtle growling in my stomach distracted me enough that I took a detour toward the parking lot. I might have a granola bar somewhere in my car. The age of the granola bar was debatable, but my quest for breakfast gave me an excuse to avoid the scene of the crime.

In the parking lot, Jerry was unloading his truck. My appetite left me.

What was he doing here? Didn't he know of Tess's murder? Wasn't it Mains's job to tell family members these things? Where was Mains?

"Good morning," he said in a cheerful voice. He didn't know yet, that much was obvious. He shut the pickup's door and walked toward the practice field. I hurried over to him.

"Jerry, wait."

He stopped. "Need help with something?"

"Can you wait here for a few minutes?"

His forehead wrinkled. "Why? I need to set up."

I bit my lip.

"Is something wrong?"

"Well . . . Tess . . . I . . ."

"Tess? This has to do with Tess? Is she here?"

"What time did Tess leave last night?" I glanced behind me, looking for Mains, for any cop, even Knute.

"I don't know. I left around seven and headed over to my forge. She was still here then . . ." He trailed off. "What's this about?"

"You mean you haven't seen your wife since yesterday?"

Jerry's eyes flashed in annoyance. "Not that it's any of your business, but I'm in the middle of working on a huge custom gate order. That means long hours and lots of noise." His face softened. "I called the house around midnight to tell her I'd sleep on my cot over there, but she must already have gone to bed. She didn't answer the phone. Why? Are you looking for her?"

I felt the blood drain from my face. "Jerry, I'm so sorry . . ."

He froze. "Sorry? Sorry for what?"

"Uh—"

"I'll take it from here, India." Mains's voice came from behind me, and I jumped.

Jerry looked from Mains to me and back again. "Who are you?"

"I'm Detective Richmond Mains of the Stripling Police Department. Mr. Ross, I need to speak with you for a minute."

Despite the chill in the air, beads of sweat appeared on Jerry's brow. "Wh-what's this about?"

I didn't move.

Mains touched my arm. "You need to give us some privacy."

I jogged back to the practice field, the granola bar forgotten.

In my haste to get away, I ran directly into Derek. His eyes were bloodshot. He knew.

"Derek, I'm so sorry." It was the best I could do, but it wasn't nearly enough.

He blinked at me.

Officer Habash stood a foot away and cocked her eyebrow at me.

I smiled at her. "I know him. He's one of my students. Derek, let's go over to that picnic table."

We sat on the bench. "Are you okay?"

"No."

I smiled sadly at the honest answer. Most people were too polite to tell you how they really feel, but not Derek.

My shoulder began to ache as it always did when I tensed up. "Who told you?"

"Detective Mains. Last night. He found me at the dorm."

"I don't know if you should be here."

"I had to come. I had to see where it happened. Not that I actually saw anything. The police wouldn't let me get close."

"That's good. You don't need to see that."

"I brought these for you." For the first time, I noticed the white bakery bag in his hand. I took the bag. Two fresh jelly donuts sat at the bottom. "I know they're your favorite. I brought them to apologize about yesterday."

"That was very thoughtful," I stammered. How could he think of bringing me donuts the morning after he learned his mother was murdered? Under the circumstances, it seemed rude not to take the bakery bag, so I decided to forgive the no-gifts rule this once. I doubted I'd be able to eat them.

"I just don't understand. The detective said she was murdered. That doesn't make any sense. No one had anything against my mom. Everyone loved her. She was so easygoing." A tear slid out of the corner of his eye, and he gruffly wiped it away.

"It doesn't look like she left last night. Her cart wasn't even packed. When did you last see her?"

"Six-thirty," he said firmly. "I offered to help her pack up, and she said I didn't have to. She was meeting someone, and it would give her something to do while she waited. I didn't argue with her. You don't know how many times I've packed her booth after a craft fair. I was happy for the excuse to leave. I should have insisted. That's what a good son would've done." He blinked at the ground.

I put what I hoped was a reassuring hand on his arm.

He looked up. "You have to find out who did this."

I removed my hand as if burned. "What?"

"Everyone knows you solved that murder last summer."

"That was different," I said quickly, panic racing through me as my mind listed all the reasons I shouldn't get involved. Lepcheck was the victim's brother. Martin College would hate it. Mains would hate it. And the list went on.

"Please?" His voice broke.

I've heard people say it's hard to lose a parent at any age. I don't doubt that to be true, but I also believed the younger the child was the harder it must be. The child didn't have a chance to prove himself before his parent was snatched away. The child didn't have a chance to become whomever he was going to be.

I looked into Derek's bloodshot eyes. At eighteen, he was on the cusp of proving himself to Tess, and he had lost his chance. Someone stole his opportunity, someone selfish who didn't consider or care about the ramifications of his or her actions. It would be a selfish person in the end who would commit murder, wouldn't it? Wasn't that what all killing amounted to? Putting one's own goals, desires, and agendas above another's?

I thought of myself at eighteen, attending art school in Chicago. When I was Derek's age, my father made a foolhardy attempt to trim a sycamore tree solo on church grounds. He fell from the tree, and we almost lost him. Dad survived, even if his ability to walk did not, but the nearness of losing him almost broke my heart in two. There was no almost for Derek. Tess was gone, at least from this earth, and Derek would never have the chance to show Tess the man he would be. He had yet to even choose his major.

"Okay," I said.

His eyes widened. "Okay?"

"Okay." My jaw was set.

Chapter Eight

Officer Habash approached us. "India, the detective wants to talk to you." She glanced at Derek. "He's over by your booth."

I stood up.

"What should I do?" Derek asked.

"Jerry is here somewhere. Detective Mains was talking to him. Do you want me to find him for you?"

Derek shook his head with a frown. "Jerry's probably as freaked out as I am. It would only make me feel worse."

I looked down at him. He looked so young. "You should go back to your dorm room. Is your roommate there?"

Derek shook his head. "He went home for the weekend, and I don't want to go back to my mom's house."

I knew he was right. Bobby was going to kill me for what I said next, but that was just too bad. "Go to the library. It should open soon. Bobby will be there this morning."

"Bobby hates me."

"He doesn't hate you."

"Yes, he does." There was a pout in his voice. "He called me a pest."

"I'm sure he was joking."

Derek looked skeptical.

"I'll walk him over to the library. Come on, Derek," Officer Habash said.

"I'll talk to you later, Derek," I said.

He nodded numbly. The hope that had flickered in his eyes

when I agreed to take the case was already extinguished. No matter what I discovered, Tess was never coming back.

When I reached the booth, Mains and his team were surveying the ground for clues, hoping to find something in the light of day that they'd overlooked the night before. If someone handed Mains a magnifying glass and a pipe, he'd look just like Sherlock Holmes. Much to my relief, Tess's body was long gone, as was the cat's head basket mold. However, when I closed my eyes, it was night again, and I could see her there face down in the grass with her head bashed in. I opened my eyes wide.

Mutt, the director of campus security, and a couple of his college cops, stood off to the side of the crime scene. I sidled over to Mutt and said hello. He was a big man who wheezed ever so slightly from walking from his office in the safety and security modular building. I rarely saw him out and about on campus.

He looked at me out of the corner of his eye. "I heard you found the body."

I nodded. "Know anything about it?"

"Nothing. The city police only tell me what they absolutely have to." He pulled a piece of candy out of his breast pocket, unwrapped it, and popped it into his mouth. "The admin is choking on this one. The summer was different. There weren't that many students on campus, and the incident could be hushed up." He shook his head. "But this happened right smack dab in the middle of the fall semester."

"Are any of the VPs coming down here?"

"Eventually. They are having an emergency powwow in the president's office."

"Do they know who the victim is?" I asked. Lepcheck would be at that meeting discussing how they would handle his sister's death.

"Not sure. They know her name. Tess Ross."

So, Lepcheck knew it was his sister by now, but by Mutt's reaction, he didn't know Tess was related to Lepcheck. I wasn't going to tell him.

Knute spotted me. "Hayes is here."

It could have been my imagination, but I thought I detected a glint of amusement in Mains's eyes when they fell on me. "Follow me, India."

I did. Mains led me a few feet away. The crafters hastily tore down their booths to move farther down the field. If I didn't start doing the same soon, Carmen would come looking for me, pitchfork in hand.

"Tell me again what happened last night. Don't leave anything out. Did you see anyone on campus? Did anything strike you as odd?" he asked.

"Other than finding Tess's body? That was pretty odd."

He rolled his eyes. "Yes, other than that."

There wasn't much to tell, so my recitation took all of four minutes.

"I suppose I should be relieved you thought to call the police before your sister."

"You know how Carmen is. If I hadn't called her immediately, she would've had my head."

"Point taken." He had a faraway look on his face, and I wondered if he'd remembered something about Carmen. His look made my stomach knot. As quickly as the expression came, it cleared. "Did you notice anything suspicious while you waited for the police?"

"Like a masked man stalking about twirling his mustache?"

Mains sighed. "Just anything that seemed out of the ordinary."

"The first odd thing I noticed was Tess's booth, which was still set up like when the festival was open." I swallowed, too vividly remembering the image of the back of Tess's head. "Before I left, I asked her why she wasn't packing up her booth.

All the other crafters were."

"What did she say?"

"She said she would when Jerry, her husband, finished packing."

He made a note in his tiny notepad.

I cleared my throat.

He looked up. "Is there something else?"

"In my estimation, Tess was killed between seven and eight-thirty last night." I looked at him like an overachiever, hoping to impress my teacher.

"Why's that?"

I took that as encouragement. "Well, I left the festival around six-twenty, Derek said he left at six-thirty, and Jerry said he left at seven. He might have been the last person to see her alive. Besides her killer, I mean." I paused. "Then I discovered I brought the wrong crate home from the festival at eight-fifteen. I was back on campus by eight-twenty and called the police at eight thirty-one. I know the exact time because I saw the time on my phone when I called." I shivered as I realized the killer could have still been on campus when I got there. I tried to remember if there were any other cars in the practice field lot. I couldn't. I'd been too focused on retrieving the face-painting money from my booth to notice.

Mains scowled. "Why do I get the idea you've been investigating?"

"Well, I'm right, aren't I?"

"It corroborates what the medical examiner said last night."

I smiled.

"India, I don't want—"

"There's something else you might not know."

"I might not know?" His tone was sarcastic. "Please enlighten me."

"Tess is . . . was Samuel Lepcheck's sister."

Mains blinked at me. "Are you sure?"

I nodded. "Tess told me herself yesterday." I debated telling Mains about the argument I'd overheard between Tess and Lepcheck. In truth, I didn't know what gave me pause. I had no reason to protect the provost. He barely tolerated me as it was, and I knew if my tenured library director, Lasha Lint, wouldn't make a huge stink out of it, he would happily not renew my faculty contract for the next school year. Maybe I wanted to keep that tidbit to myself to protect Derek from more scandal. Everyone on campus knew Lepcheck, and soon enough, everyone would know that Lepcheck was his uncle.

Mains swore and massaged his temples. Any time the Stripling Police Department had a run-in with a member of the Martin College community, it was headache for Mains. The college's policy of dealing with crime was Deny, Deflect, Defend.

In the case of Tess's death, Martin would be locked up tighter than the U.S. Declaration of Independence. So Mains, knowing what he was about to go up against, certainly had ample justification to swear.

"What do you know about their relationship?"

"Nothing," I said, which was pretty much true. I changed the subject. "Derek Welch, Tess's son, is one of my students."

Mains peered at me. "So?"

"Just thought you'd like to know for the sake of full disclosure. He's a little attached to me."

"How so?"

I bit my lip.

Mains's hazel-green eyes narrowed. "I hope you're not planning to get involved."

"Who, me?"

"Ricky!" Carmen snapped, saving me from finishing our conversation. "The festival starts in forty-five minutes. Can some of your officers help us move the booths?" She spotted me. "India, why does it look like your booth hasn't been touched?"

Mains looked heavenward as he slipped his tiny notepad into his jacket pocket. "I'll see what I can do."

My brother-in-law, Chip, stood behind Carmen and shifted from foot to foot. Chip, whose baptismal name is Cristiano, was an attractive Italian-American with dark hair and eyes.

"Good." She marched away. As she walked by her husband, she said, "Chip, find my bullhorn."

Chip jogged ahead of her.

Mains looked at me. "What were you saying about Derek Welch?"

Drat, I hoped that he'd forgotten. "It's nothing."

Over the bullhorn—apparently Chip had found it—we heard Carmen's voice. "Crafters! Listen up! We need to move, move, move! Every able body, please, pitch in to help."

"Well, I better start moving my stuff," I said relieved.

As I walked away, I looked back at Mains against my better judgment. Our gazes met. He looked confused, and I imagine my expression was much the same.

Chapter Nine

By some miracle, or Carmen's sheer force of will, the festival opened on time. All the booths were up, and the vendors and crafters were ready to start the day.

As I painted faces, the visitors seemed unaware of the early morning events. At Carmen's insistence, the police cruisers relocated to another parking lot to avoid attracting attention. Knute and Habash were stationed at the far end of the food vendors to stop any overzealous tourists from straying too far.

I was just putting the finishing touches on a purple elephant adorning a little girl's cheek when my cell phone chirped, telling me I had a new text message. I waited until the family left before reaching into my shoulder bag for the phone.

The message was from Bobby. He and Erin, my student assistant, would be stopping by the festival later that afternoon.

I put the phone back in my bag. Great, that was all I needed, I thought. And what was he doing with Erin?

Because the crafters were in tighter quarters on this side of the field, my small booth was wedged between the beaders and Lynette's tea cozies. When there was a lull in the crowd, I pulled my folding chair closer to the beaders. There were three of them. As they hunkered over their intricate work in full pioneer garb, they brought to mind the Wild West version of the three witches of Macbeth. The oldest of the group, a gray-haired lady with a pair of mother-of-pearl reading glasses perched on her pug nose, grunted. "There goes my last piece of jade."

"Where'd you drop it?" a second beader, who wasn't much older than Erin, asked. She had short purple hair peeking out from under her bonnet and a pronounced lisp.

"In the grass, where do you think? I'll never find it now," Beader Number One said.

The third beader, a rail-thin Asian woman with iron-straight black hair, stood and peered at the grass around Number One's feet.

"Forget it," Number One snapped. "You'll never find it. It's green and the darned grass is green." She looked up to find me watching them. She gave me a motherly smile. "Sorry about that. I just hate to lose a bead."

"I understand." I returned her smile.

"I'm Celeste. This is Beth," she said. "And that's Jendy." She pointed at the beader with purple hair.

Beth smiled at me shyly. "You're Carmen's sister, right?"

I nodded, steeling myself for another complaint about favoritism.

Jendy glanced up briefly from her pile of Czech glass beads. "You're the one who found Tess."

Beth opened a small tube filled with jungle green beads the size of eyeglass screws and poured them on the foam mat in front of her. Using needle-nose pliers, she picked up one of the beads and slid a fine metal chain through it.

"So what was it like? I mean, finding the body, was there a lot blood? Like on a cop show?" Jendy asked.

"Jendy, please." Beth looked like she might be sick. She shot a quick glance at Celeste, who was concentrating on her beads.

"It's not exactly like you see on TV," I said as the image of the back of Tess's head flashed in my mind.

Jendy's eyes sparkled. "Who do you think did it?"

"I have no idea. Did any of you know Tess well?" I asked.

Celeste sniffed. "I know Jerry, known him for years. If you

ask me, Tess was all wrong for him. You should have heard them fight. We're all members of the same crafter co-op. The co-op owns an old farm on Delia Road. Most of the crafters, myself included, have space inside the converted barn. Jerry has his own forge on the property."

I knew where the co-op was. It was right on the Summit-Portage county line and not far from Kent. The New Day Artists Cooperative was relatively new. It started while I was living in Chicago. I had meant to visit it after moving back to Stripling, but never got around to it.

"You see," Celeste said, interrupting my thoughts. She held up a beautiful teal and lavender glass bead. "I'm not just a beader. I make many of my own beads with glass flame work."

Jendy and Beth rolled their eyes at each other. Apparently, they'd heard about Celeste's bead-making skills one too many times.

I nodded encouragement.

"Jerry's the one who taught me how to use a blowtorch."

"Oh?" I said.

She nodded. "We are very close. In fact, he told me six months ago he was going to break it off with Tess."

I sat straighter in my chair. "Break it off how?"

Celeste paled. "I hope I'm not giving you the wrong idea. Jerry would never do anything to hurt Tess. He just wanted a divorce, or so I thought. He never said exactly what he planned to do."

Beth shook her head. "I still can't believe someone was murdered. It's so awful."

"Did you see anything out of the ordinary before you left yesterday?" I asked.

Jendy cocked her head. "That's a weird question. What are you, an undercover cop using face painting as a front?"

I laughed. "Oh, no. I'm just curious. Since I was the one who found Tess, the police have been asking me a lot of questions like that."

They shook their heads.

"On second thought," Beth said. "I left just before seven, and Tess was still here. She hadn't even started packing up her booth. I should have stopped her and asked what was going on, but I was in a hurry to get home to my kids." She bit her lip. "I remember thinking she looked like she was waiting for someone."

"Her son did mention that she planned to meet someone after the festival," I said.

Jendy nodded. "I thought that, too, when I left. I guess if the police find out who that was, they'll find out who did it."

As if it were that easy, I thought.

"Well, hello, ladies," Bobby greeted us in his most charming voice. "Those are gorgeous creations."

The three women fluttered under his gaze and compliment. Erin stood behind Bobby and rolled her eyes at me. She was a tall, lithe, natural redhead, who had the body of a prima ballerina, but she wanted to be a college professor. Go figure.

I introduced them to the group. Jendy in particular took a shine to Bobby. She asked him if he could open one of her jars of glass beads for her, saying it was on too tight. I nearly snorted.

Erin peered at me. "Do you have time to take a break? We need to talk."

I looked at my watch. It was after three, and I still hadn't eaten anything besides a pack of questionable cracker sandwiches I'd found at the bottom of my shoulder bag. There was a sizable crowd on the grounds, but no one seemed interested in getting their face painted.

I put up a cardstock BE BACK IN TEN MINUTES sign. "Let's go over to the food vendors. I'm starved."

I gravitated toward the elephant ears. "Extra powdered sugar, please," I told the vendor.

"No problem," he said with a plastic straw clenched in his teeth.

Erin wrinkled her pretty little nose. "Do you have any idea how many calories are in that?"

This concern must be why she was a size two, and I was, well, not. "Nope," I said. "What did you want to talk about?"

She waved her hand vaguely. "Oh, just that you found a dead body. Nothing major."

"Oh, that." The vendor handed me my heavenly elephant ear, and I paid him. "How'd you hear?"

"I have friend who lives in Derek's dorm."

I took a bite of my snack and noticed the elephant ear vendor was leaning toward us, straining to hear our conversation. I led Erin out of his earshot.

"I can't believe you are so calm about this," she said.

"I'm not, trust me. Does Bobby know?"

"Oh, yeah. He found out when that lady police officer brought sniffling Derek into the library. The officer told Bobby you said he'd take care of Derek."

"How'd that go over?"

She gave me a look.

"Just great. Does your friend know Derek well?"

Erin shook her head. It was like watching a shampoo commercial as her red-gold hair glistened in the fall sunlight. "No, he says no one in the dorm knows Derek that well. Not even his roommate. He's a shy kid. A loner."

"You make him sound like the Unabomber."

She shrugged. "Maybe he is."

"He's not." I paused. "He asked me to help him."

"Help him how?"

"To find out who killed his mother."

"You're kidding."

"Nope."

"All I have to say is you might want to update your résumé, because Provost Lepcheck is not going to stand for you snooping around another mystery on campus."

"There's something else. Derek is Lepcheck's nephew. Tess Ross was his sister."

Erin eyes widened. "Whoa!"

"Yeah. Well, we'd better get back."

Back at the booth, Jendy was showing Bobby her jewelry, and he oohed and aahed at all the appropriate times. When he saw me, he nodded his head to the right. I followed him to the other side of my booth. "I got your special delivery."

"Derek. Erin told me. Did you call him a pest?"

"Well, that's what he is. I can't believe you sent him over to me to babysit."

"His mother was just murdered. He had nowhere else to go."

"Speaking of the murder, you could have called or texted me about it. Instead, I found out from a cop stopping by the reference desk."

"Texted you? You want me to text you something like, 'Hey, found dead body. All good.' "

"It would have been nice to have been told by you." His eyes softened. "When I heard, I was worried. All I could think about was what happened last summer. You're not planning to get involved, are you?"

I didn't say anything.

"You are, aren't you? I appreciate what you did for me last summer, but this is different. You don't know the people involved this time. You—"

"Bobby, let's go." Erin came up from behind me.

I was grateful for the interruption. "You'd better get back to the library, or Lasha is going to send out a search party for you."

"This conversation is not over," Bobby said.

That much I knew.

Chapter Ten

At the end of the day, I packed up my car with paintings and paints to head home, but at the last second, I turned left, which was the opposite direction from my duplex, when leaving campus. The hot dog vendor in the minivan behind me made an obscene gesture as I abruptly changed my mind.

I turned into a small strip mall and parked in front of the office of Lewis Clive, Esq. Lew's office was in a storefront tucked in between a card shop and shoe store. I glanced into the shoe store's window. The snow boots were out in force. It wouldn't be long before they'd be needed.

A mechanical beep-beep sounded when I stepped into the office suite.

It was after six, so I wasn't surprised when the secretary's desk was empty. What did surprise me was who greeted me in her place. Sitting in the middle of the waiting room was none other than Zacchaeus, labradoodle extraordinaire.

Zach barked.

"Stop that confounded racket, Dog!" Lew bellowed from the back office where I knew he was smoking an unfiltered cigarette. The man was bound and determined to die of lung cancer.

I held out my hand to Zach and patted his head. That quieted him. "Lew?" I called. "It's India."

There was a pause. I could almost see him take a drag of his cigarette. "Come on back."

I wove around the receptionist's desk and down the short

hallway to Lew's office. Zach padded behind me down the carpeted hall.

"That dog had to come with you, did he?"

I patted Zach's head. "He's not so bad." Zach leaned against my leg.

Except for the framed diplomas on his walls and picture of his family on his desk, the room had as much personality as a mock-up office in an office supply warehouse. The walls were off-white. The floor was covered with industrial brown carpet, and the ceiling was dropped tile. I found the lack of color depressing.

"Take a seat." He motioned to the sofa situated underneath the lone window. Zach laid his head across my knees. Lew sat behind his metal desk, signing one legal-sized document after another at breakneck speed. "Just give me a minute. I promised my secretary I would get these signed before I headed home tonight." He signed one last document. "There."

Lew stood and patted his breast pocket. Deftly, he removed the pack of cigarettes he always kept there. He lit up, and I opened the window. A cold burst of late October air blew into the room, but it was better than the smell of Lew's cigarette smoke. Lew was a red-haired-going-to-gray, stocky, barrel-chested guy who kept my parents out of jail on a regular basis.

He pulled an armchair closer to the sofa and sat. "What did your parents do this time? Do you need bond money?"

Not for the first time, I realized most children have never heard the words "bond money" in reference to their parents. I wondered if they knew how lucky they were.

I crossed my jean-clad legs, forcing Zach to lie on the floor. He placed one of his paws firmly on my sneaker. "This isn't about Mom and Dad. As far as I know, they haven't broken any laws recently."

Lew blew out a long drag of smoke out the window. "I

imagine I will hear from them soon enough. The school board is dead set on tearing down the bell tower. Personally, I think tearing down the ugly thing is the right idea. It's a death trap. Don't tell your parents I said that."

My parents' latest crusade was having the high school's bell tower declared a historic landmark in order to stop the Stripling school board from demolishing it.

"So? What's up? Mark back in town?"

I shook my head sharply. "Maybe I should be asking you what's up. What's Zach doing here?"

Lew glanced down at the dog. "Do you know this pile of fur?"

"We met at the festival."

He focused on the Founder's Festival emblem embroidered on my polo shirt. "Oh, heck, are you involved in this mess too?"

"I discovered Tess's body," I said somewhat apologetically.

"The detective told me one of the crafters found her, but he most certainly didn't tell me it was *you.*" Lew took a drag of his cigarette as if fortifying himself. "Heck in a handbasket."

Considering Tess was a basket weaver, I wondered if Lew knew just how appropriate his curse was.

Lew looked bemused. "You sure have a knack for finding trouble, don't you?" Then his face turned sad. "Don't tell me you are going to play gumshoe again."

I shrugged.

"I'm sure Detective Mains will love that. If you're planning to crack the case, you're lagging way behind. He stopped by to drop off the dog."

"Why would he give you Zach?"

"Victor's will, of course. I imagine that's why you're here."

"Victor who?" I blinked in surprise.

"Victor Lepcheck, the deceased owner of that dog—that very wealthy dog, might I add."

"He wouldn't be any relation to Sam Lepcheck, would he?"

"Don't remind me. He was his uncle and therefore he is also Tess's uncle, too."

I looked at Zach, who had fallen asleep at my feet. "Tess took Zach after her uncle died."

Lew nodded and took another drag from his cigarette. "And the sizable trust that came with him."

"How much money are we talking?"

"Two million."

I nearly choked. "Two million dollars? And it belongs to the dog?"

"It's in a trust." He flattened his hands on his desk blotter. "Please don't tell me your parents are also mixed up in this."

"Nope. They are too busy saving the bell tower right now to take on any other causes."

His face smoothed. "Well, then, I'll write a personal letter of thanks to the Stripling school board for putting up a fight against them." He sat back.

I just thought of something for the first time. "Where'd Zach come from?"

Lew squinted at me. "I just told you. Mains dropped him off."

"No, that's not what I meant. Where was he last night? Tess was at the festival, and Jerry was at the forge. I saw him before he knew about Tess's death, and Zach wasn't with him."

"Mains told me he found the dog at Tess's house. Jerry said he dropped him off there before going on to the forge because he knew Tess would be home from the festival soon."

"So you are the Lepcheck family lawyer?"

"No, I only represented Victor and his dog by default."

"How long were you Victor's lawyer?"

"For twenty miserable years. Your parents are a walk in the park in comparison to Victor Lepcheck."

I frowned. "That bad?"

He gnawed on the end of his cigarette. "Zach's here because Victor never wrote in his will who would receive Zach and his sizable trust if Zach outlived Tess. Because Tess died before the mutt, I take possession of the dog until an agreement can be reached."

"Wouldn't Zach go to Provost Lepcheck as the surviving family member?"

"You'd be right if he were the only one. Tess also had a sister, Debra."

"You're kidding."

He shook his head. "I wish I were. Debra Wagtail. She lives in one of those new condo complexes that are popping up all over the countryside like manicured weeds." He shook another cigarette out of the pack. "And to make matters worse, Tess's husband, Jerry Ross, insists Zach should go to him since he helped care for the dog. Tess's son is also a possible heir. If they can't all come to some kind of agreement, this is going to go on for years."

I made a sympathetic noise. "Who has the best claim to the trust?"

He took a drag on his cigarette. "Both Debra and Sam have an equal claim, although they are both petitioning for sole custody of the dog and, of course, the dog's money. As if it will help them, they're both saying they'll use some of the money for charities. They can't do anything with it until Zach dies because it's for his care, but after the dog passes away the caretaker gets everything to use as he or she wants."

"What charities?"

"Sam claims Victor would have wanted him to have the money in order to support programs at Martin College. On the other hand, Debra claims Victor would have wanted her to have the money because she was Victor's caretaker during the last few years of his life. He suffered from Parkinson's. He was lucky though. He died before he lost the ability to speak or walk."

I didn't know if I would consider anyone with Parkinson's lucky.

I held up a hand. "Back up. If Debra was the caretaker, why didn't Victor leave the dog's trust in her hands in the first place?"

Lew shrugged. "He never said, and I try not to pry when my clients ask me to draw up their wills. I think the more obvious question was why he left his fortune to a dog, but I didn't ask that one, either. I wish I had."

I wished he had, too.

"Victor has the remarkable ability to be an even bigger pain in the rear in death than he was in life. That's quite an accomplishment."

"I'll do anything I can to help," I said.

A glint sparkled in his eye, and I had a sinking feeling in the pit of my stomach. "Actually, I do have a way you can help me. My wife is terribly afraid of dogs. She was bitten as a child by a neighbor's pooch."

"Was she okay?" I asked.

"Oh, yeah, she was fine. It was just a nip, really." He pointed at Zach. "However, if I bring him home, divorce is imminent. I don't have time to go through a messy divorce."

"What are you saying?" My stomach churned.

"Why don't you dog-sit Zacchaeus for me while this legal battle is going on?"

"I have no legal right to the dog."

He waved my concern away. "And that's why you should have him instead of one of those yahoos. It's only temporary. You'll be serving in the capacity of a doggie foster care."

"You said this could go on for months. I can't keep a dog for months."

"Fine, fine, can you just keep him for the next couple of days until I find a good kennel for him? Lord knows, he can afford the best."

I looked down at Zach, who was still fast asleep on my tennis shoes.

"I . . . I don't know. Ina might not be happy if I had a dog in my apartment."

"Please, you know as well as I do Ina will be thrilled."

"I have a cat."

"They'll be best buds in no time."

Yeah, right, I thought. I still had scars from the last time I'd tried to introduce a new animal into Templeton's domain.

He scribbled on a piece of computer paper. "Here. I have written a permission slip for you with the date and my signature in case you run into any naysayers." He signed the page with a flourish and handed it to me. Dumbly, I took it.

The note read, "India Hayes will be caring for Zacchaeus Lepcheck, dog of the late Victor Lepcheck, while Victor Lepcheck's estate is under dispute. Sincerely, Lewis S. Clive, Esq."

I doubted the legality of the note, but Lew knew better than I.

Lew straightened stacks of files on his desk and rose from his chair with a tired groan. "Well, you'd better be going if you want to get Zacchaeus's walk in before dinner."

I left the office with Zach on leash and a large cardboard box containing his favorite dog food, toys, and a pooper scooper.

Chapter Eleven

On the way home, Zach sat in the front seat of my car with his head outside the window, tongue flapping in the wind. I glanced over at him. How did I get myself into these things? I wondered. Oh, right. No backbone. The truth be told, I felt bad for Zach. Poor dog alone in the world without his master, and the only reason anyone wanted him was for his money. I hoped Templeton would understand.

I parked in my gravel driveway and let Zacchaeus out of the passenger seat. I thought the best recourse was to break Templeton in slowly. It was dark when I let Zach loose in the fenced backyard. I turned on my back porch light, got a couple of old dishes from the garage, and filled one bowl with water and another with kibble. Zach ate and drank hungrily, and then he was off barking at an unsuspecting cardinal who had perched on the fence. I glanced at Ina's back window, expecting to see her elfin face peering through the curtains. It wasn't there. I wondered if she was out with her crony Juliet.

I went inside my apartment through the sliding glass door. Templeton stood on the back of the couch. His eyes were narrowed, and his fangs peeked out from under his upper lip like sharp white toothpicks.

"Sweetie," I said tentatively. "I'm home. We are going to have a visitor for a couple of days."

Templeton growled deep in his throat. There was going to be heck to pay. I stroked his back, but he ran away from me to the bedroom. Absently, I wondered which pair of shoes would be graced with the regurgitated hairball this time.

I popped a French bread pizza in the oven and dug out my Summit County phonebook. I flipped to the Ws. There was only one Wagtail listed, "Wagtail, D. & D." While I still had momentum, I dialed her number. The call went directly to voicemail. I hung up without leaving a message.

The timer went off, and I was about to sit on the couch to scarf down my pizza when someone knocked at the door. Templeton, who had returned to the living room with the promise of pizza crumbs, bolted down the short hallway to my bedroom.

I recognized the knock. It was a relentless rata-tat-tat. It could be the knock of only one person.

I put my pizza down after taking a quick bite, chewing and swallowing as I made my way to the door.

Ina pushed her way in, heading straight for my rocking chair, her favorite seat in my apartment. I closed the door and followed her back to the living room with as much excitement as a pacifist heading off to war.

"Is that a dog in my backyard?" Ina asked in her baby-bird voice.

"I'm dog-sitting for a few days," I said, hoping it really was only a few days. "If you don't like it, I can take him back."

Ina grinned. "Don't even think about it. I love dogs. I would have one if I didn't have to pick up its poop. I don't do that. I hope you know that will be your job."

I nodded. Oh, joy. I returned to my place on the couch.

Ina rocked. "Oh, you're eating dinner. Kind of late, isn't it? I read in a magazine you should never eat after seven at night. It slows down your metabolism. You might be thin now, but thirty is just around the corner and you'd better start watching your figure."

I picked up my pizza and took a bite.

Ina shook her head sadly. "Juliet and I staked out the square today," she remarked as if she spoke of a garden party, although it was difficult to imagine Ina at a garden party.

I almost choked on my pizza. I put the plate on the coffee table. "Did you say 'staked out'?"

"I was on the lookout for more jaywalkers. I told Juliet what a rampant problem it was becoming and that the police weren't doing anything about it. So this morning, we decided to go over there and take a count. We counted ten jaywalkers in eight hours."

"You were on the square for eight hours?"

"There is no reason we shouldn't be. It's a public park, and we pay our taxes."

As if that were my only concern.

"I think the jaywalking upturn can easily be blamed on the public school system in this town."

Here we go.

"Children are no longer being taught jaywalking is a crime. And not only that, but they could put themselves or someone else in danger. They could be hit by a car, and what shame that would be." She thought for a moment. "Maybe I should talk to your parents about this problem. They are good at mobilizing people."

"Don't even think about it."

Ina shot me a reproachful look.

"I mean, I don't think it's a good idea to bother them right now. They're so busy with the bell tower campaign. They wouldn't be able to fully commit themselves to your cause."

Ina shrugged and rocked back in her seat. Her moccasin-covered feet dangled several inches above the scarred hardwood floor. "I'll talk to Juliet about it to see if she thinks it's a good idea."

Of course, Ina's yes-woman would be all for the recruitment of my parents.

Ina reached into her pocket and pulled out a folded piece of paper. "Take a look at this. I made these fliers up this morning. Juliet and I made copies at the public library. We made fifty, and we already need more."

I looked down at the white piece of copy paper. The original message had been handwritten in block letters. No doubt, it was Ina's handiwork; she had yet to enter the wonderful world of word processing, let alone the Internet. The message read, "Jaywalking is a crime. Keep this up, and you're going to the slammer." As a final touch, Ina had drawn a stick figure locked behind bars. Persuasive.

"What do you think?" Ina asked.

"Are you sure you're allowed to pass these out?"

"Allowed to pass these out? What do you think free speech is for?" She snatched the flier from my hand.

I picked up my pizza. "They might be perceived as threatening."

Ina harrumphed.

I backpedaled for the sake of keeping the peace. "Don't worry. My parents have handed out more-damning leaflets in their day."

Ina seemed pacified but remained in her seat. From years of experience I knew she had another bee in her bonnet, so to speak. "Was there anything else, Ina?"

She tilted her head, reminding me of Zach. "Juliet told me a terrible rumor today."

"She did?" I shook my head, fearing I knew what the rumor was about.

"She told me you were the one who found Tess Ross's body at the festival."

Leave it to Ina to lead the conversation with jaywalking, and then finally get around to murder. I put my plate back on the table. "I did."

"And you didn't tell me."

"I didn't want to worry you."

Ina made a fake sniffling sound and buried her head in her sleeve for a moment. I rolled my eyes. When she looked up her eyes were clear. "Well, what are you going to do about it?" Ina swung her legs back and forth, using her momentum to rock the heavy wooden chair.

"What do you mean?"

"Aren't you going to find the killer?"

"That's Mains's job, not mine."

"Oh, yes, and he did so well last time. If it weren't for you, he'd still have no idea who offed the Blocken girl."

I winced. "He would've figured it out eventually."

Ina snorted. "So you're going to go about your day like nothing happened?"

Templeton walked back into the room, jumped onto the couch, and curled up in my lap. I stroked his silky black fur and felt calmer. He always knew when I needed his feline support, even with a dog in the backyard.

Ina narrowed her eyes. "It's Victor Lepcheck's dog, isn't it?"

"How do you know that?"

"Please, everybody knows about Zacchaeus after the settlement of Victor's will. There was a three-page article about it in the *Stripling Dispatch* when the story was released. The question is, why do *you* have the dog?"

I opened my mouth to answer.

"I'll tell you why. Zacchaeus and his trust were willed to Tess and now that Tess is dead no one knows who should get the dog and his money." She rocked back in her chair with a smug expression on her face.

I never said Ina wasn't sharp.

"He prefers Zach."

"Who gave you the dog?"

"Lew. His wife's not a dog person."

Ina smiled. "This is just grand, a key witness right here in our midst. That's going to make it easier for us to solve the case."

I let the *us* slide. "It's just a favor for Lew. You know how many times he's gotten my parents out of a jam."

"I guess if you really are just dog-sitting, you wouldn't be interested in talking to a key suspect."

I couldn't help myself. "Who?"

"Debra Wagtail."

"Tess's sister. I was just trying to call her."

"Ah-ha!" Ina raised her fist in triumph.

"Okay, okay, you got me. Do you know Debra?"

"I most certainly do. We both volunteer for the city's garden club."

Secretly, I hoped Debra's work for the garden club was more productive than Ina's, which mainly focused on placing as many leprechauns as possible on the city's public lands. Once she even placed a leprechaun-inspired topiary in front of the public library. The library's director let it sit out there for all of five minutes after Ina left.

"Weren't you kicked out of the garden club?" I asked.

"Those monkeys have no concept of yard art. Maybe I should talk to your parents about building a case around that issue, too," she added thoughtfully.

I shivered at the very idea.

"Anyway, Debra was one of the few goofballs in the club who was nice to me. She said my leprechauns were cute."

I picked up my pizza again took a big bite. I figured if my mouth was full, I wouldn't say anything to get her going. The pizza was cold. I swallowed. "I need to talk to Debra as soon as possible."

Ina snapped her fingers. "Who do you think did it? Who are your suspects? Who have you talked to? Why are you doing it?" She jumped off the rocking chair and hopped up and down with each question.

The pizza was gone.

"Calm down. You're going to give yourself a heart attack, and I'm not in the mood to give you CPR." Ina didn't sit, but she stopped hopping.

"Derek Welch, Tess's son, works at the library. He asked me to look into the murder for him, and I said I would as a favor."

Ina plopped down on the rocking chair, sending it careening back and forth. She regained her balance. "You did?"

"Yes." I said, not feeling the need to elaborate. "And I need your help. Do you think you can call Debra and set up a meeting for me?"

"No problemo." Ina's eyes sparkled, then narrowed. "I'm coming along."

"Uhhh."

"She doesn't know you. She won't open up to you like she will to me. If you want me to call her, I'm going."

"Well . . ."

"And if you say no, I will call her and tell her not to talk to you," she said with triumph, folding her arms across her green sweater–setted chest.

What choice did I have? "Ina, do you want to come along with me to interview Debra?"

"Why, yes, India, I do. Thank you for asking."

Chapter Twelve

It was already after eight in the evening when Zach and I arrived at my mother's big brick Presbyterian church on the town square. As was tradition the Friday before Halloween, the church held its annual Fall Family Fling. The party was set to end at nine, and I debated skipping it altogether, but I decided in the long run it would require more energy to explain myself to my mother for not showing than to go.

I went to the basement of the church where the fellowship hall was located. Zach nosed the floor on every third step. Outside the fellowship hall, a large easel stood by the open doors. Zach and I paused to take it in. It was a poster asking for recruits to bear arms as part of the bell tower crusade. An eight-by-ten photo of the tower was pasted to the middle of the poster board with the question, "Do you want to lose part of your heritage?" I looked down at Zach, and we shared an eye roll.

I peeked into the room. My mother was in middle of the activity. Her long gray ponytail swayed excitedly back and forth as she made the rounds, asking the sick about their health, the young about school, and the married about their families. She always knew the best angle necessary to connect with each person. She'd give the best baby-kissing politician a run for his money. In addition to the usual church members and families from the neighborhood, the fellowship hall also contained members of my parents' bell-saving brigade. They were easy to pick out. Think "hippie meets hip replacement surgery."

Even though she was in the middle of trying to save the Founders' Festival from complete ruin, Carmen and her family were there. She and Chip, each with a baby daughter in their laps, sat with another couple from the church at one of the dozen or so round tables peppered throughout the room. A chrysanthemum sat in the middle of each table.

We stepped into the room. Instantly, the children, including my five-year-old nephew Nicholas, who was a mini version of his father, were at my feet petting Zach. "A dog!" they cried.

Across the hall, Mom folded her arms across her chest. As far as I knew there was no rule in the Presbyterian decrees that you couldn't bring a dog into a church building, but the look on my mother's face told me she thought there should be. A parishioner mercifully blocked her path for a chat as she made her way over to me.

I pulled on Zach's leash, feeling a little bit like the Pied Piper as I led Zach's fan club to a corner of the room, near the table of carved pumpkins. The pumpkins waited to be judged for the jack-o'-lantern-making contest, a contest I used to win every year until I was too old to enter. The age was capped at twelve. I tied Zach's leash to one of the legs of the long cafeteria-style table.

"Can you guys watch him for me?" I asked.

"Yeah," was the proclamation, and the kids knelt next to Zach and continued their petting and hugging of him.

"Okay," I said. "But whatever you do, don't untie him."

"We won't," they said.

I patted Nicholas's head. "I'm putting you in charge, Nicko."

He nodded solemnly. "I'll take care of the doggie, Dia."

"Good. His name is Zacchaeus."

"I know that song!" a little girl exclaimed. "We learned it in Bible school."

As if on cue, they began singing about the wee little man in the sycamore tree.

I was weaving my way to the dessert table—there was a piece of pumpkin pie with my name on it—when my mother grabbed my elbow. "India, I'm glad you could make it." She made a show of looking at her watch.

I picked up the pie plate and a fork.

"Where did that dog come from? And why did you bring it to the church?"

I sat at the closest empty table. Dad, who was trying to untangle himself from a building-fund debate with an elder, wheeled in our direction. He parked his wheelchair next to me. Dad glanced over at the dog—or what he could see of him through the mass of children. "Sure is a nice-looking dog."

Mom pursed her lips. Dad'd been hinting at wanting a dog for the last several months. He was big fan of animal rescue shows on cable television.

"Lew asked me to dog-sit. It was Tess Ross's dog. Well, sort of. It's complicated." I said this hoping she wouldn't ask me why I found it so complicated.

Mom's eyebrows went up. "Carmen told us what happened. Your father and I knew Tess, although not well. Didn't we, Alden?"

My father nodded. "Hey, is that Victor Lepcheck's dog?"

I nodded.

"I thought I recognized him."

"Did you know Victor?"

Dad shrugged. "He was an acquaintance, nothing more than that. Did you hear there was a kerfuffle about his estate after he died?"

Only my father could get away with saying "kerfuffle" in everyday speech.

"There was. There still is, in fact. Tess was the dog's trustee, and now that she's gone, it's up in the air what will happen to him."

"But why do you have him?" Mom asked.

"Lew was Victor's lawyer and executor of his estate. His wife's afraid of dogs."

"How could she be afraid of him?" Dad asked. "Look how well he's getting along with the kids?"

Mom wrinkled her brow. "It's such a shame about Tess. She was so full of life. I can't imagine who would want to do something like that to her." She sat at the table. "I want you to be careful, India. If there's some kind of crazed lunatic running around the campus . . ."

"I don't think it was a crazed lunatic," I said.

"Why not? That's what Carmen said. And it's close to Halloween. That's when the crazies rear their heads."

If it was a crazy running loose, what was I doing trying to solve the murder for Derek? I'd never be able to find such a person.

"Did Carmen get this idea from the police? Does she know something I don't know?"

"Speaking of police, is Ricky on the case?" Dad asked.

Mom frowned. "That silly boy. If it were up to him, Mark would be in prison."

I found myself defending Mains. "I'm sure he'd have come to the right conclusion eventually."

My parents looked dubious. They didn't have much faith in the *man,* especially if the man was in uniform. However, since Mains was a detective, I guess he'd be a plainclothes representation of the man.

"I'll let you get away with it this time, but no more dogs in church. You'll give the members ideas. I don't want poodles hanging around the sanctuary when I serve communion."

"I shouldn't have the dog for too much longer. Lew's looking for a kennel to place him in."

Dad's mouth turned down. "Seems a shame to put such a nice dog in the kennel. Look how he's making up with the kids."

Mom's lips drew a thin line across her face, and I finished the rest of my pie.

"You're not going to get involved in this murder like the last one, are you?" Mom asked.

"You were in involved in the last one, too."

"It involved my son. Speaking of which, have you heard from Mark?"

"Got another postcard."

Dad looked up. "From where this time?" His tone was sad.

Mom crossed her arms. "I don't know why he's sending you postcards and not us."

I shrugged and reached into my shoulder bag. I handed Mom the postcard from Mark. She read it. "All it tells us is he's in Utah. It says nothing of where he's staying or what he's doing to make a living."

Dad's mouth was downturned. "It doesn't say when he's coming home?"

Sometimes I envied Mark for running away from his life. I wondered why I couldn't do that. Weren't artists supposed to be free spirits? Where was my free spirit? And I was the youngest. Wasn't the youngest supposed to be the irresponsible one? Somewhere birth order fell apart in my family.

Screams erupted. "The doggie ate my pumpkin!"

I turned in time to see Zach wolf down the last remnants of a jack-o'-lantern.

"India!" my mother bellowed, and trust me, my mother can bellow loudly. I don't think a foghorn on an old-time riverboat could be half as deafening. "Get that dog out of here."

Chapter Thirteen

Before going to bed, I settled Zach in my tiny kitchen with an old bed pillow. He was out the moment his curly head hit the pillow. My heart went out to the lovable scruffy-looking pooch. He'd lost Victor, his beloved master, and now was being passed around Stripling like a white elephant gift.

In the morning, I wasn't feeling nearly as sympathetic. Apparently, a small apartment wasn't adequate housing for a hostile feline and a bear-sized labradoodle. During the night, Zach had knocked a glass of soda off of my coffee table, eaten my favorite pair of flip-flops, and sent Templeton into a state of continuous nervous hissing.

I found him lying on the couch in my artist's studio with a glob of yellow oil paint on the tip of his nose. My easel was upturned and throw pillows were shredded beyond recognition. Zach gave me a lazy doggie grin.

I could have sworn I'd closed the door to the studio before going to bed. I glanced back at Templeton, who was hissing softly to himself in the rocking chair. I wondered if he'd let Zach into the studio. Templeton bore his yellow-green eyes into me and let out a loud, triumphant hiss. I'd bet my life on it. Templeton had opened the door.

I cleaned up the soda and the dog and released Zach into the backyard. There was no way I was going through another night of that. I would have to find a suitable doghouse for the time being. I added "buy doghouse" to my to-do list. It sat right under "catch a killer." Why did everything seem so much more manageable once it was on paper? I wondered.

An hour later, I walked around the side of the duplex with Zach on a leash to find Ina on my glider. She wore her best green polyester pantsuit and pillbox hat and clutched a matching tote bag bursting at the seams. This couldn't be good.

I avoided eye contact. "Morning, Ina."

She jumped up and followed me to my car. She was at the passenger side door before I fobbed the car unlocked.

"What are you doing?" I asked. I could just see the top of her pillbox hat over the car's roof.

"I'm helping with the investigation."

Oh, boy.

I gritted my teeth. "We agreed you'd come with me to talk to Debra. Nothing more."

"That's not how I understood it." She adjusted her pillbox hat. "Now, are you going to unlock the door? This bag is heavy. I have osteoporosis, you know, if I hold this bag much longer, my whole arm could snap clean off."

I unlocked the door.

When the three of us were settled in the car, Ina gave me the once-over. "Where's that lovely pink dress you wore to the festival the first day?"

Et tu, Ina?

"I'd like to get me one of those. Do they have any extras?" She buckled her seatbelt.

"Umm, I don't know. You'd have to ask Carmen."

"I'll do that."

Great. I should keep my big mouth shut, I thought.

"Just give me a head start first," I said.

She gave me a perplexed look.

Twenty minutes later, we stood in front of my booth. I produced a chew bone for Zach, and he settled underneath the table with a contented sigh. Then, I unfolded the extra folding chair I'd snagged from the garage before leaving home. This had been an excellent thought because Ina had already commandeered my chair.

I handed Ina the box of paints and told her to help set up. She plopped the box on the table. "Done."

"If you really want to help, you could take the paints out of the box so the children can see all the different colors." I set my paintings on the tabletop easels.

Ina huffed. "I'm not here to be your servant. I'm a working P.I. today. I need to get cracking on this case."

It was going to be a very, very long day.

"Fine," I said. "Why don't you interview some of the vendors?"

"Really?" Ina grinned.

"Sure." I pointed at Lynette, who fussed over her crocheted kingdom. "You can start with her. She knew Tess."

Ina glanced over at Lynette, straightened her hat so the shamrock, which she'd added for a little Blarney flare, dangled over her left eye. "I'm on it." Ina scuttled away. A minute later, I heard her coo, "What lovely tea cozies you have!"

I could never say something like that with a straight face, but for Ina, it worked. I watched Lynette lay out her best cozies for Ina to peruse. I hoped they would keep each other occupied for the rest of the morning.

I finished setting up the booth, just in time for the first onslaught of children to arrive. "I want an elephant," one screamed.

"I want a butterfly. An orange one!"

"Me first!" A little boy in a yellow shirt shoved his sister out of the way. The harried mother shook her head in despair.

In the middle of playing referee as the children clamored for face paint, I lost track of Ina. When I looked at Lynette's booth again, she was gone. Carmen was going to kill me when she found out Ina was loose on the premises.

Before I could go look for her, my sister showed up. Again, she pushed the double stroller with my nieces inside. "I have a situation, and you need to fix it."

"Me? Why me?"

"Because this is your campus."

I knew it was a bad idea to have the festival at Martin. I knew I'd be the one paying for it. "What's the situation?"

"Those otter haters are in the parking lot passing out pamphlets. They're scaring festivalgoers away."

"I don't think they're otter haters. I think they're protesting because they're otter lovers."

"I don't care what they are, just get rid of them. Now."

"Did you call campus security?"

"Yes, and that Mutt person sent over a pimpled-faced teenager to do the job. The otter people laughed at him."

"You should be used to this type of thing, Carmen, considering who our parents are."

"Of course, I'm used to it, but I don't want it happening on my watch. I saw two cars drive away when they saw those kids in the parking lot."

"You don't know that's why they left."

"Yes, I do, because I saw the kids chasing them out of the parking lot waving their flyers about otter equal rights, whatever that is."

"I don't know what I can do."

"India, I can't take it. Between the murder and now these otter people, the festival is going up in flames. I will be the laughingstock of the community." She raked a hand through her hair, mussing her perfectly styled bob.

"Fine, fine. I'll go see what I can do."

"Thank you." Her eyes narrowed. "I expect you to be in your

pioneer dress tomorrow."

I put my hands on my hips. "No way. I'm not taking care of these kids, and then wearing that pink nightmare tomorrow." I sat back down to make my point.

"Fine. You don't have to wear the dress. Your breaking the dress code is the least of my worries." She pushed the girls and the stroller away.

I went off to find some otters.

Chapter Fourteen

I found the SOEC in the parking lot, pamphlets in hand. Erin said most Martin students referred to them as "So-Ick" because of their questionable hygiene.

The lone security guard shouted into the din, trying to be heard. "You must leave this area." He didn't look any older than the students he was yelling at. His skin was blotchy, and I wondered if he would break out in hives from the strain.

I almost retreated. A car turned into the lot. It held an elderly couple, who were obviously there to attend the festival. Their eyes widened when they saw the scruffy band of SOEC members. They circled the lot, threw a last regretful look at the students, then abandoned the parking lot for the open road. Although unlikely, they might have bought one of my paintings or been the source of my next big commission. Carmen was right; the SOEC crew was a problem.

I approached the person I assumed was the leader of the group by the way the female members hovered around him in a fascinated orbit. He was a white kid with blond dreadlocks and wire-rim glasses. Dreadlocks might work on some people, like reggae singers, but on this kid they resembled dirty blond sponges. By the way the girls hung on his every word, I guessed I held the minority opinion about his hairstyle.

Dreads looked me up and down. "Hey, you're in my psych class, aren't you? Want to help the cause?"

I sighed. I certainly hoped when I hit thirty years old, which I could see off in the not-too-distant horizon, I would no longer be confused with a student. I'm told I should take the confusion as a compliment, but it was most definitely a hindrance when I tried to exude authority.

The girls bared their teeth at me. Never fear, ladies. I'm so not interested, I thought.

"Uh, no. I'm not a student. I'm a librarian here."

"The library is on the other side of campus."

I tried hard not to sigh again. "I know that. I'm also helping out with the festival, and I'm going to have to ask you to leave."

"We aren't bothering anyone," a girl piped up.

"Actually, you are. You're scaring people away from the festival."

"Are you India Hayes?"

I nodded.

"Your parents rock," Dreads said. "I met them at a rally a couple weeks ago. They are awesome even though they're so old. They gave me a lot of pointers about having my voice heard."

Carmen would be so thrilled to learn we had our parents to thank for the uproar.

"They'll be glad to hear it. It would be a big help to us—to my parents even—if you could move this . . . disagreement to another part of campus."

"But this is where the community is hanging. We are spreading the word."

"That's admirable, of course," I said, placating.

One of the girls stepped forward. She was a petite Indian student with heavy eye makeup. "I heard you're going to find out who killed that woman on Thursday."

My head snapped around. "Who told you that?"

She shrugged. "Everyone's talking about it."

"Yeah," another agreed. "It's huge. This is the first big thing to happen on campus all year."

This was all said by people who weren't related to the victim, who didn't know her, who didn't find her body and crushed skull. I could blame their interest on violent television, video games, or just plain media altogether, but I suspected people had been morbidly interested in these things before the media was ever involved. It always came back to the chicken or the egg.

The Indian girl spoke up. "It totally creeped me out to think I was nearby when the murder might have been going down."

"Nearby? What do you mean?"

"I was riding my bike back to the dorm after a late class and heard some people fighting on the practice field as I rode by."

"When was that?"

She thought. "Class got out at seven-fifteen, so probably seven-thirty."

And I discovered Tess's body at eight-thirty. What the girl said fit in with both Doc's and my timetables. She probably did hear the killer.

"What did the voices sound like? Male? Female?"

"It was hard to tell. I didn't hang around to listen. I wanted to get out of there. One was definitely female. I could tell she was upset."

"You didn't call security?" There was an accusatory tone in my voice.

The girl winced. "I just thought it was some couple fighting. You hear that all the time on campus. I didn't think it was serious."

I smiled at her. "It's okay," I said, even though it wasn't. A quick cell phone call could have saved Tess's life. I didn't say that. I didn't want to put the weight of Tess's death on her thin shoulders. Truthfully, I didn't know if I wouldn't have done the same thing.

"What's your name?"

"Raka."

"Did you tell the police what you saw?"

"They never asked me."

"That's because they didn't know you were there. You need to talk to them. Your information narrows down the time of death. It will make it easier to find who is responsible."

"I don't know if I want to get involved. I shouldn't have said anything."

Dreads swung an arm over Raka's shoulder. "You have to, babe. You're cracking the case. You'll be a hero. You'll be protecting people just like we protect the otters."

The crowd of disheveled students agreed. "You're a hero, Raka," one said.

Raka glowed with the cause. I'd seen the same expression on my parents too many times to count.

"I can take you to talk to an officer now. There's one here at the festival," I said.

She nodded.

I thanked the rest of the group and suggested the library quad, which was right in the middle of campus, for their campaign. Hopefully, it wouldn't get back to Lasha that I was the one who sent them there. I wasn't sure whether the SOEC kids or the corn hole tournament would have been worse.

"She'll catch up with you guys later," I said and led Raka back to the festival.

As luck would have it, Office Habash was walking by. I waved her over. "Raka, tell her what you told me."

Habash listened carefully. "This is very important information you have. I'm going to need to take you to the Justice Center for a statement."

Raka's dark brown eyes became huge. "I don't know."

"It's no big deal," I said. "My parents are there at least once a week."

Habash smiled. "It will take a half hour at most."

"Oh, okay."

Habash looked at me. Her black eyes were questioning. "Should I tell Detective Mains you were the one who brought Raka to our attention?"

"Please don't."

"No problem."

I smiled. Was I wrong, or were Officer Habash and I becoming friends? Now, if I could just win Knute over, I thought.

Back at my booth, Ina waited impatiently. I blinked when I saw her ensemble. She wore a green gingham dress and buckle shoes as well as her shamrock-laden pillbox hat. If she wanted to be historically accurate, Ina needed to replace the pillbox hat with a mobcap. Not that I was surprised. Even on a normal day, Ina was a walking anachronism.

"Where'd you find that getup?"

"I have my sources." She wiggled her brows.

I let it go. I hoped there wasn't a naked crafter running around the premises because Ina had swiped her dress.

She held two cups of fresh-squeezed lemonade. She handed me one. Zach half-rose to sniff my drink but snorted, returning to his bone.

"Where've you been?" I asked.

"Investigating." She squirmed in the folding chair.

"How did your talk with Lynette go?"

"Just fine. She had a lot to say about the investigation."

"You told her you were investigating?" Lemonade sloshed onto my jeans. I grabbed a paper towel from the supply I kept under the table. Between the students' rumors on campus and Ina's big mouth, the whole world would know I was interested in Tess's murder before the day was over.

"No, I told her you were investigating, and I was helping out."

More lemonade splashed.

"When she goes on break at one o'clock, I'm having lunch with her to talk about the case."

I gulped the lemonade to avoid saying anything I'd regret later. My cell phone rang . . . well, it croaked. I'd found this great frog ringtone online.

Ina looked at me curiously. "There's a frog in your purse."

"It's my phone." I pulled the flip phone out of my shoulder bag and looked at the caller ID. It was a Martin College number but not from the library. "Hello?"

"Is this India Hayes?" a prim female voice asked over the line.

"Yes."

"This is Deena Beaton in Provost Lepcheck's office. The provost would like to have a meeting with you."

"With *me?*"

"Yes," she replied coolly.

"How did you get this number?"

She sniffed as if offended. "Your colleague from the library, Robert McNally, was gracious enough to share it with me. He said you wouldn't mind under the circumstances."

I'll bet he did.

"Why does Dr. Lepcheck want to meet with me?" I tried to soften my tone. It was never a good idea to irritate the provost's administrative assistant since she was the one who mailed the faculty contracts in the spring. There was always a chance she might misplace mine.

"Well, umm, he didn't say exactly." She sounded disappointed with herself for not knowing.

"I'm working at the Founders' Festival today. Could I meet with him another time?"

"Ah, yes, I remember now that Dr. Lepcheck granted you release time for that," she said as if she disapproved of the decision, which she probably did. "Nevertheless, he needs to meet with you right away. It's important."

I glanced at Ina. I might as well take full advantage of the situation she'd placed me in. I covered the mouthpiece with my hand. "Can you watch the booth for a couple of hours? I have a meeting with Lepcheck."

Ina nodded eagerly.

"I'll come to the office within ten minutes," I told Deena.

Deena cleared her throat. "The provost is not on campus today. He'd like you meet with him at his home."

"His home?" I asked dumbly.

"Yes," she said and rattled off the address and directions.

Chapter Fifteen

Lepcheck's home was in one of the newer developments in Stripling, a clustering of McMansions on postage-stamp lawns, which set my parents' teeth on edge. The house was a large affair covered with Palladian windows and dominating the end of a cul-de-sac at the edge of the neighborhood. Construction people in bright orange hardhats broke ground just beyond Lepcheck's home to plant more houses.

I rang the doorbell. It sounded a melodic chime deep in the house. The door was wide and arched, reminiscent of the entry to a medieval castle. Zach sat obediently at my side as we waited for the door to be answered. I'd thought about leaving him behind at the festival with Ina, but then I feared I'd return to a labradoodle covered in paint.

If I'd expected a butler—and part of me had—I was sadly mistaken because Lepcheck opened the door. "Thank you for coming. Won't you . . ." He stopped abruptly when he saw Zach at my side. "What is that *animal* doing here?"

I had never heard the use of the word *animal* as profanity, but Lepcheck certainly made the word sound that way in the tone he used. Zach, blissfully unaware, woofed a greeting.

"I'm looking after Zach for Lewis Clive, Victor's lawyer."

Lepcheck sniffed. "I'm well aware of who Lewis Clive is. Why did he give you, of all people, custody of this animal?"

There went the profane use of *animal* again. Seriously, Lepcheck was changing my understanding of the word. I thought for a moment before answering. Wasn't Lepcheck fighting with his one surviving sister over Zach? Didn't he want the dog in order to access the pooch's wealth? You'd think he be friendlier to Zach in that case.

"Lew's wife is afraid of dogs, and I offered to help by taking Zach until he can find a good kennel. I have a note from him, if you would like to see it?"

He sniffed a second time. "That won't be necessary."

"Then, can we come in? You did ask me to come here, not the other way around."

"You may come in, but Zacchaeus may not. I have many valuable antiques. He will break them."

What's going to stop Zach from breaking your antiques when he lives with you? I wondered. Because didn't the dog have to live with Lepcheck for him to get his hands on the trust money? Debra had to be better than her insufferable brother. I hoped Debra liked dogs.

I glanced around the front yard. It was a small patch of lush green grass with the otherworldly green glow of a recent lawn service treatment visit. Sure enough, when I looked farther down the lawn, I saw one of those little white flags from the lawn company sticking out of the yard proclaiming, "We just sprayed poison here." They probably used different wording.

"Either you let both of us in, or I'm leaving. Your lawn was recently sprayed with pesticides. If Zach is left out here, he could get sick."

Lepcheck's eyes narrowed, and for a moment I wondered if that's exactly what he wanted to happen. Had he somehow known I had Zach with me and had the lawn sprayed, all the while plotting to make the dog ill and/or possibly dead? But that was impossible. There was no way Lepcheck could know I had Zach with me. I gave myself a mental head slap.

"Very well, but if that dog breaks one thing in this house, I'm holding you responsible."

I shrugged. "He can afford it."

Lepcheck pursed his lips but opened the mammoth door wide enough for Zach and me to enter.

I blinked. The inside of Lepcheck's house was almost blindingly white. The entry was highly polished white tile. I could see my reflection in it, and the walls were high-gloss white as well. The only interruption in the monochromatic decor was an occasional piece of Greek art: clay pottery painted with black figures and bronze sculptures greened with oxidation. Zach's toenails made a soft click on the white tile, but he seemed to sense the quietness of the place and was on his best behavior. I ruffled the fur on the top of his head.

I couldn't help but compliment Lepcheck. "This is amazing."

"Thank you," Lepcheck said with obvious pride. "I have been collecting antiquities for years. You may have seen some of the Roman collection in my office."

I nodded although I hadn't been in Lepcheck's office since my job interview and hoped to keep it that way.

"My true passion is Grecian art. I especially love the Hellenistic period." He started down the hall. "This way. Remember to keep that dog under control. I don't want a single pedestal grazed."

I was too mesmerized by the pottery and sculpture to reply. Lepcheck said he'd been collecting antiques for years. Did that mean these pieces were real? The last time I had seen this much Grecian art in one place, I'd been in a museum in Athens. Apparently by being a librarian, I'd chosen a less-profitable area of higher education.

Zach's furry snout was on my heels.

The library was on the right side of the bright hallway and was another tribute to Greco-Roman culture. I peered at the Etruscan sword under glass.

"Please sit," Lepcheck said and pointed to a leather armchair. He sat in an identical armchair across from me.

Zach put his head on my knee and looked up adoringly. I could get used to his adoration, until I remembered my half-eaten flip-flops at home.

I looked at Lepcheck closely, hoping to see some indication of grief, such as red-rimmed eyes, balled up tissues, or nervous gestures. I saw nothing. Lepcheck was cool and collected. It was like any other meeting I'd had the displeasure of experiencing with him. He was as cool as ice—in control, and he wanted me to know it.

He cleared his throat. "I know we've had our differences in the past, Ms. Hayes, but I wanted to speak with you about the small misunderstanding you witnessed between my sister and me on Thursday. You can see, due to the sensitivity of this topic, why I would not want discuss this in my office."

I nodded, still confused by the fact he felt he needed to explain himself to me at all. Not that I was complaining. This meeting certainly gave me an excuse to interview Lepcheck, who was a prime suspect.

I knew Lepcheck was married. I'd met his wife at different functions at the college. She was a professor of history, if I remembered correctly, at a rival college in Cleveland. However, from what I'd seen of their house there was no hint of a woman's touch. It was hard for me to imagine a woman living in this space, but perhaps Mrs. Lepcheck was as austere as her husband.

As if he could read my mind, Lepcheck said, "My wife's teaching a semester in England. Sadly, she won't be back for the funeral." He crossed his legs and wrapped his hands around his knee. "She was very sorry she couldn't make it." By his tone, I wondered if that was true.

"I'm sorry for your loss. Although I'd just met Tess, I liked her very much."

Lepcheck stood abruptly. "Of course, you would." He walked to the window and stood by it. "My sister and I had little in common. We'd had our misunderstandings, but I didn't want her to die. You may hear differently, which is why I wanted to talk to you."

"To me?"

"I know my nephew thinks a lot of you. He has spoken of you often when I've seen him."

"He has?" I cringed. I hoped that Derek didn't tell Lepcheck I was his special friend. How horrifying.

"He was fascinated with that business last summer."

I knew he was talking about the death of my childhood friend on campus and my part in finding her attacker.

"So putting those two clues together, it would not be a stretch for me to conclude Derek may come to you and request your assistance in finding his mother's killer. To, how do you say, snoop."

I didn't confirm or deny his assumption.

"I take by your silence he's already approached you." He returned to his chair and sat.

"Who would say you wanted Tess dead?"

"Her husband for one. Possibly my other sister, Debra."

"Does this have anything to do with your uncle Victor's estate?"

Lepcheck looked at Zach, who had fallen asleep at my feet. His forepaws twitched, and I wondered if he dreamt of chasing a cat. Preferably not Templeton or it would be another long night. "If you have the dog with you, you must know of his ridiculous will. To leave everything to a dog, and, what's worse, entrust that dog to Tess of all people."

"Who should he have left Zach to?"

"Oh, I don't care who he left the dog to. He shouldn't have

put all his money in a trust to him."

I scowled.

"I'm not an animal hater, Ms. Hayes. My uncle had enough money to make Zacchaeus very comfortable as well as the rest of the family."

"Why did you think Tess shouldn't be trusted with the dog?"

"You met my sister. She spent her weekends hopping from art fair to art fair with her arty friends. They're a flighty bunch. She was flighty. I'm not saying my sister wasn't talented at her trade. She just wasn't someone you put a lot of responsibility on. She meant well but couldn't handle the responsibility that came with the trust."

I was surprised at how candid Lepcheck was being. I decided to press my luck with another question. "Why would Jerry think you killed her?"

He steepled his fingers. "We've had some heated discussions over the last few months about the trust. I felt that even though she was the one in charge of the trust, she'd be reasonable. Share the money within the family. She wouldn't. She said once the dog received his care, she'd donate a large portion the money to that co-op she was a member of. She thought Uncle Victor would approve because he'd helped start it. She could donate some of the money there of course, and it would still be more money than they could ever imagine. But they certainly did not need all of it."

"Was that New Day Artists Cooperative?" I asked.

"Yes. And then, she planned to give another large portion to an animal shelter," he almost spat out. "She said Uncle Vic would have liked that, too, because of Zacchaeus."

Yes, clearly not an animal hater, I thought.

"What's the name of the shelter?"

"Hands and Paws. It's in Uniontown."

I knew of it. My parents, as local champions of the underdog—in this case literally—had attended a fundraiser there in August.

"And your sister Debra—why would she think you'd hurt Tess?"

"Same reason. Debra knows how I feel about the will and that I planned to contest it. She was joining me on that front. She was the one who nursed Uncle Vic through his last illness, but he left her nothing."

Debra had just moved up my list of people I needed to talk to.

"Are you going to go through with it?" Lepcheck asked.

His words shook me from my thoughts. "Go through with what?"

"Playing at gumshoe."

"You're the one who invited me here, Provost, not the other way around."

"I'll take that as a yes." He stood. "My family is like any other. We have our problems. I trust you won't spread anything you dig up around campus. That would be detrimental to *both* of our careers."

I rose too and woke Zach in the process. He opened his eyes and woofed gently as if to ask permission to leave. Permission granted. I had no desire to stay in Lepcheck's presence inside his cold house one second longer.

"I'll show you out," Lepcheck said.

As I was loading Zach into the car, my cell phone croaked. It was Ina. "You got to get back here. Now."

"Why? What's happened?"

She disconnected. Ina didn't have a cell phone, and I called the number she used from my cell, but it rang and rang without response, not even voicemail.

Chapter Sixteen

When I got back to the booth, I half expected to find Ina hovering over another dead body. Instead I found Ina, Mutt, and Derek standing around my booth. They made a strange trio. Derek and Mutt's backs were to me, but Ina, who faced me, did a little finger wave from across the field.

I suspected the other crafters found the trio a little odd as well. Jendy and Beth watched them from the beaders' booth. All the while their deft fingers sorted colorful beads. I noted Celeste was away from the booth. A few booths away, Lynette scowled at me before showing an elderly couple a raccoon tea cozy, or maybe it was a moose tea cozy. It was hard to tell. I wondered what the scowl was for. I thought she and Ina were friends, but apparently Lynette's friendship didn't extend to me.

Zach pulled on his leash, and I let it go. He ran ahead with a woof, directly to Derek. Zach leaned on Derek's leg and whined softly.

Slightly out of breath, I asked, "What's going on?"

Derek and Mutt turned around. Mutt looked as churlish as ever, but Derek looked like he'd gone three rounds with a champion boxer. Both of his eyes were black, but the left was worse than the right with a cut in the eyebrow. He had a fat lip and his nose was bleeding. Derek patted Zach's curly head. The dog looked concernedly up into Derek's bruised face.

"For goodness sake, someone give Derek a tissue," I said.

Ina rifled through her industrial-sized purse and produced a crumpled tissue. "It's clean," she said. "Probably."

I tried not to think about the condition of the tissue as Derek pressed it to his nose.

"What happened?" I demanded.

Mutt adjusted his belt. "Your buddy started a brawl in his dorm. I got a call to run over there and break it up, and you know how much I like to run."

I looked at Derek. "Why?"

"Why don't I like to run?" Mutt asked.

"No." I directed my question to Derek. "Why'd you start a fight?"

Derek's eyes flicked at me before he returned his gaze to the ground. His right eye was beginning to swell. If he didn't put some ice on the bruise, his eye would be swollen shut within the hour. When he didn't answer, I looked to Mutt.

"I can't say I blame the kid. Apparently, he overhead some riffraff in his hall making fun of his mother's murder, and he snapped. You should see the guy Derek decked. I hope his parents have dental insurance to cap his teeth," Mutt said.

"You punched someone's teeth out?" Ina said, her voice full of respect.

I hoped she wouldn't consult Derek for street-fighting pointers.

"Okay," I said slowly. "Why'd you bring him here to me?"

Mutt shrugged. "I had to get him out of the dorm. Those knuckleheads were set on pulverizing him, and I knew you were around. I really don't have time to babysit. I thought you wouldn't mind."

Mutt's radio crackled. "Chief? Chief? You there?"

"Ten-four. I'm here."

"Hey, chief, one of these punks threw a chair through the window." The kid security guard's voice squeaked. There was the faintest sound of yelling in the background.

Mutt patted his breast pocket. Despite the fact it was late October, he wore a short-sleeve black T-shirt with MARTIN SECURITY printed across his chest, and he was sweating. I knew he searched his pocket, hoping to find the candy bar he usually kept there. When he came up empty, he sighed. "I hope I don't have to throw anyone out of the window today. I'm really not in the mood."

I blinked. "That rumor is true? You really did throw a frat boy out of a window?"

Mutt smiled. "I'll leave Derek in your capable hands. It would be best if he didn't come back to the dorm for the rest of the weekend. He should let those dunderheads cool down a bit."

Derek didn't respond but scratched Zach behind the ear.

After Mutt lumbered away, Ina inspected Derek's face more closely. "That's a serious shiner. I hope you aren't planning to be in any pictures any time soon."

"Ina, give us a minute?" I asked.

She crossed her thin arms across her chest. "I'm not going anywhere. This is obviously related to the case, and I'm the sidekick. You can't get rid of the sidekick. Did Sherlock Holmes say 'get lost' to Watson?"

"Ina, please." I was certain Derek wouldn't talk to me about the fight with Ina there to chime in every three seconds.

She sniffed. "Fine. I have some leads to follow up on my own." She waggled her penciled-on eyebrows and adjusted the bag on her shoulder. As she stomped away she resembled a leprechaun training for the British royal guard. Not that I'd ever tell her that. Ina'd be horrified I compared her to anything British.

I sat in one of the folding chairs. "Sit down, Derek."

He sat, and Zach snuggled beside him, resting his head on Derek's knees. "What's Zach doing here? I thought Lew took him. That's what Jerry said."

"He did, but then Lew gave him to me to take care of. His wife doesn't like dogs."

"Oh," he said as if that were explanation enough.

I reached under my table for a bottle of water and my roll of paper towels. I poured water on a wad of paper towels before handing them to him. "Put this on your cut eye. It won't stop the swelling, but it might help. You need to get some ice."

"I don't care about my face," Derek said glumly.

"You will when you see yourself in the mirror. Trust me. You look awful." I felt the beaders' gazes. I glanced over, and the beading pair quickly looked down at their work. I lowered my voice. "Tell me what happened."

He shrugged. "I was walking down the hall, and I heard some guys making cracks about my mom. I don't really know what happened after that until Mutt came and hauled me out of there."

"Did they know Tess was your mom?"

"I don't know. It doesn't matter. She was someone's mom, sister, daughter, or whomever, and they shouldn't have been joking about her murder."

"You're right, they shouldn't have, but you're lucky Mutt showed up. You could have been seriously hurt."

"I don't care about that," he said.

I folded my arms across my chest. "Well, I do."

He looked up at me. His left eye was almost completely swollen shut. He needed an ice pack badly. In the one eye I could see clearly, I saw a glint of hope. I probably shouldn't have told him I cared about him. He would more than likely get the wrong idea, but he needed to know someone worried about what happened to him. I changed the subject. "I just met with your uncle."

Derek made a face. "What did he want?"

"To tell me he had nothing to do with the murder. Apparently you gave him and a lot of other people the idea I'm looking into the crime."

"I shouldn't have?"

I sighed. "It does take away the element of surprise."

"Oh."

I lowered my voice even further. "Who do you think did it?"

"I have no idea. Definitely not my uncle. He'd never do something like that on campus."

I noted Derek conditionalized Lepcheck's innocence with the murder being on campus, as if that were the only circumstance to stop the provost from killing another person.

"It had to be someone she knew," I said. "You said yourself she was waiting to meet someone that night. I'm willing to bet all the books in the library that person was the killer. Lepcheck mentioned Tess was part of the New Day Artists Cooperative. Tell me about it."

"They opened it when I was a kid. They converted this old horse barn into the main building. The horse stalls are artist workshops now. Both she and Jerry were members of it. My mom loved that place."

"She planned to donate some of Victor's money to the co-op?"

"Yeah, she said she wanted to do something good with the money after Zach goes." He fondled the dog's ear in apology. "She was going to give money to them and to an animal shelter. She wasn't giving it all away. She said there would plenty left over to pay for my school and support us."

"The animal shelter is Hands and Paws?"

He nodded again.

"Did the shelter know about the donation?"

He shrugged.

"Did anyone disagree with these donations?"

"Jerry was upset about it. He thought Mom should keep the

money. And my aunt and uncle were upset, too, because they thought she should give them some of the money."

I didn't think Derek realized it, but he had just revealed motive for three suspects. "Anyone outside your family care?"

He shrugged again.

"How'd your mom and Jerry get along?"

"Okay, I guess. They'd been arguing a lot lately about Uncle Vic's money, but before that they were fine."

"How do you get along with your stepfather?"

"He's okay." A resounding endorsement indeed.

"Tell me more about the co-op. Are there crafters here who are members?"

"Oh, yeah, I think all of them are here. They tend to do the craft fair thing together."

"Who are they?"

"Ummm . . . there's my mom's best friend, AnnaMarie. She's a broom maker. There's David the papermaker, Ansel the weaver, Celeste the beader." He looked over at the beader booth. Beth and Jendy were entertaining customers and didn't see him looking. "Celeste isn't over there right now."

"I've met her. Who else?"

"Carrington makes these crazy hats like the kind rich ladies wear to the Kentucky Derby. I don't know what she is called."

"A milliner," I said.

"Oh." There was a pause. "And my mom and Jerry."

"That's it?"

"Those are the full members. There are a lot of other artists who are in and out or rent space for a short period of time."

"Okay. So we're talking about six members plus Tess."

He nodded.

"Did your mom have problems with any of these people? Any little spat you knew about?"

He shook his head.

"What does that head shake mean? No, or I don't know?"

"I don't know."

"What wild animal attacked you?" Bobby asked, interrupting our conversation. Erin was standing beside him on the other side of my booth. The two looked awfully chummy.

CHAPTER SEVENTEEN

Derek reddened.

"There was a fight at the dorm," I said.

"I heard about that," Erin said.

"How in the world did you hear about it already?" I asked.

She reached into her pocket and pulled out her smartphone. "Campus text alerts."

I pulled out my phone and looked at it. "I didn't get one."

Erin rolled her eyes. "The unofficial text alert system."

"Oh."

Zach crawled out from under the table. Bobby jumped. "What is that?"

Zach yawned in reply.

"That's a labradoodle," I answered.

Erin's eyes widened. "That's not *the* labradoodle, is it?"

"It is." I told them how I'd gotten temporary possession of the dog.

Erin scratched under Zach's chin. "He's adorable. I did a lot of research on designer dogs last night."

Bobby squinted at her. "When I was your age, I didn't spend my free time researching topics that weren't required."

Erin ignored him and kneeled next to Zach. "Did you know that when breeders started to breed designer dogs like a labradoodle, they bred a poodle to a lab. That's the difference from purebred dogs, because a pug breeds with a pug to make a pug."

"Fascinating." Bobby gave an exaggerated yawn.

"And even though designer dogs aren't recognized by the kennel clubs, they sell for as much as purebreds, sometimes even more. I researched labradoodle breeders in the state, and there are only three. The least expensive labradoodle went for seventeen hundred bucks."

"Good Lord." Bobby put his hand to his chest. "Seventeen hundred dollars for a mutt."

"It's not like Victor didn't have the money. He left two million to the dog."

Bobby blinked and looked at me. "Is that true?"

"Yep," I said.

Bobby scrutinized Zach. "He seems like a nice pooch, but why would he leave a dog all that money?"

"That's a good question," I said.

Derek, whose red face was now a shade of pinkish orange, which complimented his bruises nicely, chimed in, "Uncle Victor really loved his dog. He's always loved dogs and has had one or more for as long as I remember. He wanted to make sure Zach was taken care of."

Bobby looked dubious. "Isn't that a little bit of overkill?"

Derek frowned, and I changed the subject. "I'm glad you two stopped by. Can you take Derek back to the library and put some ice on his eye?"

Bobby sighed. "I suppose so."

Erin glared at him. "We don't mind, India."

"Thanks." I turned to Derek. "When you're feeling up to it, you should go home."

Derek shook his head. "I can't go to my mom's house yet. I'll go back to the dorm. It's Saturday night, and I'll be able to sneak inside my room unnoticed while everybody else is out at parties and on dates.

I bit my lip.

Bobby smacked Derek on the shoulder. "Sounds like a good plan. Until then we'll stash you away in the library, preferably somewhere Lasha won't see you."

I smiled my thanks at Bobby.

After Erin and Bobby left with Derek in tow I had an onslaught of children wanting their faces painted. A half hour passed quickly, it wasn't until the last youngster skipped away with a pumpkin on her cheek that I noticed Zach was missing. Great. I'd lost a two-million-dollar dog. I stepped over to the beaders' booth. I noticed Celeste was still MIA, so I asked the two remaining beaders. "Have you guys seen Zach lately?"

"He ambled that way a little while ago," Jendy said and pointed to the right.

I thanked her but thought, Why didn't you tell me?

Several church vans had dropped off their blue and gray haired parishioners, so the crowd was thick with slow-moving patrons. I wove through the festivalgoers' canes and walkers. A spot of hot pink trampled into the grass caught my eye. It was a ball of yarn. Next to it was a tangle of orange. My stomach dropped. Bits of a yarn were strewn in the grass like tossed spaghetti. Then, I saw the half-eaten body of Lynette's elephant tea cozy. Not good. Not good at all. I followed the destruction.

The screams came. "Get that monster away from my booth! How could you?" The cry of outrage ended in a strangled sob.

I pushed through the crowd, which had grown with Lynette's outburst. When I was finally within view of the booth, she pointed her gnarled finger at me. "You! This is your fault."

The scene wasn't pretty. Zach lay on top of Lynette's booth with several former tea cozies hanging from his mouth. There was yarn everywhere, and Lynette's teapots she used to show how well cozies worked lay in the grass. One was missing its spout, another its handle.

I held my hand to my chest. "Me?"

"Yes, I saw you bring this dog here today. This is no place for a dog. What are you doing with him anyway?" She frothed at the mouth and was at a real risk of stroke, especially at her age. "Damages! I'll sue you for damages."

"Excuse me. I said excuse me," I heard Carmen tell the crowd as she barreled her way through.

Oh, no. Could this get any worse? I wondered.

Carmen appeared, pushing the twins in their double stroller, and the crowd gave her a wide berth. "What's going on—" Her eyes narrowed as she spotted Zach on the table.

The labradoodle yawned and displayed a piece of green yarn tangled in his back teeth.

"I'm ruined. Do you realize how many months it took me to make all those cozies, and that monster destroyed them in less than five minutes. I left for a minute to warm up my tea, and I came back to this." Lynette broke into a sob.

Carmen looked at me. "You brought this dog here."

"I—I, well, you see . . ."

Carmen closed her eyes and looked heavenward. She was going to blow.

"It's your sister's fault. I knew your nepotism would come to a bad end. I earned my place here, and since you let her in, look what's happened."

Out of the corner of my eye, I noticed a gap-mouthed campus security guard radioing for help. He looked like he was a middle school student, not someone who was packing heat, and when I say heat, I meant a large flashlight. It was the most weaponry Martin would allow its security to hold.

Mutt didn't have to make a path through the crowd. People moved out of his way before being asked. When he got a load of the scene, he bent over in a belly laugh. "Oh, oh," he chuckled. "This is too good. Seriously, Hayes, this job would be a complete snore without you around."

I gave him my best withering glare. "You're not helping."

"Are you going to arrest her?" Lynette demanded. "She destroyed my property."

Mutt picked up one of the uneaten cozies. I think it was supposed to be a giraffe. "You make a living off these?"

She ripped it out of his hand. "Yes, and I demand she be punished for this."

Mutt eyed me.

"Don't even think about it," I mouthed at him.

Carmen white-knuckled the baby carriage. "India, do something with that dog. Now!"

I scurried over and pulled Zach off the table.

"Get him out of here. No animals allowed, period."

I nodded, stopping short of saluting her.

The SOEC kids were there. "You have no right to keep a pet. That dog should be free to run wild. This is what happens when you tame nature—it backfires," Dreads said.

His cohorts agreed.

I held Zach by the collar. "I'll find someone to take him for the day." I pulled Zach to my booth and stashed him under the folding table.

As I got my cell out, I told the dog, "Zach, that was very bad, very bad behavior. Carmen was not pleased, and neither was Lynette." Truth be told, I feared Carmen much more than I feared Lynette. I still had scars from our scratching matches as kids.

I called the only people I could think of to come to my rescue.

Twenty minutes after my urgent call, my parents showed up. Mom pushed Dad's wheelchair across the lumpy grass. Her thick silver ponytail bobbed on the back of her head as they approached.

"We meant to stop by the festival today to route the petition anyway, so we don't mind dog-sitting for a bit," Mom said.

Dad held out his hand, and Zach immediately put his big fluffy head in Dad's lap. All puppy-dog eyes. Dad fondled the dog's ear.

"Petition? What petition?" I asked.

Mom made a disgusted sound. "The petition to save the bell tower. We need to get a levy on the ballot to do it."

Oh, right.

Mom reached into her ever-present backpack and pulled out a clipboard. "You can be the first one today to sign."

"The judge granted us a restraining order to stop the school board from demolishing the bell tower before we had sufficient time to route a petition," Dad said.

Mom grinned. "They don't know who they're messing with."

I signed rather than argue. "I don't think Carmen will like it if you walk around the festival propositioning people for signatures. Trust me. She is not in a good mood."

"We'll be discreet," Dad assured me.

Ha, I thought. That would be the day.

"Hello, Mr. and Reverend Hayes," Mains said as he approached the booth.

I inwardly groaned. Mains would show up when my parents were here, wouldn't he?

Mom sniffed. "Ricky. I hear you have another murder on your hands. Please try not to arrest any innocent persons this time."

He was nonplussed. "I'll do my best."

Dad lifted his clipboard up to Mains. "We'd like your support on saving the high school bell tower. Will you sign?"

Mains took the clipboard and read over the petition slowly. Mom's eyes narrowed. Mains looked at me and gave me a half-smile. He signed the petition and handed it back to Dad.

Mom pursed her lips but didn't say anything. I think she'd been hoping he wouldn't sign it, so she could give him a lecture.

"India, we'll be on our way," Dad said to me. He took Zach's leash, and the three of them set off in search of more signatures.

Mains sat in Ina's chair uninvited. "Don't tell me that was Victor Lepcheck's dog with your parents."

"Okay, I won't." I opened my cooler. It looked like I would need some fortification for this conversation. It was after three, and I'd yet to eat my packed lunch. After Ina's you're-going-to-be-thirty-and-slow-metabolism speech the day before, I decided to lay off the fried food for the rest of the festival. I opened the bag of baby carrot sticks and offered them to Mains. Peace, brother. I come bearing carrots.

He took a carrot, and I figured that was a good sign.

"And why do they have Zach?"

I liked that he called Zach by his name instead of "dog" or the other things I had heard the labradoodle called over the last couple of days. I also liked how there was the faintest hint of a smile in his eyes. Relax India, I warned myself.

"Well . . ." I blushed, realizing I was staring at him. I swallowed. "Lew gave him to me until things are settled. His wife's afraid of dogs. It's temporary. And we had a small mishap with the festival earlier, so I asked Mom—"

"Mishap? That wouldn't be the tea cozy–eating incident, would it? Knute told me about it."

"It would," I muttered.

"Uh-huh." Mains crossed his arms. "And you were the only person in town Lew could have given the dog to?"

I shrugged. I wasn't entirely sure if convenience was Lew's only motivation for entrusting me with Zach.

"Are you up to something?"

"What do you mean?"

"I have a feeling you're tampering with my investigation. Again." Mains took some more carrots from the bag and our fingers brushed.

I popped a carrot in my mouth. Chewing gave me time to think. I ignored his question. "Do you have a prime suspect?"

Mains frowned, and I thought he was going to ignore *my* question. "We are looking at everyone associated with Tess, but there are some who have more motive than others."

"You suspect Lepcheck?"

"You know I can't answer that." His tone became serious. "This isn't like last time, India. I let you have your fun then because your brother was involved. But this has nothing to do with you or with your family."

I felt my face grow hot. He *let* me? I silently fumed. As I recalled, he fought me every inch of the way to the point of even throwing Mark in jail.

"I'll arrest you if I have to." Mains stood, squeezing my arm as he passed me. I watched him walk away, wishing my arm didn't tingle from his touch.

As I painted faces throughout the remainder of the afternoon, I thought much more about my conversation with Mains than about Tess's murder.

Ina scurried back to the booth as the festival was closing. "I have great news."

"What is it?"

"There's a crafter party tonight in Tess's honor, and we're invited."

"Really? Where's it at?"

"Some artist co-op near Kent. Do you know it?"

"I know it."

Chapter Eighteen

The wake—if that's what it could be called—at New Day Artists Cooperative wouldn't start until eight that evening. When the festival ended at five, I told Ina I was going to follow up another lead. She insisted on coming along. After a quick stop at home where I changed out of my festival polo shirt, we headed out. Ina did not change her clothes. She refused to take off her pioneer dress.

Like the co-op, the Hands and Paws Animal Shelter was on the outskirts of town. However, it was in the opposite direction in Uniontown, a small rural community in northern Stark County, Summit County's neighbor to the south. It was only a twenty-minute drive via the interstate.

"Where are we going again?" Ina asked as I exited off the highway and onto a county road that didn't amount to much more than boarded-up, forgotten businesses and a few farmhouses.

The sun was beginning to set, and I was relieved when the shelter came into sight. There were no streetlights, and the shelter sat far back from the street. Despite my SUV's headlights, I was sure I would have driven by it in complete darkness.

"Hands and Paws Animal Shelter," I said for at least the third time. "This is one of the organizations Tess planned to donate some of Victor's money to."

"Why?"

"We are here to find out why."

I shifted the car into park. When we opened our doors, we were greeted by a thousand barks.

"Sounds like the Hound of the Baskervilles in there," Ina said.

There was a doublewide trailer in the front portion of the property, and we could see a large modular building in back. Since that was the source of most of the barking, I assumed it was the kennel.

As we approached the trailer, a woman, who looked a touch older than my sister and had a long sleek blond ponytail, greeted us. "Can I help you?"

Her tone gave me the impression the kennel was closed for the day. It was almost seven after all.

I gave her a big smile. "I hope so. We're friends of Tess Ross, and—"

As soon as I mentioned Tess's name, the woman's face crumpled. She stuck a hand in her jeans pocket and withdrew a tissue. Ina scurried to her side. "There, there," Ina murmured.

Only Ina could say such a clichéd platitude and sound sincere.

"I'm sorry," the woman said as the porch and security lights flicked on, apparently triggered by the twilight. "I heard the news yesterday about her passing. Her sister, Debra, called me. It's such a terrible loss."

"Loss in donation for the kennel, you mean," I said.

Shock registered on her face. "How—how did you know?"

"Her son, Derek, told me," I said. "My name is India, and this is Ina. You are?"

"Meredith Dern. I run Hands and Paws." She looked from Ina to me and back again. "Are you police detectives?"

Before I could say anything, Ina jumped in, "We're of the private variety. Derek asked us to look in on the case."

I wanted to step on Ina's foot to shut her up, but she was out of range. She knew me well.

Meredith's brow wrinkled. "Oh," she said dubiously.

"How long have you known about the donation from Tess?"

Her face reddened. "I'm not just upset about the donation. Tess was a great lady. She even volunteered here a few times. She told me about the donation she planned to make a month or so ago. I was shocked and grateful."

"Why Hands and Paws?" I asked. "There are a lot of animal charities to which she could have donated."

"Because Victor got Zach from us about eight years ago, I think. Tess thought it was fitting to give some of Zach's money back to us."

I was surprised that Victor's dog came from a shelter. I thought mistakenly a man with that much money would have bought a dog. I liked Victor a little better, knowing he took in a dog who really needed a home. It was truly a canine rags-to-riches story.

"What were you going to do with the money?" Ina asked.

"Let me show you. The kennel's out back." Meredith shoved the tissue back into her pocket.

We followed Meredith around the trailer and into the kennel. When we stepped into the building, a medium-sized black and white dog with floppy ears greeted us. I guessed he was some kind of spaniel-lab mix. He was a good-sized dog that came up to just below my knee. He trotted directly to me.

"That's Trufflehunter," Meredith said. "He's a doll."

He most certainly is, I thought. I held out my hand to Trufflehunter. "Is he up for adoption, too?"

The dog licked my hand, and his feathered tail wagged crazily when I scratched him under the chin.

Meredith nodded. "All the animals here are. Truffie is such a dear and so well trained, I let him wander around the shelter until bedtime. His owner's house was foreclosed a few years back, and he had to give him up. It's a sad story and all too common lately."

The kennel was clean and brightly lit but clearly overcrowded. There were three to four cats in a cage and even some of the dogs were double bunked. The noise from all the meowing and barking was almost deafening.

Ina immediately gravitated toward a cage full of five adorable striped kittens. They really were darling with their colored stripes accented by white bibs and paws. No, India, no, I told myself. It had been proven again and again that Templeton was not interested in having a new roomie, feline, canine, or otherwise.

"As you can see, it's tight. I have a great group of volunteers, most from a liberal arts college in Canton, but we really needed the money. We were going to use it to expand. Not only to make room for the animals we have but to bring in more. Maybe even take in farm animals in need of homes."

Meredith showed us the rest of the shelter, and we met more of the inhabitants. All of the animals seemed to be content even if they were cramped. As we moved through the building, Trufflehunter never strayed from my side. I was happy to see the kennel and to learn how Zach came into Victor's possession, but it was most definitely a dead end in the case. There was no reason I could think of for Meredith or anyone at Hands and Paws to want Tess dead. Her passing left behind a lot of disappointed dogs and cats. We said our goodbyes, and I knelt, giving Trufflehunter a hug before I left the kennel. He licked me up one side of my face and down the other. He'd make someone a great pet, just not me, or so I kept telling myself.

When we were back in the car, Ina sighed. "I could really go for one or two of those kittens. My, they were sweet."

"You have Theodore, remember?"

"That's true." Ina chewed on her lip. "I do love Fella, and it's hard enough to keep him in food with the amount he eats. You don't think your brother will want him back when he gets back to Stripling, do you?"

"I don't know," I said honestly. I glanced over at her. Her forehead was wrinkled with worry. I started the car. "Don't worry, Ina, I don't see Mark coming home any time soon. He's too busy living his big adventure."

Ina smiled. "You're right. But it would sure be hard to give Fella back, even if he's an ornery old soul."

Chapter Nineteen

By the time Ina and I arrived at the co-op, the three-quarters moon and the security lights lit the way down the long gravel driveway. Maple trees marched along the drive and gathered around the gray barn like sentinels, offering up their few remaining leaves to every rustle of wind.

Ina wiggled in her seat. She smoothed her green gingham pioneer dress and adjusted her shamrock-laden pillbox hat. "This place gives me the creeps."

I had to agree. There was something spooky about being out on a country road at night with no streetlights. Ina and I were both very much city girls. It didn't help that Halloween was only a few days away.

The parking lot was full. I parked my little SUV in the grass adjacent to the parking lot. The land the co-op was on used to be a large horse and hobby farm, and I'd visited there as a kid on school field trips to pet the goats, alpacas, and of course the horses. The animals were gone, but the barn and outbuildings remained. The weathered barn served as the co-op headquarters, just as Derek had told me earlier that day.

New Day Artists Cooperative opened seven years ago while I had been an art student in Chicago. I'd been back in Stripling over four years, and I wondered why I hadn't been out there sooner if I wanted to make inroads with the artist community and establish myself as a member. It came down to another commitment. Between my job, my family, and my painting, there wasn't enough time to do everything I felt I needed to do. But then again, maybe I just didn't try hard enough to do everything I thought I needed to do. Obviously, if I wanted to be successful even locally, I'd have to dedicate the time. If not, I might be working for Martin much longer than I would like. The only plus side was Lepcheck was over twenty years my senior, so he'd retire first. Unless he planned to die in office like a Supreme Court justice or the pope. That was a depressing thought.

Ina bounced and rubbed her palms together. "What's the game plan?"

"Try to talk to as many of Tess's friends as you can. Find out if any of them had a problem with her or knew someone who did. Do you have the list?"

She held it up. I'd written a list of persons of interest for each of us before leaving for the party. Ina liked the "persons of interest" title. She said it made her feel like a TV police detective. The list contained the names of the people Derek said were full co-op members. I hoped to talk with all of them that night. Also before leaving, I called my parents and asked if they could keep Zach for a few days. Luckily, I got Dad on the phone, and he readily agreed. Despite how much Dad enjoyed Zach's company, I made a mental note to call Lew the next day to ask if he found a kennel or if he was even looking for one, which I was beginning to doubt.

The barn was a weather-beaten white-gray, but the security lights illuminated the last remnants of red paint that clung to wooden boards like ladybugs. Intricately carved jack-o'-lanterns sat on hay bales outside the barn's wide-opened doors. Their tiny flames flickered back and forth with the breeze. Music and cheerful orange-yellow light flowed out onto the path from the co-op. If the upbeat folk music was any indication, this evening sounded more like a square dance than a wake. From the little I knew of Tess, I guessed she would have liked that.

Inside, I was able to appreciate the mammoth size of the building. The former horse barn had housed as many as thirty horses in its prime. Seconds after crossing the threshold, Ina took off. I hoped she'd be discreet during her portion of the investigation, even though I knew it was too much to wish for.

The place was packed. There were at least forty people milling around a buffet table plus the folk band in the center of the barn. I had no idea how I would find the names on my list. There was no sign of Ina. As she was five feet tall in her Sunday heels, I usually lost track of her in a crowd. Laughter and chatter floated up to the bare rafters, nearly beating the musicians in volume.

The horse stalls had been combined into large rooms. The artists' names were painted on the stall doors with their handicrafts underneath. Each stall was decorated by the owner, who displayed his or her craft to the best advantage. The first stall belonged to Celeste Berwyck, the beader, which reminded me I should talk to her again. Her low stall door was bedecked with colorful beads, and the inside of the empty stall had dozens of Celeste's jewelry pieces hanging from tiny iron hooks set in a specially made grid on the wall. I suspected Jerry made those hooks for her and wondered, not for the first time, where their relationship stood.

I paused in front of what had been Tess's studio. No one seemed to pay any attention to me as I stepped inside Tess's stall.

At the festival Tess struck me as a bit flighty, but her studio stall proved me wrong. The space was well organized and everything was put away in its proper place. I felt bad for misjudging her. The side of the stall was lined with blond wooden cubes full of basket-making supplies. Each cube was labeled. A Pegboard of wool hung on the back wall next to the small window, illustrating the different natural dyes she used for her basket weavers. Walnut for black, indigo for blue, marigold for yellow, and finally cochineal beetle for red. Tess's weaver tripod, many of her basket molds, and baskets were missing as they sat in the evidence room at Stripling's Justice Center. Enough remained to tell me Tess was not only talented but loved her craft.

"Looking for anything in particular?" a friendly voice asked.

I turned to see a big man, built like a lumberjack, not a pillow, standing behind me. He had a Santa beard, and his thumbs were hooked in his blue suspenders. I introduced myself.

"I'm David Berring," he said. "I'm the papermaker here and president of the co-op. Are you a friend of Tess's?"

I nodded. I did consider her my friend in a way.

David Berring. He was one of the names on my list. I smiled wide.

"I took a papermaking class in art school. It's hard work," I said.

He smiled. "That's right. Most people don't know that. Making paper the old-fashioned way is labor intensive. So you're an artist then?"

"A painter, mostly oil and acrylic. Watercolor for a commission."

That made him smile a second time, and then his brow wrinkled. "I thought I knew all the local artists in town. What did you say your name was?"

I told him again.

"Are you related to Lana Hayes?"

I inwardly sighed. "She's my mother."

"She never told me she had a daughter who was an artist. I've met her at different events in town. She's . . ." He paused as if searching for the right word. "Passionate."

I grinned. "That's true." I stepped out of the stall. "I'm still working on my career, building up a following. That and juggling a day job until I can strike out on my own."

"I know what that's like. It took me a good fifteen years before I could walk away from my desk job. The day I did was the best day of my life."

"Actually, I'm interested in the co-op. I'm just noting the members' names, so that I can speak to them to find out how it all works. What do you have to do to join an organization like this? What are the benefits, that sort of thing? I understand there are different types of membership."

"That's right. We have seven full members—well, six now, with Tess's passing. The full members are like partners in a law firm. They have full voting rights on all the co-op decisions and approval of any new projects. Right now, we don't have any apprentice members, but those are artists who are petitioning to be full members. We require they be an apprentice member for two years before becoming full members. We want to know they are committed to the co-op. Finally, we have a revolving door of ten to twelve artists at a time who work on special commissions with us or rent studio space in the barn for a short while." He blushed. With his red cheeks, he looked even more like St. Nick. "That's probably much more than you wanted to hear."

"Oh, no," I insisted. "I'm very interested, and it gives me an idea of the commitment required in case I decide I want to pursue joining a co-op."

"I'd be happy to meet with you sometime to tell you more."

I thanked him. "You mentioned there are six full members in addition to Tess."

"That's right. There's myself, Celeste Berwyck, AnnaMarie LaRue, Ansel Levi, Carrington Snowden, and Jerry Ross, who is Tess's husband."

The names David rattled off matched Derek's list perfectly.

I nodded. "I've met Jerry. Is he here tonight?"

"I saw him earlier but didn't get a chance to talk to him. I haven't seen him since. He's taking it hard."

"I'm sure he is. The whole co-op must be taking it hard."

David's bright face drooped. "We're all still shocked at the news. In the co-op we're like family. It was like losing my sister, truly."

"I'm so sorry. My booth was right next to hers at the Founders' Festival. It was a surprise when I learned what happened to her." I didn't share that I'd found the body.

"We're all having trouble absorbing it."

"Do you know why anyone would want to hurt her?" I hoped I sounded casual.

He cocked his head as if he thought the question was odd. "None at all. Like I said, we all loved Tess. Jerry mentioned once they were in the middle of a row with her family, but I don't know the particulars. I'm guessing her death was a random thing, some crazy walking the campus at night. Stripling's not as safe as people want to believe. Nowhere is."

"Maybe," I said, but I didn't think so. Whoever killed Tess knew her. I'd bet on it. Derek said she was meeting someone on the festival grounds that evening.

"Painting booth?"

"Huh?"

"You said you have a booth at the festival. Was it a painting booth?"

I nodded and didn't tell him it was face painting.

"Well if you want to learn about the co-op, you've come to the right place. I'm not just the co-op president, I'm also a founder. I'd be happy to show you around and introduce you to folks."

"That would be great, thanks."

I was about to follow David and be introduced to the other co-op members when Ina appeared at my arm. She plucked on my sleeve. "I need to talk to you. Now."

I gave my excuses to David.

Ina pulled me into the weaver Ansel Levi's empty stall. "He's here."

"Who's here?"

"The jaywalker."

Chapter Twenty

Momentarily, I blanked. "The jaywalker?"

Ina made an exasperated sound. "The person who nearly ran over Juliet and me on the square. He's here. I saw him. He went out the back door. We're going after him."

Before I could protest, Ina was halfway across the barn. I stumbled after her as she slipped out the door.

The grounds behind the barn weren't as well lit as the front. The only light to speak of was the moon, which was half shrouded behind a cloud and the yellow light pouring out of the barn's windows. I paused to let my eyes adjust. I spotted Ina's shadow creeping across the grass in the direction of one of the half dozen outbuildings peppering the back of the property.

Ina bounced from tree to tree like a super spy, or at least the comedic movie version. I hurried to catch up with her. "What do you think you're doing?"

"Tracking a criminal. I saw him go into that building." She pointed a wrinkled finger at a large shed the size of a one-car garage. It stood roughly thirty yards from the co-op headquarters.

"Are you sure it's the jaywalker?"

"Of course, I'm sure," she said in a harsh whisper. "I have a memory like a steel trap. Do you think we should call the police?"

"No," I said quickly. I'd had more than my fill of the police over the last two days. "They have enough to worry about with

Tess's murder."

"Are you saying this crime isn't worthy of their time?"

"In comparison, yes, that's exactly what I'm saying."

"Then, we need to make a citizen's arrest." She hopped to the next tree. I followed quickly behind.

There was an orange glow coming from the small barn. The door was cracked opened. Ina was peering into the crack. I tiptoed beside her. "It's him," she whispered.

I motioned for her to move and placed my own eye to the crack. I found myself looking into a blacksmith's shop. Sharp pieces of iron hung from every wall and surface. An anvil sat in the middle of the room with a sledgehammer resting on top of it. A wooden bucket of water sat beside the anvil. Behind the anvil, Jerry fed charcoal into the forge's flaming mouth.

I pulled Ina back from the crack. "That's Tess's husband."

"It is?" She tapped her chin. "He must be the killer then."

I pulled her farther away from the smithy. "Keep your voice down. You don't know Jerry's the killer just because he jaywalked in front of you."

"One crime leads to another. Let's go in there and take him down."

"We are not taking anyone down. We're not going to accuse him of anything. We're going to talk to him."

"But he is a suspect."

Reluctantly, I nodded.

"And a ruthless jaywalker."

I looked up at the moon and mentally counted to ten in French. For some reason, I found French soothing, although the only things I could do with it were to count to ten, say my name, and recite the colors of the French flag.

"Let's go," Ina said.

I knocked on the smithy's door, wondering about the wisdom of talking to Jerry in the smithy. What if Ina was right and he was the killer? With all the sharp objects around, not to mention the deadly forge itself, there were many ways he could silence a couple of busybodies like Ina and me.

"Hello," I said tentatively.

Jerry spun around. His dark eyes were red-rimmed and his cheeks were white-streaked with tears.

I don't know if Ina noticed his obvious distress because she pushed passed me into the room. "I'm onto you, Bub."

"Who are you?" Jerry asked.

"I'm the defenseless little old lady you almost mowed down on the square."

"What are you talking about?"

"Oh, you're going to play dumb, are you?"

Jerry looked to me. "What is she babbling about?"

I winced. "Ina thinks you're the jaywalker who nearly collided with her a few days ago."

"Early Thursday morning, to be exact," Ina piped in. "You were carrying a huge box and not minding where you were going. I could have been killed."

I thought I saw Jerry pale ever so slightly. "I don't know what you're talking about."

"Don't even try to deny it."

Jerry picked up a small hammer. "Listen, lady—"

I stepped between them. "Ina, you might be mistaken. Remember, you can be forgetful at times."

"I am not—"

I gave her a hard look and, for once, she snapped her mouth closed. I turned to Jerry. "I'm so sorry about this. I know you don't need us barging in on you, especially at a time like this."

He lowered the hammer. "I came in here to work. It helps."

I nodded. "Painting usually helps me when I upset."

Ina pouted.

"Are you going to come into the party?" I asked.

He shook his head. "Those are Tess's friends. Not mine. Half of them think I killed her."

I saw Ina open her mouth, and I stepped on her toe.

"Yow!"

Jerry jumped. "Did you poke yourself on something? There are a lot of sharp objects in here."

She gave me an accusatory glare. "No."

"Why would they think you'd hurt Tess?" I asked.

His shoulders sagged. "I can be hotheaded at times." He threw more charcoal into the forge, and sparks flew. Ina and I jumped back. "And someone told the cops I was planning on divorcing Tess."

"Were you?"

Another piece of charcoal flew into the forge's fiery mouth. "No."

"Then why would they think that?" Ina piped in. She gave me a triumphant look as if to say *I can ask a question as well as you can.* I didn't doubt it.

Jerry pulled the chain controlling the billows and pumped air into the fire. The flames grew. Ina and I stood there mesmerized. "A few months back I was upset about something stupid. You know how married couples fight over silly little things. I came into the co-op that day really steamed and might have said I was thinking of leaving my wife. I didn't mean it. It was a dumb comment to make. I know that."

"Who heard you say this?"

"I was mad and wasn't making a secret of it. Anyone could have heard me say it." Whoosh, whoosh went more air into the fire. He let go of the chain. "I'm sure Celeste Berwyck was there. She's always following me around the co-op."

"Why would she do that?" Ina asked.

Jerry grimaced. "I don't know. She's crazy." He paused. "I'm sure everyone in the co-op hopes I did it, so they'd have grounds to kick me out. I've been a member for two years, and they only let me in because of my wife."

"Oh, for some reason I thought you and Tess had been married for a long time," I said.

He shook his head. "We've only been married for three years."

"Do you know anyone in the co-op who would have a grudge against you or Tess?"

Jerry selected a ten-foot pole of iron and stuck it into the forge's mouth, burying it in the blazing hot charcoals. He looked me straight in the eye for the first time, and his gaze was just shy of menacing. "What's it to you? I thought you were a face painter. You a cop or something?"

I gulped. "No. I'm a friend of Derek's."

Jerry brow furrowed. "You're that librarian my stepson said was going to find my wife's killer." He snorted.

Ina straightened to her full four-foot-ten height. "Oh, she will. She solved a murder last summer."

Jerry squinted at me as if trying to imagine that. It would be a stretch for the most imaginative person, I was sure. "I think our conversation is done here. I have work to do."

"We'll be on our way," I said. "So sorry to bother you."

Ina looked ready to protest, but I nudged her toward the door.

"If you find out who killed my wife, be sure to tell me who it is so I can repay them." Jerry sent another puff of air through the billows into the fire, and the flames sparked.

I didn't say a word, just dragged Ina from the smithy.

When we were out of the smithy's earshot, Ina said, "I can't believe you portrayed me as a senile old lady."

"It seemed like the right move at the time."

Ina sniffed. "He's lying about the jaywalking. I *know* it was him."

"I believe you, but we weren't in the position to force the issue."

"Should I call that mouthy Officer Knute to check him out?"

"I'm sure Jerry's already on the police radar where Tess's death is concerned." I paused. "He's hiding something. That's for sure."

"Do you think he's the killer?" Ina asked excitedly.

"I don't know. You said he was carrying a box."

Ina nodded. "Yes, a big one, and it looked heavy."

"I wonder what was in it. My best guess is he doesn't want us to know. Why else would he deny the jaywalking?"

"Jaywalking is a crime," Ina said, aghast.

"Yes, I know, but not one people are afraid to admit to. Also I think there is something more to his relationship with Celeste. I know she has strong feelings for him. I wonder if they were reciprocated."

"You think they killed Tess so they could be together."

"Wouldn't it be easier to get a divorce?"

"If Jerry divorced Tess he wouldn't get any of Zach's money. Maybe he thought it would go to him if Tess died, since he's her next of kin."

"From Lew's explanation, that's not how the trust works."

Ina shrugged. "Yeah, but Jerry probably didn't know that."

That wasn't a half-bad theory, I thought. Hoping not to encourage Ina too much, I only said, "Maybe. Let's see what else we can find out at this party."

Ina grinned, and I suspected she was having a little too much fun with this.

CHAPTER TWENTY-ONE

When Ina and I entered the barn, David appeared at my elbow. "Is everything all right?"

"Um, yes," I said a little startled.

"Good, good. There's someone I'd like you to meet. I was just telling her you were Tess's booth neighbor at the festival." David led me to one of the stalls.

I glanced behind me to see if Ina was following, but she had disappeared again. Her vanishing act was becoming an annoying habit.

David led me straight to the broom maker, AnnaMarie LaRue. She was yet another crafter Derek had included on the list. AnnaMarie was a head shorter than me and near Tess's age, late forties. She had thick, frizzy strawberry blond hair with long bangs that covered her eyebrows. If it weren't for her hair I wouldn't have recognized her. She was the woman who ran away from the group when Carmen announced the murder to the festival crafters.

AnnaMarie sniffed. "You'll have to excuse me. It was a bad idea for me to come here tonight."

David patted her arm. "Tess would have wanted you here."

"You're right. You're right."

"Did you know Tess well?" I asked.

"Oh, yes, she was my dearest friend. I don't know what I'll do without her. She was an angel to me during my divorce, even let me stay with her until the house issue was settled."

"She was quite a lady," David agreed.

"Ever since I spoke to the police . . ." AnnaMarie spoke in a distant way. "I've wracked my brain trying to think of anyone who would hurt her. No one comes to mind."

I blinked. "You spoke to the police?"

"Yes, a very nice detective. His name was Mains. He couldn't have been kinder. He said I could call him if I thought of anything. He gave me his cell number."

David grimaced. "They were here this afternoon. They searched Tess's workspace and questioned the co-op members who were around. Since most of the members were at the festival, I imagine the police interviewed them there."

AnnaMarie nodded. "That's where they talked to me. It was just awful staying at the festival, knowing what had happened there. I forced myself to stick it out because I knew Tess would've wanted me to."

David smiled at her. "She most certainly would. Tess had great faith in your talent."

"I know," AnnaMarie moaned. "Without her support I wouldn't have joined the co-op. It's so nice to see all these people coming out to celebrate her life. She was a wonderful person, just wonderful."

"I really know her son better. I'm a librarian at Martin, and he works in the library," I said.

AnnaMarie teared up again. Mascara streaked her face. "Poor Derek. He's such a sweet kid. It's a tragedy this happened to him again."

"Happened again?"

"You don't know?"

I shook my head.

"Derek's father, Tess's first husband, died when Derek was a little boy. He was walking home from work when a car hit him."

"When was this?" I knew my tone was sharp.

"Ten years ago. Derek was eight at the time."

Why hadn't Derek mentioned this before? He'd hung around me at the library for months telling me every little detail of his life. I knew his roommate's name, his class schedule, and the professors he liked and didn't like, but he never mentioned this? Then I remembered he never mentioned Lepcheck was his uncle, either, and that certainly would have been more likely to come up in conversation than his father's death. I realized Derek and I had never spoken of anything with any real depth. We chatted. Actually, he chatted until I shooed him away from the reference desk. Was it because I held Derek at arm's length, hoping to keep a professional distance? How well did I know Derek, really?

I pushed back the guilt that crawled up my throat and tried to focus on AnnaMarie. "That's horrible. Where did her husband work?"

"He was a personal accountant. His office wasn't far from the square."

"And someone hit him and ran?" I was still in a state of disbelief.

AnnaMarie looked pained to think about it. "He worked late that night and was walking home. Since he lived so close to his office, he walked almost every day. Stripling is a safe place. There never seemed to be any reason to worry. He was crossing a side street when he was hit just a block from home. It was late, and he wore a dark suit. The police thought the driver didn't see him until it was too late."

"What was his name?"

"Oh, I'm sorry. I should have mentioned that before. His name was Seth Welch."

"Who was the driver?"

Sadly, she shook her head. "It's still an unsolved hit and run."

I felt my stomach tighten. Poor Derek, I thought. He'd lost both of his parents, and he was only eighteen. It was a lot for anyone to deal with, not to mention a teenager.

AnnaMarie checked her watch. "I can't believe I've been here this long. I need to get home. I told my husband I'd only be an hour."

"Are you sure you can drive?" David asked. "I'm sure someone can give you a lift home, and you can pick up your car tomorrow."

"I'll be fine." She looked around, taking in the whole room. "This was nice. Tess would have been touched." AnnaMarie choked a sob. "If you'll excuse me . . ."

David placed a hand on my arm. "I'm sorry about that. This has been so hard on AnnaMarie."

"No need to apologize. I feel horrible that I didn't know about Derek's father."

"I've known Derek since he was a child. He's a quiet but resilient kid. Now I'd like you to meet the other members of the co-op." He led me across the barn to a couple standing next to the buffet table. A large punch bowl sat at the end of the table. Disposable plastics cups full to the brim with red-violet punch lined the end of the table like sentinels. "Ansel? Car? Meet India Hayes. She's a painter living in Stripling, and she knew Tess."

The woman had a small afro with an elaborate hat placed upon it and tethered down with flowered hatpins. The man was about my height and had silky brown curls flying in all directions. He held out his had. "I'm Ansel Levi. I weave. This is Carrington Snowden. She's our resident milliner." That explained the outlandish hat. Carrington didn't extend her hand. "It's nice to meet you."

A waiflike woman in a peasant skirt tapped David on the arm. "David, one of the musicians has an electric violin, and she wants to know where she can plug in her amp."

David looked reluctant to leave. "All right, where's she at? I can show her. If you will excuse me, India."

I smiled, happy to see him go. I was relieved because I planned to question Ansel and Carrington about Tess's murder. I feared David would think it odd when I asked more questions about Tess and less about joining the co-op.

I picked up a cup of punch from the table. The punch smelled strongly of alcohol, much stronger than I was accustomed to. It wasn't something I would drink before getting behind the wheel of a car, and I would be driving Ina and me home later that night. I thought it would look rude to slide it back on the table, so I just held it. "Have you been full members of the co-op long?"

Ansel shook his head, causing his dark curls to bounce in tandem. "No, not in comparison to David or Tess. I joined three years ago, and when did you join, Car?"

She bent the edge of the plastic cup with her long manicured nail. "Just after you. The co-op was expanding at the time, and we were the two selected."

"That's right. I remember now. There was some stiff competition. I think ten or so talented artists were finalists. We were lucky enough to be the ones chosen."

"They must have been impressed with your work," I said.

Carrington laughed. "I don't know about that. I think they were impressed with our client lists. Ansel and I each had quite a loyal following before we joined the cooperative. Since members contribute a portion of their earnings to the co-op at large, they wanted to select artists they knew would bring in good money." She paused and continued to pick at the rim of her cup. "Not that I am complaining. The advantages of being a member here far outweigh the disadvantages. I would never be able to afford the kind of studio space I have here or the networking reach to gather more clients. For me, it's been a great move."

"Me, too," Ansel agreed.

"Jerry mentioned he recently joined, too."

Carrington wrinkled her nose. "He joined about two years ago."

Ansel brow furrowed. "Car, you voted like almost everyone else to let him in."

"Of course, I did. As a blacksmith, Jerry could pull in some major commissions the rest of us could never dream of, and it's what Tess wanted. We all did it for her even if we didn't much care for him."

"I think the vote was five to one in favor of adding Jerry."

"Oh that's right. Celeste was adamantly against it."

"Celeste Berwyck?" I asked, as if there might be another Celeste in New Day Artists Cooperative.

Ansel nodded.

"Did Celeste say why she didn't want Jerry to join?"

"I don't think she ever did. Do you, Car?"

Carrington shook her head.

Ansel ran a hand through his brown curls, causing them to spring in all directions. "I suspected the other members knew, though. All the full members beside Car and me go way back. I don't know the details, but I think there is a lot of emotional baggage there."

"I don't want to know," Carrington said. "I don't have room in my life for their drama."

"I'm sure you will miss Tess around here," I said.

Ansel frowned. "Oh, we will. She was just a bright spirit. She was always so upbeat."

"She was nice to have around even though her cheerfulness got a little old at times," Carrington said.

"Car—"

"Well, it did," she said matter-of-factly.

Ansel shook his head.

"It's awful what happened to her. The police are saying she was murdered," I said.

"I heard that," Ansel said. "It's hard to believe. Despite the fact Car thought her cheerfulness annoying." He shot the milliner a look. "Everyone liked Tess. I can't believe anyone would want to hurt her."

"She shouldn't have stayed on campus alone after the festival closed." Carrington sipped from her cup and made a face at the taste. "That practice field is so far on the edge of campus it can't be as well monitored as the main quad."

"I heard she was meeting someone. Do either of you know who that might be?" I asked.

Ansel's eyebrows rose. "Beats me."

"Me, too," Carrington agreed before taking another sip of her drink.

Chapter Twenty-Two

I said my good-byes to Ansel and Carrington, discreetly deposited my full punch cup in a wastebasket, and went in search of Ina. It was getting late, and I was ready to go home and stew over everything I'd learned. I found Ina with a half-empty punch cup in hand, standing in the middle of the three beaders near the barn's main entrance.

"Your pal here can really drink," Jendy said with reverence. "I hope I can toss them back like that when I'm her age." Jendy straightened her dress. I noted she'd traded her pioneer frock and buckle shoes for a sweater dress and calf-high leather boots.

Beth wrinkled her nose.

"Jendy, really," Celeste said. I looked at Celeste closely. It was the first time I'd seen her, or any of the beaders for that matter, outside of the pioneer garb and in normal street clothes. Celeste wore elastic waist jeans and an oversized pullover sweater. Her hair was pulled back from her face by a bead-covered barrette, and a long beaded necklace hung from her neck. She looked normal enough, but her gaze flicked around the room as if she were looking for someone.

Ina grabbed my arm. "We're having the loveliest time, India. Celeste told me she and Jerry were engaged."

I was glad I'd already thrown out my drink because if it had been in my hand I'd have dropped it. "Engaged?" I squeaked.

Celeste blushed. "It was a long time ago. A lifetime really."

Ina peered at her. Her look was sharp. I suspected she was

not nearly as drunk as the beaders thought. As Ina says, every Irish woman should be able to drink her weight in Irish whiskey without falling down. She takes a nip, as she says, of whiskey every night before bed. "How interesting you ended up working at the same co-op. Did you start together when you were engaged?"

Celeste cleared her throat. "No, I joined long before Jerry did."

Ina cocked her head. "Oh, well, you must have parted on good terms if you can work so closely together."

Beth pointed at the buffet table. "Oooh, look at that cheesecake, Celeste. It looks delicious. You like cheesecake, don't you? Let's get a piece."

"I'm not hungry," Celeste snapped.

Ina cocked her head the other way. "Did Jerry and Tess join at the same time?"

"No. Tess has been a member from the start along with David and me."

"Hmmm . . ." Ina said.

I was afraid Ina was playing her part a little too dumb, but I decided to let her finish.

"So Tess married Jerry after the co-op started."

Celeste nodded.

To herself, Beth was muttering about the cheesecake, as if Celeste might change her mind and eat it. I suspected Beth wanted to get Celeste out of Ina's clutches. Beth was nobody's fool.

"That must have been awkward," Ina said.

Beth stepped on Jendy's foot. "Ouch," the younger woman yelped. Apparently those boots weren't as thick as they appeared. She shot daggers at Beth with her eyes. Beth raised her eyebrows back.

"Celeste," Jendy said. "You promised to show us those new

beads you flamed this week before we left. The ones with the semiprecious stone set on the inside."

Celeste's face cleared. "Oh, that's right. Let's go look now. They turned out beautifully."

"You wouldn't mind if India and I joined, would you?" Ina asked. Beth looked like she wanted to kick Ina, but before she could object Ina said, "I'm looking for a present for my niece's birthday. A bead necklace with her birthstone would be just the thing. She loves folk art."

Let it be known that Ina was an only child and does not and never has had a niece. The lie slipped off her tongue like sweet Irish cream. Ina had never been to Ireland, but she surely did not need to kiss the Blarney stone to tell a story, be it true or false.

Celeste smiled. "What's her birthstone?"

I bit the inside of my lip.

Ina looked at the ceiling as if trying to think. "You know I can't remember. I'm sure I'll be able to recall it when I look at the stones."

"I don't have all the birthstones set in beads. I only have semiprecious stones. None of the precious stones like diamonds or rubies."

Ina smiled wide. "Oh, it's definitely not a diamond or ruby. I'd have remembered right off if it had been one of those."

Beth cleared her throat. "We wouldn't want you to have to look at the beads if your niece's birthstone isn't among them. We can figure out her birthstone very easily. In what month was she born?"

Ina gave everyone in the group a sheepish grin in turn. Her impish face was endearing; I knew better than to trust it. "I'm sure I will remember that, too, when I see the beads. Celeste, if you will lead the way."

Five minutes later, Ina, the three beaders, and I stood in

Celeste's horse stall–cum–studio space peering down at her worktable. The table was covered with a black cloth to show the beads to their best advantage. The beads sat in a black velvet–lined case. The stones were enveloped in clear glass and looked like drops of rainbow-sprinkled rain. They varied in size from my pinkie nail to my thumb nail.

Ina pointed at a garnet bead. "That's the one. That's Suzy's birthstone."

Great, now her fake niece had a name, I thought.

Beth smiled. "Oh, she's an April birthday then. It must be nice to have a birthday in the spring."

Ina said triumphantly, "Oh, no, the garnet is January's birthstone. My niece was born on January ninth. How could I have forgotten?" She grinned and held up her drink. "I best take it easy on any more of these, huh?"

Beth looked like she wanted to pinch Ina, and Jendy looked like she was ready to burst out laughing.

With tweezers Celeste picked up the garnet bead from the case, and it twinkled as it caught the light. Celeste placed the bead on the black cloth and began choosing beads to be placed with it.

"Your beads are gorgeous, Celeste," I said, ogling them.

She smiled.

"You mentioned before that Jerry was the one who taught you to use a blowtorch."

She frowned. "Yes. He taught me many years ago when we were together." Her brow creased. "He'd have been much better off if he'd married me instead of Tess."

"Celeste," Beth said, clearly horrified. She looked over her shoulder as if to make sure no one else overheard.

Celeste crossed her arms, still holding the tweezers in her hand. "He didn't need all the drama Tess and her family brought. He's usually so punctual, but these last three weeks, he was behind on a huge commission."

"Is that the gate he's working on? I saw part of it in the smithy. It's gorgeous," Jendy said.

Ina yawned. This, too, I suspected was for show. She was an impressive little actress when she wanted to be. "Why'd you break up?"

Celeste clenched her jaw. "I don't think that really matters, now does it?"

Ina, all innocence, cocked her little bird head full of white soft grandma curls. "If Tess was the reason for the breakup, I would say, yes, it does matter."

"We broke up long before Tess and Jerry met, and she was married then. Now, about the necklace," Celeste said. "It starts at fifty dollars and goes up from there. However, since this is my first necklace with this type of semiprecious stone bead, I really want it to be seen. Would your niece wear it often?"

Ina fingered the beads as if seriously considering purchasing a necklace for her fictitious niece. "I'm sure she'd wear it every day."

Celeste grinned. However, what Ina said next made her face fall. "Let me think about it, and I'll call you about the necklace. Do you have a business card I can have?"

Celeste reached into her straw purse and produced a card. She handed it to Ina. Ina tucked the card in her colossal tote bag. We said good night to the beaders and headed to the exit.

As we stumbled through the parking lot to the lawn where I had parked, a now completely sober Ina whispered how jealous her friend Juliet would be, having missed the party. "I play a pretty good drunk, don't I?" she asked.

"You were a casting director's dream," I said. As I spoke, I noticed a car in the parking lot. It was an old but well-kept sedan, and its interior light was on, illuminating the driver inside. The driver watched the party as it slowly emptied out, and I locked eyes with him. Mains. He nodded, but I didn't nod back.

Chapter Twenty-Three

"This is way too early," I told Ina at six the next morning when I met her on our joint front porch. It was still pitch black out, and we only had the porch light to direct us to my car. "I can't believe you're not tired at all. It's not normal. You stayed up as late as I did last night, so you should be tired."

"Stop complaining. You do want to speak with Debra, don't you?"

I yawned. "I need coffee. Lots and lots of coffee. Straight from the carafe, please. No. Wait. Intravenously would be best."

"This was the only time she would agree to. She's at her wits' end planning for the funeral."

"You know, the last time I was up this early, I flew to Europe. I think you shouldn't get up before six unless you're about to embark on an international excursion. And even then, it better be a great deal."

Ina helped me down the steps. "Do you want me to drive?"

"No!" I came wide awake.

I had on hiking boots, jeans, a thick sweatshirt, and hooded jacket, just as Ina had instructed me to wear the night before. Ina wore a similar outfit. "Where are we meeting her?" I started the car.

"In Maple Park on the north side of town."

"Maple Park? But there's nothing there except woods and a couple of trails."

"Debra chose the place. She goes there every morning to do

her counting."

"Counting?" I sensed Ina enjoyed my confusion.

"Bird counting. Debra's an avid birder. She's been one for years. She's even gone on birder vacations to the Galapagos Islands."

"Haven't all the birds flown south by now?"

"Not all birds fly south, India," she said in an exasperated tone.

I yawned and thought of Zach, who was still at my parents' home. He was much better off there. At least he could wake up at a normal hour. Templeton was happier last night with Zach out of the apartment, but I knew my mother wouldn't want to keep the labradoodle for long. I made a mental note to call Lew ASAP. I'd wait until the sun came up.

The gravel ground crunched under my tires as the car rolled into the small Maple Park parking lot fifteen minutes later.

A light frost covered the fallen leaves of the trees. The limbs and few remaining leaves on the trees were also covered with frost and looked like they were fringed with gray lace.

There was one other car in the lot and a woman, who looked to be making the downward slide toward sixty, got out of the car. She had steel gray hair, a squat body, and a no-nonsense expression. However, when we got closer, I saw Tess in her face. The sisters had the same small noses and high cheekbones.

"Did you bring your binoculars?" Debra asked without preamble.

Ina held out her pair. "India doesn't have a pair."

Maybe because I don't spy on my neighbors like some people do, I thought.

"I have an extra." She held out her hand to me, and we shook. "Debra Wagtail. You must be India."

I nodded. Debra had a mean handshake.

"Let's go."

Was it smart to follow a murder suspect into the woods? I wondered.

Debra opened her backpack and pulled out a clipboard. "This is the list of bird names. When you spot a bird, identify it, and mark it on this list.

I nodded. My parents were also birders, so this wasn't my first bird count. Nor did I think it would be my last if they had any say in the matter, which I hoped they wouldn't.

"I keep records of the number of birds in these woods just in case."

"Just in case of what?" I asked.

"In case they ever decide to turn this last piece of Stripling wilderness into a shopping plaza," she said with heat.

I wondered if I should introduce Debra to my parents. They'd get along famously.

"We have to be quiet on the inside, so don't speak louder than a whisper."

I shot a look at Ina, who was diligently adjusting her binocular strap around her neck. If anyone could spook birds into flight it would be her. Then again, maybe the birds would think Ina was one of the flock, with her baby-bird voice.

Into the woods we went. Our footfalls muffled on the leaf-covered dirt path. The sounds of twittering unseen birds and chattering industrious squirrels preparing for the long winter welcomed us. We continued to walk in silence for a few moments. To the east the sky began to lighten from black, to midnight blue, to gray.

I inched my way up until I was walking beside Debra. She spoke in hushed tones. "Ina tells me you're investigating my sister's murder."

"Derek, her son, is one of my students," I said.

"Derek's a sweet boy, if a little odd."

This seemed to be the general consensus about Tess's son.

"If you work at the college, then you've probably already spoken to my brother."

"I have."

"Pompous jerk. You can tell him I called him that, too. There's no love lost between us."

"Your brother disagrees with the terms of your uncle Victor's will and seemed concerned the police will consider that a motive."

"Why wouldn't they? Two million dollars is quite a motive, wouldn't you say, even if you get the dog along with the dough."

"Just saw a blue jay," Ina said in a loud whisper.

"Excellent," Debra loud-whispered back. "Mark your list." She hopped over a log. "And yes, before you ask, I was upset with Victor's decision too. I was the one who cared for him in his final illness."

"He had Parkinson's?"

"Yes, but he died of pancreatic cancer. It's a horrible way to go."

"How awful. I'm so sorry."

"Don't be. It was a relief in the end. Uncle Vic was a hard man to live with, and an even harder man to care for."

"Why'd you do it then?"

"I'm a nurse. I took early retirement a couple years back. Someone had to do it, and my brother and sister certainly weren't about to volunteer. No matter how ornery Uncle Vic was, he was family, and you take care of family."

I wondered if I could do the same. "Did anyone know about the trust before the will was revealed?"

"No one but Victor and, I suppose, his lawyer. We were shocked when we got the news. Sam was particularly upset."

"Oh?"

"He made some claim that Victor planned to leave money to Martin College in the Lepcheck name. I was with Uncle Vic the most, and he never mentioned any gift to the college to me."

"Did Victor ever mention his will when you were with him?"

"No. Never. I'm not surprised he left the money to his dog. He dearly loved that dog."

"Tell me about Zach. How old is he?"

Debra peered through her binoculars into the nude canopy. Only a handful of hardy oak leaves clung to the skeleton-like branches. "I'd say he's ten, maybe eleven. He was already an adult when Uncle Vic brought him home. My uncle was an animal lover. He always had a dog, but he particularly liked Zach. Probably because the pooch loved him even though Uncle Vic was a grumpy old curmudgeon. That dog adored Victor. He slept at the foot of his bed every night." She made a notation on her list. "House finch."

"Zach came from the Hands and Paws Animal Shelter?"

"If you say so. I don't know where Vic adopted Zach from." She shrugged. "I was afraid when Victor passed, Zach would be depressed, and he was for the first couple of months. I do have to admit Tess took good care of the dog. She took him a lot of places with her, including her co-op. It helped Zach to be out and about. He's a very social animal and didn't get to see many people when Uncle Vic was ill. I'm sure he still misses that old dodger though." She turned her binoculars to the right. "Cardinal, female." She marked her list. "How many birds have you counted?"

I looked down at my uncheckmarked list. Would it be wrong to count the female cardinal on my list as well? Cardinals were everyday occurrences in Ohio. It wasn't like inflating a bird count for an endangered species, was it? I wondered.

Before I could make up my mind, Debra took the clipboard from my hand and shook her head. "I think we should do less talking and more looking." She handed the clipboard back to me.

"One more question. Tess's first husband was killed by a hit-and-run driver?"

Debra let go of her binoculars for the first time, allowing them to hang from her neck. "Yes," she said slowly. "I don't know what that has to do with my uncle, his dog, or my sister's murder."

"I don't know, either," I admitted. "I can't even imagine what Derek is going through. He's awfully young to have so much tragedy in his life."

"There is no minimum age for loss," Debra said in a knowing voice. She lifted the binoculars back up to her eyes. "The whole family was devastated by Seth's death. Tess the most, it goes without saying. Her first husband was a good match for her. He was smart and had an excellent head for figures. His left brain balanced out her right brain. She was the one who wanted to adopt Derek, but it was Seth's organization that made it happen. He was a much better fit for her than Jerry, if you don't mind me saying. Tess and Jerry were too much alike. Two scatterbrained artists under one roof is a recipe for disaster if you ask me."

The sky began to brighten from gray to a dusty bluish pink. The trees were no longer just gray statues. The greens, browns, reds, and oranges shone on their rough bark and resilient leaves. Maybe I would come here another day in the morning with my paints and easel.

"He was an accountant," Debra said, interrupting my thoughts.

"Oh?"

"Yes. In fact, he was Victor's accountant. He helped him with his investments, that sort of thing. We have Seth to thank for Victor's large estate." She paused and marked her list. "See? There's a goldfinch. He should have made his way south by now, poor thing. I hope there's nothing wrong with him, making him miss the trip. Although with climate change, more and more birds aren't making their annual migrations south anymore. It's a real shame. You can see robins in January around here. It wasn't always that way."

I wanted to bring Debra back on track. "Seth worked for Victor?"

"Didn't I just say that?" she asked.

The dawn was bright enough that we no longer needed our flashlights to see the path. I clicked mine off.

"Psst! Psst!"

"Is that some kind of bird call?" I asked, looking up into the trees.

Debra looked around. "That's no bird."

"Psst!"

I looked behind me, and the path was empty. "Where's Ina?"

Chapter Twenty-Four

"Ina!" I called. The park wasn't that big nor the forest so thick that we were cut off from civilization. At most, Debra and I stood a quarter mile from the parking lot, and the sound of traffic was clearly audible. It would only take a minute to run to the road, flag down a car, and throw together a search party. What was I thinking? My cell phone was in my pocket. I'd just call Mains, and he'd have the police department mobilized within minutes.

"Shhh!" Ina's head peeked out from behind a bush.

"Where have you been?" I demanded a little more harshly than I intended. I would never admit it to her, but she gave me a fright.

"Follow me," she whispered and disappeared back behind the bush. Debra followed her through the shrubbery faster than I would have thought possible, and I found myself alone on the path. I hurried after them.

When I stepped out from the bush, Ina and Debra stood beneath a denuded sycamore tree with their necks bent back, looking straight up.

"Shhh!" They both looked at me with a finger to their lips.

"What is it?" I hissed.

Debra pointed up. I looked up. Way up at the very top of the tree was a large blob. It had to be a bird, but it was huge. It was much larger than the red-tailed hawks that so commonly perch on power lines in town. I lifted the binoculars to my eyes. It was a bald eagle. My breath caught. I'd seen a bald eagle in the wild many times, but never in my hometown of Stripling.

"The Cuyahoga River isn't far from here," Debra said, her voice barely above a whisper and answering my unspoken question. "He was probably scouting it out for fish."

"Does it live here?" I asked.

Debra shook her head. "I think he's one of the pair that lives in Cuyahoga Valley National Park. It's only ten miles from here by car, a lot closer by how an eagle flies."

I agreed. Suddenly, the huge raptor spread his wings and took off. We followed it with our three sets of binoculars, tracking it until it was out of sight.

I was glowing from the bald eagle sighting when I walked onto the practice football field two hours later, rolling my blue cart of paintings behind me. It was Sunday, and Ina had gone to church, so she wasn't playing my Watsonesque wingman this morning. I'd usually be there myself, sinking into my pew as my mother told yet another embarrassing story about me, my family, or both from the pulpit. She says we make excellent sermon illustrations, but I'm convinced she just likes to see us squirm. Because of the festival, I'd gotten a pass that Sunday morning. Well, if not a pass, at least a believable excuse.

My glow faded when I saw Jerry there setting up his booth for the day. Jerry tested the heat of his blowtorch against an iron hook.

David walked over and stood beside me. "He said he couldn't stand being at home or at his forge any longer," he said as if reading my mind.

I bit my lip. I wondered if I would have the strength to entertain the public after losing someone as close to me as Jerry had. I doubted it. I doubted it a lot.

David patted my shoulder. "I'll be sure to stop by your booth later to see your work. Who knows, maybe we can find a place for you at the co-op."

Tess's place, he meant.

I was setting up my booth for the day when Celeste and the two other beaders arrived. The trio chatted away until Jerry came into view. Celeste dropped her bags by the beader booth and ran over to him. Jerry, who was hanging iron kitchen hooks on a large Pegboard, grimaced. They were on the other side of the field from me, so I couldn't hear their exchange. I meandered in their direction, trying my best to look inconspicuous.

"I don't need your help." Jerry's tone was gruff.

Celeste was crestfallen. "I—I'm sorry."

"You've been waiting for this, haven't you?" Jerry snarled. "I wouldn't be surprised if you were the one who killed her."

Celeste's mouth fell open.

The whoosh of a prairie skirt grazing the grass came from behind me. I turned to see Beth approaching at a fast trot. "Celeste, we need help setting up the booth."

Jendy was a few steps behind Beth, twisting the hem of her pioneer skirt.

With tears in her eyes, Celeste kicked the ground. A tuft of grass bounced off Jerry's cart. "No, I didn't like her. She stole you from me."

"I never belonged to you, not like I belonged to Tess." Jerry turned his back to her and resumed hanging hooks.

Celeste stumbled into the arms of her fellow beaders as if he'd slapped her. She threw her companions aside and fled. Jendy went after her, and I slunk back to my booth.

Fifteen minutes later, Jendy returned without Celeste. She and Beth held a whispered conversation in their booth.

"Is everything okay?" I asked.

Jendy's purple hair peeked out from under her mobcap. "Yes, everything's fine."

They went back to whispering.

Later that morning, I folded dollar bills into my fanny pack from my most recent face painting, a Frankenstein's head on a seven-year-old's cheek. It was the last day of the festival, and with all things considered, it had been a success. The festival had attracted a record turnout. The question was if that was because people wanted to learn the history of their town and buy some crafts from local artisans or if they came in hopes of seeing a crime scene. Either way, Carmen was pleased. When she stopped by my booth later that morning to tell me the good news, she didn't even yell at me for not wearing my pink gingham nightmare.

During the lull in the crowd, I called Lew.

"Have you found a kennel?" I asked.

There was a hoarse sigh on the other end of the line.

"Lew."

"I knew I'd rue the day I gave you my cell number."

"Did you find a kennel for Zach or not?"

Instead of answering, he yelled into my ear. "Careful with that. It's worth more than you make in a year."

"Ouch," I complained.

"My apologies. I'm dealing with a pack of butterfingers here."

"Where are you?"

"Victor's house. Your provost's lawyer dropped by my office yesterday. He requested a full inventory of Victor's possessions before the estate can be settled."

"Wasn't that done after Victor's death?"

"It was." I heard him take a pull from a cigarette. "What a nightmare."

"Why do you say that?"

"There are some small but very expensive pieces missing from the house."

"Were they there during the first inventory?"

"Yes, I'm positive. We took digital pictures." Lew groaned.

"What's missing?"

"Valuable coins, small medals, and a few antiques."

"Sounds like a lot. Tess was in charge of the trust. Maybe she sold some of these items."

"She'd better not have. The trust said nothing could be sold or removed from the house by Tess until after Zach's death. The trust was very specific on that point. Victor wasn't going to let anyone out of caring for his dog."

"What do you think happened?"

"Isn't it obvious? Someone stole from the estate and fenced the antiques."

"Was everything missing photographed?"

"You're thinking whoever took the items used the photographs as a key to what was valuable?"

"Makes sense."

He sighed. "I already thought the same thing. It has to be an inside job. The items stolen were too specific, and all were photographed for the last audit. Unfortunately, a lot of people knew about those photographs: the auditors, photographers, lawyers, and family members. We are talking thirty people plus."

"Yes, but who had access to them to note their value?"

"I don't know if the auditors and photographers kept copies, but I imagine they did. Also Sam Lepcheck and his lawyer each got copies. I gave copies to Debra Wagtail as a courtesy. Tess had copies of course, because she was ultimately responsible for the items."

"Which means her husband and son had access to the photographs, too."

"Probably," he agreed.

"Where is the house? Is it secure or easy to break into?"

"It's a huge gray Victorian not far from the square."

"Lew, there are at least six gray Victorians in and around the square. Be more specific."

"It's five-four-five Roland Street."

"Roland Street?" I paused. "We used to say that house was haunted when we were kids."

If I remembered correctly, the house in question was a massive affair with a turret and huge front porch. It was regularly the target of middle school pranks, which amounted to toilet papering and sometimes even egging. Not that I had ever done either of those delinquent misdemeanors, or at least I'd never gotten caught. I didn't know where the haunted story came from, but it was just accepted as fact by kids growing up in Stripling. Could it be because Victor was an elderly man living all alone in that big house? I hadn't known whose house it was when I'd tossed my rolls of toilet paper into the trees as a part of seventh-grade initiation.

"It still might be. Anyway, the house is secure. There's an alarm system, and it's intact. No sign of forced entry. Your buddy Officer Knute is here. We called the cops when we discovered it was more than one or two items missing."

"How will this affect Zach?" I felt my shoulder begin to ache, a sure sign of tension. It was doing that a lot lately.

"It might take longer to settle everything than I first thought."

"You are trying to find him a kennel, aren't you?"

"I'm still working on it. It's not just a matter of finding the kennel."

"I don't think I'm going to like this."

"One of the stipulations of the trust states Zach cannot be in a kennel for any extended period of time. I'm sure Victor built this in to keep his family members from stowing the dog somewhere, then spending its money. I have it with a judge right now because of the extenuating circumstances, but she's yet to make a ruling."

"What is an extended period of time?"

"According to the trust, no more than four hours."

"Four hours." I ground my teeth. "Why didn't you tell me this before?"

Lew inhaled in my ear. "Can't say I remembered the stipulation at the time."

"What kind of trust did you write for Victor anyway? Could you've made it any harder?"

His voice took on an edge. "I write what my clients ask me to write. I can advise them, but they don't have to listen to me. Trust me, Victor never did."

"You have to make other arrangements for Zach. He and my cat are at war. Right now, he's with my parents."

Lew groaned. "They didn't take him to a peace march, did they?"

"No, but I can't promise they won't. You've got to take him."

"I'll see what I can do. I'll put some pressure on the judge and maybe get an answer soon." His tone was dubious.

"I want those answers today, Lew. Or I'm dropping Zach on your doorstep."

Lew laughed. He knew I would never do it. I was too much of a softie when it came to animals. I'd taken Mark's troublesome cat Theodore in after all. Okay, Ina took him in, but I was the one who'd found him a good home.

Crash sounded through the phone receiver.

Lew grunted. "India, I have to go. Your friend Officer Knute is making a point to break all the antiques we have left."

"What about Zach?"

"I'll see what I can do," he said, clearly finished with our conversation. "In the meantime, don't let your parents do anything drastic to him, like tie-dye his fur." He disconnected before I could respond.

Chapter Twenty-Five

The crowd was pretty light as I mulled over my conversation with Lew. It was just after noon, and most of the festivalgoers had moseyed over to the food vendors for lunch. I realized this was my opportunity to question some of the crafters more thoroughly. I had one particular crafter in mind.

I told the beaders, who amounted to Jendy and Beth—Celeste had not returned after her run-in with Jerry that morning—I was going on a lunch run, and they agreed to watch my booth. On the way to AnnaMarie's broom booth, I stopped and bought an elephant ear. It was part of my cover, so I felt obligated. I could have found a healthier lunch option at the festival, but in times of stress, sugar is always my go-to drug. I made a point of forgetting my pledge to eat healthier for the remainder of the festival.

A small cluster of people gathered around AnnaMarie's booth as she stitched a broom with a needle as hard and thick as a roofing nail threaded with thick hemp-like twine. It was a round broom and clenched in an iron vise.

If she noticed me joining folks around the booth, she gave no indication. She tapped the uneven bristles of the broom, still covered in broomcorn seeds. "This is a hearth broom. It's also known as a round broom. It's called a hearth broom because women in pioneer days used it to clean out the hearth after cooking. When I finish sewing it together, I'll cut the end with this blade." She placed her hand on a contraption that looked like a medieval version of the library's paper cutter. "The ends will be so even the broom will be able to stand on its bristles without falling over. If it can do that, it's the sure sign you have a good handmade broom." She picked up the round broom from the table next to the vise and stood it on end. The group applauded.

After the onlookers disbursed, AnnaMarie smiled at me. "I remember meeting you last night, but I'm sorry I can't remember your name. I'm so bad at names, and I was so upset."

"India."

"What a pretty and unusual name. I should've been able to remember that." She frowned as if disappointed in herself.

"Nothing to worry about," I assured her. "I just wanted to stop by and say hello while on my lunch break." I held up the elephant ear as evidence. "Your brooms are beautiful. I tried my hand at broom making once. It's hard work. I remember my hands hurt for days afterward."

She smiled. "You get used to it after a while, and it builds up your hand strength. There isn't a bottle or jar I can't open myself. My husband asks me to open jars for him, not the other way around." She sat on a folding chair she had behind her booth. "Looks like most people are off in search of lunch. Why don't you come around and have a seat?"

I shuffled around the booth, offering her part of my elephant ear as I sat.

"No, thanks. I'm not much for sweets." AnnaMarie didn't make eye contact. Instead, she looked across the field. Following her gaze, I noticed for the first time she was directly across from David's papermaking booth. He was in the middle of a demonstration but caught us staring. He smiled and gave us a half wave. "David's been so supportive," AnnaMarie said finally.

The way she said it made me wonder if there was a story of unrequited love there.

"He seems to believe in the co-op."

"Oh, he does. It was his vision. He wanted Stripling artists to have a place they could work within the community. David's a strong believer in community-building."

He should talk to my parents, I thought. On second thought, a very, very bad idea.

She met my gaze. "I want to apologize for how I behaved yesterday. I was such a mess."

I swallowed my bite of elephant ear. "There's nothing to apologize for. You'd just lost your friend. It's completely understandable."

She shook her head. "Derek's the one who's suffered the greatest loss. He's a sweet boy, especially considering everything he's gone through."

I nodded. "Do you remember anything in particular about the day Tess was killed?"

She winced slightly but answered my question readily. "Nothing out of the ordinary. We've done hundreds of these craft fairs or festivals. It's always the same drill, generally the same clientele. There were more young people about this year, but I think it's because we were on campus. Usually there're only a handful of those. I left at five. I had to pick up my daughter from band practice. She goes to the middle school. The only small thing I remember . . ." she paused.

"Yes?"

". . . was Tess bringing Zach here."

I took another bite of elephant ear to hide my disappointment. Powdered sugar puffed around my head in a sweet-smelling cloud, my idea of perfume.

"When I saw him with her that morning, I told her she shouldn't have brought him."

"Why's that?"

"Because this was her brother's turf and bringing the dog

here was like, well, like rubbing his nose in the fact that Victor left her the money."

"How'd she take that?"

AnnaMarie bit her lower lip. "She laughed and said I was silly to worry. Now, I'm not so sure."

"About what?"

"Maybe he was so upset she brought the dog, he did something."

"You think her brother killed her? Is that what you think?"

"I . . . I don't know. I just can't think of anyone else who was upset with her. Sam really wanted that money."

I stuffed the remainder of the elephant ear in my mouth. I'd certainly seen Lepcheck mad before, but mad enough to kill his own sister? I couldn't buy it, and he most certainly wouldn't do it on campus. Talk about bad press for Martin, and Lepcheck loathes bad press.

"Tess really loved Zach," AnnaMarie said reflexively. "After the initial shock of course."

"Shock?"

"Over the trust. She had no idea why her uncle would leave the trust and Zach in her care. At first she didn't want to take the money. It was too much responsibility. Tess was a free spirit. She didn't want to be tied down, most especially by money."

"I suppose she could have turned down the trust."

"She almost did, but in the end she felt she couldn't, not really. She had to think of what was best for Derek, too. Private college tuition is expensive, and with the economy in the tanker, there's no guarantee Derek will be able to pay off his loans after graduation. Zach can't live forever. Don't get me wrong, he's a great dog, and I'd hate for anything to happen to him. But after Zach passed on, Derek would've been well taken care of. I don't know what will happen to either of them now."

"I heard she planned to give a portion of the money to the co-op."

"She did. A quarter of it at least, which is more money than the co-op's ever seen. It would have been nice, too. We'd use the money to renovate the rest of the outbuildings. We could add more artists and pay someone to improve our website. One of the outbuildings would be transformed into a gallery with a shop to sell our pieces. It would have been fabulous and put us on the bus tour route if done right. So many plans flew around the co-op when Tess made her announcement."

"She announced this?"

"Yes, at the last members meeting. It was the first Monday of October. All members meetings are on the first Monday of the month."

"Didn't that seem a tad premature? Why did she make that announcement when Zach could live for many more years?"

She shrugged. "That's Tess for you. When she got an idea in her head, she went for it."

"Was everyone happy with the news?"

"Well, no. Jerry was upset and stomped out of the meeting."

"Do you know why?"

"He didn't know about Tess's decision."

"She didn't tell her husband before she made the big announcement?"

"It probably didn't occur to her. I'm not saying Tess was insensitive, but she didn't always think things through before running full speed ahead."

"Did he feel better about it when he cooled down?"

"You'd have to ask him, but I don't think so." She thought for a minute. "I don't think he believes in the co-op as much as Tess did. He was a successful independent blacksmith before becoming a member. He joined the co-op after he and Tess were married. David and the others weren't too keen on letting him in but agreed in the end because they knew the large commissions a good blacksmith could bring in. A portion of whatever we make through selling our works or through commissions goes to the co-op."

"Were they reluctant because of Celeste's history with Jerry?"

AnnaMarie reddened. "You heard about that?"

"That they were once engaged? Yes."

AnnaMarie looked away from me. She watched David again. He clothespinned freshly made paper on a clothesline strung from one end of his booth to the other.

"And how long has Celeste been a member of the co-op?" I asked.

"Since the beginning. She, Tess, and David were the three founding members."

"Was it awkward for Tess to be in the same co-op with Celeste?"

"There was tension, yes. Celeste and Jerry were engaged when the co-op started." She blushed slightly. "I believe that's how Tess met Jerry—through Celeste."

No wonder Celeste wasn't one of Tess's biggest fans. "That must have been uncomfortable."

AnnaMarie shook her head. "Tess didn't let that type of stuff bother her. She always claimed Jerry was the one for her. I think it was hard for Celeste though. She made no secret about how she felt about Tess."

"How so?"

"She'd make a snide remark about Tess's baskets or talk behind her back. Petty things like that. She never said anything much to me because Tess and I were such good friends, but I heard it from other people."

"Who?"

"I can't remember exactly," she said vaguely.

I let it go for the moment. A little chat with Celeste was

overdue. I stood and thanked AnnaMarie for her time.

She grabbed my wrist. "I don't want it to seem as if Tess was a man stealer. It's just when she saw Jerry, she had to have him."

Unfortunately, a man stealer was exactly what Tess seemed like, and people have killed for far less.

Chapter Twenty-Six

When I returned to the booth, I found Ina painting my nephew's smooth cheek. "Hi, Dia!" Nicholas greeted with his usual enthusiasm.

I flopped on a lawn chair. "Where's your mom?"

Nicholas shrugged.

Ina, wearing her green pioneer dress, looked up from her handiwork. "She's looking for you."

I gulped. "She saw you here? Have you been painting faces?"

Ina peered at me. "What was I supposed to do? There was a line five deep of children waiting to get their faces painted with you nowhere to be seen. I did the neighborly thing and pitched in."

"I'm sure Carmen was surprised to see you." That was putting it mildly. I was in for a tongue lashing when Carmen found me.

"She did seem a little taken aback."

I bet.

"Where were you anyway?"

Nicholas, who was painting spirals on the vinyl table cloth, asked in a shout, "Do you like my shark?" Shouting was his normal speaking volume. He tilted his head so I could get a better look at his cheek.

I looked at the blob, trying to envision a shark's fin. It was tough going. "It's great." I turned back to Ina. "I just had an interesting conversation with AnnaMarie, one of the co-op members."

Nicholas wiped his hand across his cheek, smearing blue paint from cheek bone to the bottom of his chin. The shark, if that was what it really was, didn't appear any worse from wear. It looked like Celtic war paint streaked along his face. I wondered if that had been Ina's intention all along.

I reached under the table for my paper towels and began to clean him up.

Ina hopped out of her chair.

"Where are you going?" I picked dry paint out of Nicholas's bangs. Then I spotted Juliet standing in front of Jerry's blacksmith booth and knew my answer. Juliet was a bit older than Ina, a few years on the other side of eighty. She had sky-blue curls, always wore panty hose even when wearing pants, and used a four-prong cane she held in a death grip. She still had her own car and drove herself everywhere. She'd flattened two of Ina's leprechauns recently, so I wondered how much longer the state would let her keep her license. It should be noted the leprechaun flattenings were not reported to the police. If it had been anyone other than her best friend, Juliet, Ina would have certainly gone to the cops.

Ina stood beside Juliet, and white and blue curls mingled as they consulted each other.

"Whoa!" A collective yell rose up from a group of preschoolers who watched Jerry's blowtorch presentation.

The two older ladies nodded as if they had reached a decision. This was bad. Ina muscled her way through the children toward Jerry. "I know what you're up to buster."

I swore.

"Dia, you said a bad word."

I winced.

Nicholas ran the dirty paper towel on his right cheek so that now both cheeks were blue. "Is Ina going to hit the blacksmith?"

"No, of course not." I jumped out of my seat.

"Is she going to go to jail like Grandma and Grandpa?"

That one I wasn't so sure of.

I was out of the booth and hurrying toward the escalating scene. Ina was threatening Jerry with one of his own iron kitchen hooks.

"Should I call the lawyer?" Nicholas called.

Now, that was a kid raised in my family.

Preschoolers ran screaming in all directions. A harried teacher held a hand over her head in the universal teacher attention-getter and yelled, "Class! Class! Form a line!"

Ina was oblivious to all the commotion she stirred up and shook the iron hook in Jerry face. Thankfully, Jerry had the good sense to turn off the blowtorch.

"Class! Class! Over here! Come away from the crazy lady."

"You nearly killed me! What right do you have to jaywalk across the square? Don't you have any concern for your elders?" Ina shouted.

"Ina, what are you doing?" I asked dismayed. "I'm so sorry, Jerry, I don't know what's gotten into her. She's not usually like this."

Okay, the last part was a lie.

"Is she your grandmother or something?"

I gave an involuntary shudder. Good heavens, people thought Ina and I were related? Why was I surprised, with all the other kooks in my gene pool?

"Just because I'm old you think I'm a grandmother, is that it? To you 'old woman' instantly equals grandmother. There's respect for you." Ina did a good impression of an angry pirate as she thrashed the hook about.

"Ina, please."

The teacher grabbed the last member of her class, and she

hurriedly ushered her brood away. As she crossed the yard, I saw her stop Carmen and gesture violently at Ina. Uh-oh! Carmen glared at me.

"Ina, we discussed this last night. Jerry said you must have been mistaken."

"That's right," Jerry said. "Leave me alone. You've scared away my customers."

"No, no, young man, I'm sure you were the jaywalker. I saw the whole incident." Juliet said meekly. She adjusted her thick glasses.

Ina looked triumphant. "See, two eyewitnesses."

"Two crazy old bats," Jerry muttered.

"What did you say?" Ina balled her fists.

"I said you were a crazy old bat."

Carmen marched across the yard, punishing the ground for our misbehavior.

Nicholas scrambled out of my booth and showed my sister his cheek. Carmen tilted her son's face up, and her eyes narrowed.

Oh, it gets worse and worse.

"What were you doing last Thursday morning running like a banshee across the square? Someone would think you'd just knocked over a liquor store. Were you running away from the scene of the crime?"

Ina continued to harangue Jerry, but all my thoughts pooled into her last phrase, "running away from the scene of the crime." Thursday morning. My conversation with Lew just a few hours before played over in my mind. The missing antiques. Lew's assessment that it must have been an inside job. If Jerry could steal from Victor's estate, which I was sure he had, could he murder his own wife? Maybe Tess had found out about it. Maybe he'd needed to silence her.

I looked at Jerry. His upper lip was sweating, and I didn't

think it was from the heat of the blowtorch, which was no longer firing. A knot grew in my stomach.

Jerry's gaze met mine. Was that understanding I saw in his eyes? I didn't have a chance to find out because Carmen was upon us.

"India, is it your mission to destroy this festival?"

Nicholas was right behind her. My nephew pulled on Jerry's pant leg. "Can I see your blowtorch?"

All the adults shouted a collective, "No!"

"Whatever argument you're having, it can wait," Carmen said in her most authoritative voice, sounding just like our mother. "There are only a few hours of the festival left. Let's not ruin them."

Ina gave Jerry another beady look. "Fine, but I'm going to find someone to arrest you after the festival. Come on, Juliet." Ina stomped off, and Juliet hobbled behind.

Carmen dragged a protesting Nicholas, who eyed the blowtorch enviously, away from the blacksmith's booth.

I watched them go, wondering if I could be right. Did Jerry steal those antiques? I had no evidence, just a hunch based on a phone conversation with Lew and suspect eyewitness accounts from Ina and Juliet. If it had been Juliet alone who claimed Jerry was the jaywalker, my suspicions wouldn't have even occurred to me. However, Ina was involved, and despite all her idiosyncrasies, Ina had a sharp memory. If she was that certain the jaywalker was Jerry, then Jerry was the jaywalker.

"Can I help you?" Jerry asked, stirring me from my jumbled thoughts. I still stood just outside the blacksmith's booth staring off into space.

"Actually, I think you can."

Jerry frowned.

"I spoke to Lew on the phone a few minutes ago. He said he was conducting an inventory of Victor's estate and some of the coins and small antiques were missing."

"So?"

I shrugged as if unconcerned. "I just wondered if you'd heard."

"Not that it's any of your business, but I hadn't." Jerry hung the kitchen hook Ina had threatened him with back on the Pegboard. "I don't know why this is your problem anyway."

"I'm taking care of Zach while the trust is being settled. I thought Lew told you."

"He said he'd found someone to take in Zach. He didn't say it was you."

"It's only temporary. Lew's looking for a kennel," I said, even though I knew the kennel idea was becoming more and more unlikely. I got back to the subject I really wanted to talk about. "Lew thinks someone must have known about the antiques because a lot of the most valuable items were stolen."

Jerry grunted and started packing some of his tools—the festival would be closing soon.

"I just wonder if Ina's jaywalking story is connected to this. Victor's house isn't far from the square. Ina said you were carrying a big box . . ."

"You think you have it all figured out, don't you?"

"No, not all," I said honestly.

"No one was using those things. I needed the money. Blacksmithing is an expensive trade. I only sold a few things from Victor's house, some small antiques that wouldn't be missed."

"You used the photographs from the inventory to choose those items?" I asked.

He hung his head.

"You stole from Tess?"

"Tess?" He laughed bitterly. "They belonged to that damned dog. He didn't need them. Two million dollars to a mutt. It's the most ridiculous thing I ever heard of. What's a dog going to do with a horse-head clock or a silver teapot?"

"Did Tess find out?"

"No, she never knew, I swear." Jerry's head shot up, and he eyed me dubiously. "You think I killed her, don't you? I'm telling you I didn't. I loved her."

"You stole from her," I reminded him.

"I stole from the dog, not her," he said in a harsh whisper.

Ina returned with a reluctant Officer Habash in tow. Juliet brought up the rear.

"There he is. Arrest the man," Ina said.

Officer Habash smiled at me before turning back to Ina. "Ma'am, it's your word against his. I can't write him a citation on hearsay."

"I have a witness. My friend, Juliet, was with me at the time," Ina said.

Myopic Juliet nodded enthusiastically.

I opened my mouth. Jerry looked at me pleadingly. I snapped my mouth closed.

Two hours later, Nicolas and Ina wheeled paint supplies to my car as I folded up the church tables. A couple of members from church would be there soon to pick up the tables and take them back to the church. The festival was over. Tomorrow, I'd be back behind the reference desk.

Jerry stopped by the booth. "I wanted to thank you for not saying anything to the police."

"It doesn't mean I won't." In truth, I wanted to talk to Lew before telling the police.

"There's something else I have to tell you."

I waited.

"But I can't tell you here. Come to my forge tonight."

"What's it about?"

"The murder."

"Do you know who did it?"

He looked nervously back and forth. "I might—no—I'm not positive."

"But you are suspicious of someone."

He nodded.

"Tell me who it is now."

"I can't. I need to be sure. I should know by tonight. I can tell you then."

"I don't think that's such a good idea," I hedged.

"Please. I need to tell someone."

"You should go to the police. Or I could go to them and tell them you know something."

"Don't do that. I'm only willing to tell you because you kept my borrowing"—he paused—"secret."

"I don't think what you did would be qualified as borrowing."

"Please."

I needed to know what he had to say. "What time?"

"Eight at the co-op. In my forge. I'll be waiting."

"I'll be there."

"And come alone."

That I did not agree to.

As Jerry walked away, David ambled up. "I'm surprised Jerry is here today."

"I think work keeps his mind off of things," I said.

David looked dubious. "I'm glad I caught you before you left. I'm really impressed with your work, India. You have a signature style. I can see it in these landscapes of the town."

"Thank you. That's very nice of you to say."

"I'm sure you want to paint more than just landscapes and portraits of people's pets."

"I do, but these seem to be the paintings I'm able to sell at the moment."

"Most people wouldn't know a real piece of art if it bit them in the behind. If we had a place for you in the cooperative, you'd have the freedom to paint more of what you wanted than what sells the easiest. I'll talk to the members tonight to see what they think about you joining."

I thanked him, and he left. I knew I should be excited by David's potential offer, but I was too preoccupied with my meeting with Jerry.

I hoped I wasn't making a mistake.

Chapter Twenty-Seven

Maybe I should have brought Mains along to Jerry's forge that evening rather than Ina. Shoot, even Bobby might have been a better choice. I didn't ask Mains to come along because he was a cop, and Bobby was working the late shift at the library, which left me with Ina.

Ina didn't disappoint with her outfit, either. She wore the kelly green trench coat over a lime green polyester pantsuit, taking a neon approach to detective noir. Instead of pairing the ensemble with a gentleman's detective hat, she wore the mobcap from the festival. She called the look, "pioneer meets sleuth." More like pioneer meets frog, if you asked me. I was sure Ina's look would be all the rage in London and Milan the next fashion season.

She squirmed in her seat, giving the small SUV a little extra hop to its roll. "Juliet is going to die when I tell her you brought me along to face the killer."

"Ina," I said for the umpteenth time, "Jerry might not be the killer."

"Pshaw! He's the jaywalker, isn't he? And he confessed to stealing antiques from Victor's house. Small crimes lead to big ones. It was only a matter of time before he moved on to murder. Tess must have found out about the antique thievery and threatened to report him to the police. And whammo! He hits her on the head with the basket mold to shut her up."

Is it even legal for someone over seventy to use the term

pshaw? I wondered.

I'd followed the same logic myself, although a little less exuberantly. Her summarization of Jerry's motive and opportunity made sense, but he'd insisted he didn't kill his wife. I don't know if his earnestness amounted to much. I'd been lied to before. And if I suspected him of murder, seriously suspected him, why was I meeting him at night at his forge with a geriatric sidekick when I should be calling the police?

"I doubt there is any direct correlation between jaywalking and murder," I said, trying to talk both of us out of thinking Jerry was the murderer. "Remember, we are just here to talk, not to accuse him. Whatever he asked me to come out to his forge to hear, he's not going to share it if you go in there in attack mode."

The trees bent in the glare of the co-op security lights. They had an eerie skeleton glow about them. I shivered. I was letting my imagination run away with me. It was close to Halloween. Perhaps I could blame my trepidation on that.

Ina glanced out the window. "Looks like a storm is coming in."

I leaned over my steering wheel and deduced that she was right.

"The weather girl said it would rain," Ina offered. As soon as she said it, a crack of thunder rocked the car. "At least she was right, for once." She grinned and pointed up beyond the co-op. "There's his forge. I see the smoke coming out of the chimney."

The rain came, pelting the windshield in pinball-sized drops. "I'll drive closer to the forge. There's another small parking lot behind the co-op."

In the small members' lot, I put the car in park. Ina rifled through her expansive bag.

"You wouldn't want to get your mobcap wet," I commented, watching the rain. "We're going to get soaked."

"What? Are you going to melt?" Ina questioned. "Don't be such a sissy."

I glanced over at Ina and was amazed to see she'd already traded her mobcap and trench coat for a new getup. Ina was decked out in full-on hurricane gear: slicker, puddle boots, rain hat, and umbrella. All green. She looked like a stout plastic frog. Luckily, I knew better than to say this aloud.

"That's easy for you to say," I said.

"It's your own fault for not watching the weather report. You should be more prepared for the weather." The smile on her face took the bite out of her words. It always did.

"Yeah," I muttered. I wore a wool sweater, barn coat, jeans, and running shoes. I'd look like a drowned rat, smell like black mold, and probably have a serious case of chafing before I reached the forge.

"Here." She handed me her umbrella.

As I watched the rain roll down the windshield, I began to have second thoughts. "This is a really, really bad idea. What if Jerry is the killer, and he's waiting to finish us off? We should call the police and let them sort it out. Or at least we could call Mains."

Ina snorted. "I'm not letting that Englishman take all the glory." She jumped out of the car and scuttled across the lawn. She could move pretty fast for her age.

I followed. A rumble of thunder shook the air, but no lighting came. The eye of the storm was a long way off. Hopefully we would be back at the duplex by that time.

I caught up with Ina as she slipped on wet grass. I caught her before she fell.

"For crying out loud, be careful. I don't want to have to drive you to the hospital with a broken hip."

Ina waved my complaint away.

I pulled the umbrella low over my head, as Ina and I trudged over the soggy ground. "Careful." I advised. "Watch out for gopher holes."

Ina glanced down. "Gopher holes?"

What did I know? I was a city girl. "Just watch where you're going."

Despite the umbrella, my legs from the knees down and my sneakers were soaked through by the time we reached the forge. I felt my toes curl from the dampness and the cold. I hated wet feet.

The smithy barn doors were wide open, letting white plumes of smoke escape. Smoke also rose out of the roof through an aluminum chimney.

Once inside, Ina shook off her raingear like a dog. Most of the flying raindrops landed on me. The smithy was warm. Inside the mouth of the forge, coal smoldered red-hot. A bar of iron stuck out of the coal. Tools sat in disarray on the workbench. On the anvil a decorative shepherd's crook for the garden waited cold and incomplete.

"Jerry?" I called.

"Doesn't seem responsible of him to leave with his fire going, if he's not here," Ina mused.

"Something is not right." I said. My skin tingled.

Artists might have a bad rap for being forgetful and disorganized, but really that wasn't true. When it comes to our tools, we artists take meticulous care of them because they are so expensive to replace. One misplaced fan brush could set me back fifty dollars. I knew Jerry wouldn't have left his forge in its current state.

Above us, the rain danced on the centurion shingles.

"Stay here," I told Ina, and for once she listened to me.

I stepped around the workbench and found Jerry.

He was lying face down on the gravel ground, a sledgehammer gripped in his hand and bloodstain on his back.

I froze, unable to scream.

A groan snapped me out of my gruesome study.

"Is someone else here?" my voice squeaked. I gripped my furled umbrella like a saber.

The groan came again.

"Is someone here?" I tried to hold back the panic rising in my throat.

Ina poked her head in. "What's going on?"

"Stay out. Jerry's dead. I think someone else is here. Go to the car and call the police."

"But . . ."

"Go!"

To my surprise, Ina went.

The groan came again. I walked further into the forge. The heat radiating from the furnace was almost too intense to bear. When I rounded the corner of the large anvil in the middle of the room, I saw Celeste, lying on her side, holding her head. In her other hand, she held a bloody iron spike.

"Don't move," I said, showing her my umbrella. Not that it was much of a weapon compared to all the sharp objects in the room.

Celeste rolled over and threw up on the dirt floor.

Chapter Twenty-Eight

Ina rushed back into the forge a few minutes later. Celeste lay on her side and looked as if she'd be sick again at any moment. I kept my umbrella trained on her. "Did you call the police?"

"Yep. Oh, my!" Ina exclaimed when she saw Jerry's body. Much of her bravado evaporated. The color drained from her small face, making her look like all of her seventy-odd years.

"Come over here," I said.

Ina stumbled in my direction. She looked down at Celeste, who still had the spike firmly gripped in her hand. "Is that the beader?"

"Yes," I said and handed her the umbrella. "Watch her while I check on Jerry."

She took the umbrella and held it like a baseball bat. "He looks dead to me. Really dead."

I touched the side of Jerry's throat, searching for a pulse. I didn't feel one. Not that I expected one with the wound on his back, but I didn't want to be reprimanded for not checking, as I had been when I discovered Tess's body.

Ina recovered quickly. "Juliet is never going to believe this. I bet none of her fabulous grandkids have found a dead body."

I wasn't sure what to do about Celeste. She was still lying on the floor behind the anvil. I told Ina not to get too close.

Ina tsked. "Lost her cookies, did she? Well, that's what you get for killing somebody."

Luckily, I heard sirens and wasn't forced to make a decision.

My plan was to give my statement, hand the whole mess over to the police, and get out of there. It was my second dead body of the week, and I was through playing super sleuth. It wasn't nearly as fun as it seemed in books.

Two Stripling Police Department cruisers, an ambulance, the medical examiner's black car, and two SUVs from the sherriff's department pulled into the members' parking lot. Behind them, I saw Mains's unmarked sedan.

The techs and deputies got right to work and booted Ina and me out of the forge. "Careful," Ina advised. "There's a murderess in there."

Ina and I stood under the small overhang just outside of the forge's barn door. It did little to keep the rain off. Cold rainwater fell in rivulets from the cracks in the weathered wood and into the collar of my coat. Ina in her El Niño getup looked perfectly comfortable though.

When Mains stepped out of his car in a tan trench coat, he jogged through the rain and under the overhang. He shook the excess water off of his coat and onto me. "Thanks," I said. Not that I could get much wetter at this point. I was already soaked to the skin.

He misunderstood my meaning, which was just as well. "I got here as quick as I could. I see I didn't beat the cavalry though."

"Yup, I'm expecting Custer to gallop up next."

"Are you okay?" He squinted at me in the dim light.

"Peachy."

"Really?" He was dubious.

"I'm fine. Shocked, but fine. You'd think I would be getting used to this kind of thing."

"When you get used to it, then I'll get worried." Mains ran his hand through his rain-soaked hair. "This is going to be a nightmare. The case started in Stripling, but this far out of town the county guys are sniffing around, and maybe the state troopers will want a piece."

I was glad it wasn't my headache.

All business now. "Give me the outline."

So I did. I told him about Jerry asking me that afternoon to stop by the forge because he had something to tell me about Tess. Ina interjected every couple of minutes when she thought I needed correction.

Mains grimaced at this. "So you brought Ina?"

Ina adjusted her rain hat so that the water collected there fell onto Mains's shoes. "I resent that, Mr. Detective."

Mains ignored her. "Why didn't you call the police or me?"

"Because you would have insisted on coming along, and then Jerry wouldn't have told me anything."

Irritation crossed Mains's face, but like the gentleman he was, he pushed it back. "I'd better get back there and fight for my piece. Anything else I should know before I head back?"

I told him about Celeste and the bloody spike.

Mains's eyes widened. "Geez, you should have led with that. That's my arrest."

"You think she did it?"

Mains gave me a look.

"I'll take that as a yes."

Ina shook her head. "That's what I told her. Celeste has to be the killer. The evidence is pretty damning."

"You two wait here. I'll send out Knute to record your statements."

It would have to be Knute, wouldn't it?

Knute appeared at our side and was not too happy to be assigned to witness-recording when there was a fresh dead body and a suspect caught literally red-handed within fifty feet.

Ina was in the middle of a longwinded version of our adventure when one the sheriff's deputies came out, holding a handcuffed Celeste by the arm. Celeste, fully conscious, had tears streaming down her face. "I didn't do it. I wouldn't do it. I loved him! I love him!"

The officer didn't even blink as he pulled her along. He loaded her into the back of his cruiser, and they drove away. Knute finished with us and went back inside the forge.

I shivered as a cold trail of rainwater slid down my collar.

The plastic of her raincoat crackled as Ina moved. "What's wrong with you?"

"I'm fine," I said without emotion.

"You're not fine," she insisted.

A tear slid down my cheek. "What if it's my fault?"

Ina grabbed my hand. "Your fault for what, honey?"

"What if it's my fault Jerry's dead? I should have let the case go. Why do I always get involved where I don't belong?" Another tear followed the first.

Ina's face was stern. "First of all, if this Jerry character was going to get himself killed there was nothing you did or didn't do that would have caused it. You didn't stick him, did you?"

I shook my head.

"And second of all, you poke where you don't belong because that's the way you are. That's the way you're made. I'm the same way. It's better if you just accept it than fight your nature."

Was that supposed to make me feel better? Because it was doing one heck of a job, I thought.

Mains came out with two other cops. "Next of kin?"

"Just the stepson, sir."

The stepson, I thought. Derek. How much more could the kid bear? How much more could anyone bear in a situation like this, no matter what their age? This was the third parental figure for him to lose in violent death.

Mains sighed and echoed my thoughts. "Poor kid. I'll tell him. You guys get everything you can on Ms. Berwyck. We need this to stick."

I cleared my throat. Mains looked at me. "You and Ina can go home. Stop by the station tomorrow morning to sign your statement."

The crime scene techs wheeled out the body bag on a gurney. I looked away, but Ina followed them to the ambulance, peppering them with questions about chain of evidence and rigor mortis.

"I think it will be easier for Derek if I'm there when you tell him. That's where you are going, isn't it?"

He nodded. "Does this include your sidekick?" He gestured to Ina.

"No."

He sighed. "I'll swing by your house on my way there. It might be pretty late."

"I'll stay up."

Mains smiled, and I felt my shoulders ache.

Chapter Twenty-Nine

Over two hours later, I watched for Mains's sedan through my kitchen window in a dry set of clothes with my purple raincoat and dog-print puddle boots on. Templeton sat on the kitchen table, looking just as intently out the window. His plume of a black tail twitched anxiously across the oak tabletop. I ran a hand along his back, hoping to calm him, hoping to calm myself.

Headlights turned into the drive, and I was out the door before the car came to a complete stop.

"Are you sure you want to do this? It's going to be tough," Mains said as I fastened my seatbelt.

"I'm sure." I wiped the rain from my face with the hem of my sweatshirt.

He backed out of the driveway. I hoped Ina was asleep, because I didn't want to face her questions about this late-night meeting the next day.

We drove in silence until Mains turned onto Martin's campus.

"He's still staying in the dorm?" I asked. I thought Derek may have moved back to Tess's house by now to avoid another fight with his dormmates.

Mains nodded as he drove through fraternity row, which was quiet. It was a Sunday night, after all, and the majority of Martin's students leaned more toward being bookworms than party animals. Along the row, the garish Halloween decorations were lit up with orange, yellow, and red twinkle lights. Some of the houses had so many of them, I wondered how the occupants slept. The rain made the experience even more surreal, blurring the lights into movement.

"Are you sure we can simply waltz into one of the dorms and talk to a student? The dorms are locked, and security will throw us out."

"They can't throw me out. I'm a cop, and I've already called ahead. Mutt has already woken Derek and taken him to the dorm office so we can speak to him in private and not disturb any of the other students."

"Oh," I said.

Derek lived in West dorm, named for one of Stripling's early families and located on the east side of campus. Go figure.

Mutt waited outside when Mains parked in the handicapped spot. Mutt arched an eyebrow when we approached. "I could give you a ticket for parking there."

"You could," Mains agreed.

Mutt took a slug from the can of pop in his hand. "Ahh, were you out on a date? Nice to see you again so soon, India."

I returned the greeting.

"I brought Ms. Hayes along because she knows the student."

Mutt shrugged as if it was no concern of his.

Mains gestured toward the building. "After you."

Mutt turned and led us inside without further comment. Stepping inside the all-male freshmen dorm, the first thing to hit me was the smell. It was a powerful mixture of dirty bathroom, feet, and bicycle tires. The bike tires were explained immediately, as there were half a dozen bikes chained to various pieces of furniture in the lounge.

I had a brother, so I recognized the scent of boy, but had never been subjected to the smell on that level. I covered my nose. Mutt laughed. "Little different than the smell of moldy books, isn't it?"

"A little," I agreed.

Mutt led us down a short hallway that held only three dorm rooms. As we walked by the rooms I heard the exclamations of video games being played inside. There was an animated version of gunfire followed closely by a curse word.

The last door on the hallway opened into an office. The room was crammed full with extra toilet paper, cleanser, and paper towels. It appeared the resident director shared his office with the janitor's closet. And I thought my office was low-ranking.

Inside the tiny space there was a worn metal desk, much like my own in the library, a desk chair held together with duct tape, and two mission-style wooden chairs with stained cushioned seats. Derek, who wore a gamer T-shirt and sweatpants, slouched in the desk chair.

The one saving grace was that the RD had a window. It looked out onto the parking lot, but it was still a window, so that was something. I was starting to understand why the resident life staff was a revolving door of recent graduates. I didn't think anyone could stand a place like this for long.

Derek blinked when he saw us step into the room. Mutt stayed in the hallway. There wasn't enough room for his bulk. He said he trusted we had everything under control and was heading home for the night. Mains didn't argue with him. If we needed anything, we could call the security Cub Scout on duty.

Derek stared at me. "What are you doing here?"

Mains sat on one of the stained seats. I sat on the other and tried not to think about the source of the stains. Mains put his elbows on his knees. "We are here to talk to you about Jerry."

Derek shook his head as if coming out of a trance. "Jerry? What about him?"

"I'm sorry to tell you this, but Jerry is dead."

"Dead?" Derek blinked. A shadow of pain crossed his face.

"He was killed this evening. We believe he was murdered, and we already have a suspect in custody."

Derek swallowed several times before answering. "I can't believe this. Is this for real?"

I looked him directly in the eye, ready for any signs I should get him some help. "Do you want me to call your uncle or aunt?"

"No. Uncle Sam wouldn't care. He never liked Jerry. It's too late to bother Aunt Debra." He leaned forward as if to reach me, but the desk separated us, for which I was grateful. "It means so much to me you would come here in person to tell me."

I could see the hero worship back in his eyes, and I wondered if I had done more harm than good by coming. Now that the case was over and Celeste was arrested for the murders, I wasn't obligated to help Derek any longer. "I'm sure Debra wouldn't mind under the circumstances. You shouldn't be alone. It's a lot to absorb in a short period of time."

"I could stay with you," he said.

I jerked back. "That . . . I—"

Mains came to my rescue. "That's not a good idea." He gave Derek a stern look.

Derek looked crestfallen. He took a deep breath. "You said you have someone in custody. Did that person kill my mom?"

"We are still building a case," Mains said.

"So you think so."

"Nothing about your mother's case is certain yet."

Derek turned to me, his eyes wide with wonderment. "You did it, didn't you? You solved the case. I knew you would."

"I didn't really do anything, Derek," I said, feeling horribly uncomfortable. "I just happened to be in the wrong place at the right time."

"A lot," Mains muttered under his breath.

Derek's reaction wasn't what I expected. I thought I would be coming into a situation of tears and gnashing of teeth, but he took our news with a strange amount of, well, I wouldn't call it joy, but it was close. "Let me call your aunt."

Derek looked at me. His expression made me shift in my seat. "No, no. I'm fine. I'll be fine."

Mains rose and pulled a card out his trench coat pocket. "Here's another copy of my card. Call any time."

Derek took the card without a word.

"We'd better get going," Mains said, and I stood as well.

Derek popped out of the desk chair. "I'll walk you out."

Derek paused at the dorm entrance. "I'll see you at the library tomorrow, India. I'm working there in the afternoon."

"It's okay to take some time off to process everything, Derek."

"No, no, I'll be all right. The library is my favorite place."

That's what I was afraid of.

Mains and I drove the short distance back to my apartment in silence. I worried over Derek's lack of a reaction to Jerry's death. Was it possible he'd been afflicted by so much trauma in his young life that events like his stepfather being murdered weren't worthy of tears? That was hard for me to believe, no matter what might have happened to him before.

"Do you have to do that a lot? Tell people about the death of a relative?" I asked Mains as he walked me to my front door.

He didn't seem surprised by my question. "More often than I'd like."

The rain had stopped, and the street glistened under the streetlight. Beads of water reflected the porch light as they rolled off the hats and foreheads of Ina's leprechauns. I should have gone immediately inside my apartment. I could feel fatigue seeping into the marrow of my bones. I'd been up for over twenty hours, and my shoulders ached from the tension of the day. Tomorrow, I had to be at work bright and early in the morning. I hoped I didn't have any classes to teach, since it was pretty clear I wouldn't be on top of my game. I put my key in the lock, gathering the strength to turn it.

Mains broke the silence. "Derek has a thing for you."

"I don't know what to do about it," I said, worry creeping into my voice. I'd been hoping I had imagined Derek's extra attention. "He's just a kid."

Mains shrugged. "He doesn't think so."

"I feel so horrible for him. Do you know what happened to his dad?"

Mains nodded. "He hasn't had an easy time."

"I wonder what will happen now. Will he have to leave school? Will Debra or Lepcheck take him in? I suppose they don't have to because he's eighteen and of legal age, but one of them should look after him."

"One of them should," he said. His tone was quiet, almost hushed. "I imagine his uncle could pull a few strings to keep him at Martin and afloat until Derek gets his act together."

"If he would." I grimaced.

"You don't have to help him because of your brother."

"My brother?" I looked Mains square in the face for the first time since we'd left Martin. "What does my brother have to do with this?"

"He's not here, and you need someone to protect."

Was it true? I wondered. Was I helping Derek because he reminded me of Mark? Was he some type of weird brother surrogate as Mark was off globetrotting on his own? I'd always been Mark's guardian.

"I'd better go in. We don't want to wake Ina."

He had a wry grin. "No, we don't." He leaned closer to me, and I felt my body tense up. "It was nice of you to come. I know it meant a lot to Derek."

"He's a good kid," I said. My speech sounded short, as if I didn't have enough air.

"It meant a lot to me too. It's always hard to tell a family member that a relation has been killed. Thanks for sharing the burden."

"You're welcome," I whispered.

"You know, you can't really blame the kid for liking you," Mains said, looking down at me.

"You can't?" I asked.

He tweaked my ponytail, and the moment passed. I stepped into my apartment tired and confused, perhaps as confused as Derek.

Chapter Thirty

On the way to work the next morning, I stopped by the Stripling Justice Center to sign my statement. To my relief, Mains wasn't there. I'd spent half the night wondering over the ponytail tweak and what it meant, and the other half worrying about Derek.

I slid behind the reference desk just as the library was about to open. Lasha was waiting for me. Lasha was a big black woman who loved to wear bright colors. She also loved to call people the nicknames she assigned to them. She called Bobby "Looker," much to the appreciation of his already inflated ego. Even though I'd worked at the library for over four years, she hadn't yet settled on a nickname for me. Instead she preferred to try out the names of developing countries.

She placed plump elbows on the reference counter. "Sri Lanka, a little bird told me you used the dumbwaiter as transportation."

I remembered seeing Jefferson, the cataloger, when I exited the dumbwaiter last Thursday. My brow went up. "Some little bird?" Jefferson was a hulking man who looked like he was better suited for professional wrestling than cataloging for a college library.

She smiled as if she could read my thoughts. "Fine. A great big bird. Don't do it again. You and Bobby give the students too many ideas for new ways to get in trouble. I'd much rather they get in trouble on their own. Understood?"

"Yep."

"I also heard you had a bit of excitement at the festival."

"You could say that, and there's more." I proceeded to tell her about Ina's and my discovery the night before. "I'd be surprised if Derek comes in to work today. He said he would, but it's a lot for a kid, for anyone, to deal with."

Lasha nodded. "If he comes in, I'll pull him aside and talk to him. Try to find out where his head is at. We can certainly get along without him for a few weeks." She tapped the reference desk with her sharp nails. "Interesting to see Lepcheck involved in this."

"Have you seen him lately?"

"No. He canceled last Friday's deans meeting. Understandable, of course. You think he did it?"

"No," I said.

"Me neither," she said, sounding disappointed. "If he killed someone, it would be way off campus. There's too much risk to his career here."

I agreed.

After Lasha returned to her office, I pulled up the database containing the old issues of Stripling's newspaper, the *Stripling Dispatch.* The paper came out three times a week and was too small to have its own morgue. So the back issues were housed in the Ryan Memorial Library. The library's offering of space was another one of those community relationships of which Lepcheck was so fond.

First, I looked up the hit-and-run accident involving Derek's father. The *Dispatch* had only started storing digital copies of its articles four years ago. Anything older than that was saved in clippings in the library's basement. It wasn't a place I went often if I could avoid it. The basement was dusty, dark, and smelled of rotting paper. Lasha had complained about it for years, arguing that the newspapers and journals stored there would eventually disintegrate if the temperature and humidity issues weren't addressed by the college. So far, no one who could do anything about it had paid much attention.

Before venturing into the basement, I looked up any information the paper had about Victor's death. There was his obituary, and then two weeks later, an article about Zach's trust. The details of the trust weren't listed, but it did name Tess as the sole trustee and noted that the other heirs, Debra and Lepcheck, were left out of the will.

Building my courage, I took my scrap of paper with the clipping's numbers on it and told Andy, the student working at the checkout desk, I needed to go to the basement to pull a clipping.

He grinned. Andy knew how much I detested the basement.

The basement was off limits to library patrons, so I used my key to enter the stairwell. When I reached the bottom floor, the rotting paper smell hit me immediately. I wondered if the library could apply for a grant to get the humidity in the basement fixed. I made a mental note to mention the idea to Lasha next time we met.

The *Dispatch*'s morgue was in a small room behind the stairwell. That door was locked, too, but my universal key got me in.

The clipping was right where it should have been. I knew this was thanks to our anal cataloger, Jefferson. I wouldn't be surprised if he dreamed about alphabetizing things at night.

I decided to read the clipping while in the morgue, so that I wouldn't have to make another trip back down to refile it.

I didn't learn anything new from the article. It was just as AnnaMarie related. Seth Welch had been hit by an unknown driver while walking home from his office late at night. The article ended with, "Police are asking for anyone with any information about the crime to come forward." Apparently, no one ever did.

A grainy photograph beside the article struck me. It was a picture of Tess, Seth, and a young Derek. It was a family portrait probably taken at one of the photo studios at the mall. In the picture, Derek was missing his two front teeth and grinning at the camera with a smiling parent on either side. Out of the smiling faces in that photograph, he was the only one left.

I filed the clipping back in its place. As I stepped out of the morgue, "Boo!" was shouted into my ear. I screamed and jumped three feet straight up. Bobby was bent over laughing at me.

"Jerk," I said, after pushing my heart back behind my sternum.

Bobby gasped. "I—I couldn't resist. Andy told me you were down here."

"You know, patrons are going to think someone else was murdered on campus because of my scream."

"Yeah, right," he said. "They'd never hear you down here."

"That's cheerful."

"What are you doing anyway?" Bobby asked.

I told him about Derek's father and the clipping, and then I proceeded to tell him about last night.

Bobby squinted at me. "If Mains has the murderer in custody, what are you doing wasting your time down here looking up an old crime?"

"I guess I was curious."

"I, for one, am happy that Mains made an arrest. I don't like the idea of you chasing after a killer." He frowned.

I blinked in surprise. "Wow, Bobbo. Thanks."

"I like having you around. I mean who else is going to pick up my slack around here when I want to goof off? I'm sure Jefferson is not willing to pitch in."

I snorted. "Touching, really."

"Aww, India, you know I love you."

"Yeah, I know. Now, about picking up your slack, I'd like to renegotiate."

Bobby rolled his lovely baby blues at me, and I followed him back upstairs. Andy and Bobby shared a high five at my expense when Bobby related my basement hysterics, and I returned to the reference desk, making a point to ignore them both.

By mid-morning, I could hardly keep my eyes opened as the late night was catching up with me. A pretty African-American girl approached the desk with a big smile on her face. Her smile put me on my guard. In my experience, students who approach the reference desk rarely smiled. They winced, grimaced, and chewed their fingernails. The reference librarian was the last resort before they threw themselves on to the mercies of their professors for an extension.

"Are you India Hayes?"

"Yes, can I help you?"

"You can. I'm Angela Darren, and I would like to interview you about the murder on campus. My sources tell me you caught the murderer red-handed."

"What is this for?"

"Oh, right, sorry. This is my card." She handed me an embossed ivory business card with the name of the college's student newspaper in the center. Under Angela's name, there was the phrase INVESTIGATIVE REPORTER.

"I don't think this is a good time."

"I have a deadline. I need a comment from you to finish my story by eleven."

I looked at the clock behind the checkout desk. It was a quarter after ten.

I hemmed and hawed and was relieved when I saw Erin walk up behind Angela. Erin leaned on the reference counter. "What are you doing here, Angela?"

The student reporter's eyes narrowed. "I'm interviewing Ms.

Hayes about the murder."

"Buzz off about it. She won't tell you anything."

"This has nothing to do with you, Erin. Why don't you go off with that guy librarian I always see you with? Now that would make an interesting piece for the paper."

Warning bells went off in my head. I definitely needed to talk to Bobby about his relationship with Erin. I didn't relish the idea of the argument to come, but from Angela's statement, they had gone too far, even if everything was perfectly innocent, which I suspected it was.

Erin tapped her tapered nails on the counter as if sharpening them before administering a scratch.

"Angela," I interjected into their glare-off. "I'd rather you kept me out of the article altogether."

"No way," she said. "A crime-solving librarian. That's good stuff. It's the heart of my story."

I winced. "Just put down 'no comment' for me."

Angela looked from me to Erin and back again. "Have it your way." She walked away.

Erin had heard about my adventure the night before. Despite telling Angela I wouldn't talk, Erin wanted all the gruesome details. I gave her the gist, then shooed her away.

The reference desk phone rang.

"Hello, Ms. Hayes, this is Deena in the provost's office. I have the provost on the telephone for you. Please hold one minute."

"Uh, what—"

Before I could finish my question, Lepcheck came on the line. "I wanted to thank you for your part in my sister's case."

"Thank me?" Unease settled over me like an itchy wool blanket.

"Yes, I suppose my nephew was right to ask for your help. Detective Mains stopped by my office this morning to personally tell me the news."

"The news?"

"That Celeste Berwyck was arrested for the murders of my brother-in-law and sister."

"They're sure Celeste's the murderer of Jerry and Tess?"

"That's what the detective said." Lepcheck sounded annoyed. He wasn't used to thanking people, and I prolonged his agony with my questions.

"What will happen to Derek?" I asked, pressing my luck.

"What do you mean?"

"He's lost all of his parents. Will you or Debra take him in?"

"He's legally an adult. He's far too old to adopt."

"I'm not suggesting adoption, but he needs a family to look after him, especially right now."

Lepcheck's tone bristled. "It is none of your concern, Ms. Hayes, how my family deals with private matters. You've helped us, yes, but I will kindly ask you to butt out." He hung up the phone.

The minute I replaced the receiver in its cradle it rang again.

"We have a situation." Mains voice said over the phone.

"A situation."

"It's your parents."

"Okay," I replied, knowing full well I wouldn't like what I was about to hear.

Mains swallowed hard. "They've chained themselves to the bell tower."

"Geez." We were the middle of fall semester, and the library was busy. It would be hard for me to get away, and I told Mains so. "Why don't you try Carmen? She's not working right now."

"I'd rather not. She's still mad at me over the festival."

"I'll see what I can do."

Chapter Thirty-One

The scene at the high school was one I was all too familiar with—my parents in the middle of a media circus. Mom leaned out of the top windows of the tower, waving to the crowd below—a cluster of high school students, teachers, and police. Dad, restricted to his wheelchair, had chained himself to the tower's entrance, barring anyone from entering and reaching Mom at the top.

Mains spotted me immediately. He stood among a cluster of amused police officers and livid school board members. He waved and hurried over.

"I wish I could say I can't believe this. But then I'd be lying," I said.

Mains shook his head. "Do you think you can talk any sense into them?"

I laughed. "I can try."

Mains ran his hand through his dark hair. "Your dad won't let anyone inside the tower."

I nodded, knowing my parents' method of operation. "What brought this on? I thought they were happy with their petition."

"The school board moved up the wrecking date to this coming Saturday. A wrecking company offered to come in and demolish the tower at a substantial discount."

"What about the restraining order?"

"The judge overruled it, saying the wrecking deal took precedence because it would save the city money."

"Great." I squared my shoulders. "Wish me luck."

Officer Knute stood in front of Dad with his arms crossed over his broad chest.

"Knute, can you give us a minute?"

"I was told to stay here and watch the perp." Knute eyed Dad.

Dad shook his fist. "Perp? Perp? I'm not a perp. I am a concerned citizen trying to save our cultural heritage from cretins like you. If you had your way, the world would be one big mini-mall."

Knute grinned. "Doesn't sound like a bad idea to me. Does the mini-mall have a smoothie shop? I love a good smoothie."

I blinked. Did Knute crack a joke? Would wonders never cease?

Dad glowered. I guessed he didn't find it quite as amusing as I.

Mains called from a few feet away. "Knute, over here, please."

I smiled at Knute as he slunk off. Mains shot me a pleading look before returning to his group of cops and board members.

After he was out of earshot, I said, "Daaaad."

"Don't lecture me, India. The judge's decision was a pure violation of the restraining order. He had no right to overturn it. Your mother and I had no choice."

"But . . ."

"This bell tower was here when your grandfather went to high school, when I went to high school, when you went to high school. I will not let the board tear it down when it's a town landmark. We're trying to get it declared as a historical site, but do you know how long that takes? Years! We don't have years. We don't even have weeks. They'll have the wrecking ball here in three days."

"But did you have to go to this extreme? Couldn't Lew have handled this legally?"

"Of course we have Lew on the case, but a bunch of lawyers jabbering back and forth isn't going to bring the public's attention to the problem. This will."

It certainly did that. A local news van pulled into the high school parking lot.

"Where's Zach?" I didn't see any sign of the large labradoodle, which I'd put in my father's care.

"Oh, he's fine. He's at the church with the secretary. He's a very nice dog. Reminds me of Riley."

Riley was Dad's childhood pet, praised to mythical proportions by my father. Before he could wax nostalgic about Riley the super dog, I asked, "Can I go in and talk to Mom?"

"Of course, honey." He rolled his wheelchair away from the door and let me squeeze in behind him.

The inside of the bell tower was dark. The only light shone from the open-air windows at the top of the tower, where the bell and my mother waited. The school board had long ago cut off electricity to the structure. Probably when that happened, the writing was already on the wall for the tower's future.

"Mom?" I called, looking up the three stories of winding wooden stairs. I had an eerie feeling I was looking at a scene out of a gothic novel.

"Up here! Are you alone?" My mother's head peeked over the top banister. Her gray pigtails flapped in the breeze.

"Do you really think that Dad would have let anyone else pass?"

"No. Your father is good at keeping back dissenters."

"I'm coming up."

"Okay." Her head disappeared.

I started my way up. The first step creaked and gave a little under my weight. This was going to be great, I thought sarcastically. Each step after that creaked with my slow progress. At the first landing, I looked up. My mother's head appeared again.

"What's taking so long?"

I gritted my teeth. "I'm almost there. I don't want to crash through one of these steps and plummet to my death."

"You're exaggerating. The staircase is perfectly safe. Hurry up, and we can have a snack."

"You packed a snack?"

"Well, how am I to know how long I will be up here?"

I doubled my speed, hoping the steps would hold. My mother may have food covered, but I wondered about other personal niceties. I doubted there was a bathroom up by the bell. Afraid of the answer, I didn't ask.

When I reached the final landing, Mom sat cross-legged to the right side of the bell. A backpack lay open beside her with her Bible, a half dozen mystery novels, a bag of organic mini-bagels, and a jar of peanut butter. She was committed to the long haul. She patted the wooden floor beside her. "Have a seat."

I sat.

Mom handed me a peanut-butter-slathered bagel. I ate half of it before I began my argument. "Don't you think it's time to go down? The news crew is here. I think you've made your point."

Mom shook her head, and her gray braids flew back and forth. "Now is the time to hold firm," she replied like any true revolutionary. "Some days I wonder if your father and I successfully instilled our values into our children. Mark is goodness knows where, Carmen is so provincial, and you . . ." She trailed off wistfully.

"This has nothing to do with values. I agree the bell tower should be saved if it can be done safely. And think about it, what would happen if the tower fell on the marching band? Do you want that on your conscience?"

"What are you saying?" My mother scowled. "That your

father and I want to be responsible for the death of children?"

"No, that's not what I'm saying." I grimaced. "Have you considered the issue from both sides?"

"Of course we've looked at the problem from every angle."

Uh-huh.

"You make it sound like we haven't saved a building before. What about the old library that's now a senior center? Or the old farmhouse on the county line? What about those?"

"But the levy—"

"We know the levy might not work, and we are in the process of applying for grants to restore the tower to ensure its safety. We brought licensed contractors in, four in fact, from different firms, and they all agree the bell tower isn't in danger of falling down any time soon. We took those findings and the contractors to the school board, but they wouldn't even listen. Instead, they were perfectly happy to rely on the opinion of their one-horse contractor—who partially owns the demolition firm, might I add. Well, is it any surprise he thinks it's unsafe?"

I shouldn't have tried to argue. I shoved the rest of the bagel in my mouth.

Mom polished off her bagel and started another. She could eat and eat and never gain an ounce. It was disgusting and oh so unfair. "How's the investigation coming?" She gave me a beady-eyed look.

I looked out the open-air window. I had a clear view over the high school's football stadium to the square in downtown Stripling, where my mother's church quietly waited for Sunday morning. It probably wouldn't be a great idea to leap through the window just to avoid my mother's questions. I'm sure I'd regret it the minute I cleared the windowsill. "What investigation?"

"Debra Wagtail gave me a call and told me about your birding expedition."

Nothing in Stripling happened without my mother knowing about it.

I sighed. "It's over." I related the events of last evening.

"Celeste didn't do it." She it said matter-of-factly.

I blinked. "Do you know her?"

"I think I've met her before, but no, I don't know her well."

"Then why do you say she didn't do it?"

"Because, don't you see, it's too easy with her lying there holding the bloody spike. Come on."

"The scene was pretty convincing."

"Staged."

"Mains didn't think so."

"What does he know? If he had his way, your brother would be in prison." My parents might have forgiven Mains for arresting Mark last summer, but they certainly hadn't forgotten. Another reason to forget whatever I thought Mains's intentions were the night before on my doorstep.

I shifted uncomfortably, grinding splinters into my backside from the rough wooden floor.

"Lana! It's Lew! Come to the window!" Lew's voice ricocheted off the bell, giving me an instant headache. Forgetting our quarrel, Mom and I hurried to the window and leaned out. The crowd was still there. Lew stood beside Dad. He waved a piece of white paper in the air. "I got another judge to turn over the ruling. The restraining order against the school board is back in place. Come on down."

When we were back on ground level, reporters waited for my mother at the front door, eager for the evening news sound bite or quote for the local paper. While she was so engaged, I caught up with Lew, who was already heading back to his car. He didn't have my parents' taste for drama and had learned long ago it didn't do any good to advise my parents as to what they should and should not say to the media.

"Lew!" I called as he opened the door to his SUV.

He turned. "I see you were called to the rescue."

"I didn't make much progress reasoning with them."

"No one ever does."

"How true," I paused. "Have you found a kennel?"

Lew slid into his seat, but left the door open. "I've been a little busy, India. Jerry was killed last night."

I swallowed. "I know. I found him."

"You—" He closed his eyes and patted his jacket pocket for his pack of cigarettes. When he found the cigarettes, he lit one and took a long pull.

"Actually, Ina and I found him. I thought the detective would have told you that."

Lew narrowed his eyes in Mains's direction. Four school board members, waving their arms wildly, surrounded Mains.

"You are looking for a kennel, aren't you?"

"It's tricky. I told you about the four-hour limit in a kennel that's written into the trust."

I had a sinking feeling. "How long do you think it will be before the trust is settled between Tess's family members?"

"Cases like this are tricky. They can be settled in a few hours if one of the parties bows out. If everyone holds their ground, it takes longer. Add a couple of murders on top of it, it could take years."

"Years! I can't keep Zach for years!"

Lew slammed the door. The driver side window was down.

"What are you going to do with Zach? Mom will never agree to keep him indefinitely, and I can't either. I'm sure my cat has it in for him. We are talking about dogicide here."

He gunned the engine. "You'll figure something out."

"Me?" I cried, but he didn't hear me because he had already pulled away.

Chapter Thirty-Two

I headed back to my car, which was parked on the street. As I unlocked the door, I heard footsteps jog up from behind me. I turned to find Mains a foot away.

"Thanks for coming down," he said.

I smiled. "No problem. You should thank Lew, though. There was no way she was leaving that tower for me."

He laughed. It was his awful guffaw, which my sister had grumbled about when she and Mains were high school sweethearts.

I found myself smiling.

"Are you hungry?"

"What?"

"I'm starved. Would you like to go to lunch"—he paused—"with me?"

I felt my eyes widen. "I should get back to the library."

"You get a lunch hour, don't you?"

"Well, yes."

"Great. Knute can handle the clean up. Let's go get a bite."

My mind said: Say no, say no.

My mouth said, "Okay."

I gave myself a mental head slap.

He grinned. "Great. How about Byron's?"

I agreed but insisted on driving myself. Byron's was a vegetarian restaurant just outside campus grounds. It was midafternoon and most of the lunch crowd had been and gone. There were several students sitting at tables studying alongside monster mugs of free-trade coffee. The SOEC kids clustered around their favorite table in the back of the restaurant. I wondered if they were planning their next move since the festival was over.

Raka caught my eye and waved. I waved back.

Byron's, which was not named after the Romantic poet but after the owner's favorite dog, had pictures of the owners and Byron shaking hands with local celebrities, including my parents, on the walls. Since Halloween was only days away, the walls and their adornments were covered with a thin layer of cotton spider web, and tiny plastic black spiders marched up and down its length. Softball tournament trophies stood in the windows, and bumper stickers decorated worn table tops.

I sat at a table in the front window, so I could watch Mains approach. I didn't have to wait long. He expertly parallel parked his sedan on the curb into a spot between a Smart Car and a VW bug, a space that I would never even dream of attempting to park in. His floppy dark hair fell over his face as he reached across the car to get something from the passenger seat. I tried to look away. I didn't want him to see me studying him, but I couldn't resist. This wasn't the time to try to sort out my conflicted feelings about Mains. I'd thought after the incident with my brother that maybe Mains and I would be, at the very least, friends. However, after everything was through and Mark drove off into the sunset, I didn't see Mains again until we met over Tess's body. Why then did I agree to have lunch with him? I groaned. The student studying at the next table looked up owl-eyed from his laptop.

Some twenty-first-century woman I was. I could use a telephone just as well as Mains, but I figured it was his move. He knew where to find me. After last summer, he knew more about my family and my life than some of my closest friends, and he chose not to call. I wondered if the Hayes package, because we do come as one quirky set, was too much for him. In the end, it wasn't because I was a girl. It was because I was a wimp that I hadn't called him. So what was I doing here? I wasn't sure what to make of it, if there was anything to make of it. Or maybe I should for once just see how it would turn out on its own without worrying about the outcome.

Mains came inside and sat across from me. We chatted as we both perused the menu. I settled on the wild mushroom bisque, and Mains chose a veggie burger.

"Separate checks, please," I told the waitress. She nodded and took our orders back to the kitchen.

Mains grinned but didn't say anything.

I started with the only topic I felt safe to speak with Mains about: Murder. "What did Celeste say after the arrest?"

Mains sighed. "That she found Jerry lying there. The spike, which it turns out is part of a gate Jerry was making, was on the ground beside him. She picked up the spike and fainted."

"Who would be stupid enough to pick up the murder weapon? Doesn't she have a television?"

"You'd be surprised, but we are pretty sure it's a story. She definitely still had feelings for Jerry. We found her journal in her station in the co-op. She wrote some pretty heated words in there about Tess."

"She might have just been venting."

"Is 'I wish she were dead,' venting?" He arched an eyebrow.

I rolled my eyes. "Obviously, you've never seen a teenage girl's journal. You would be scandalized with the number of threats found there."

"Celeste wasn't a teenager."

Point taken. "I can see her going after Tess, but Jerry? Wouldn't that defeat her agenda?"

The waitress brought our food and left.

Mains took a bite of his burger and chewed thoughtfully.

"Maybe his rejection at the festival that afternoon was too much and she snapped. Who knows? People kill their lovers all the time."

Remembering the scene at the festival, I conceded. "She was upset." The soup was near scalding, and I blew on the spoon. "What about Victor's money? Did you look at the case from that angle?"

"Of course I did. It turned out to be pure coincidence," he said.

"Did you know Jerry was stealing from Victor's house?"

"Not until I read your statement." He eyed me.

I swallowed hard. "Well, was it true?"

Mains nodded. "Jerry had several business loans called due because of the recession. He was selling antiques from Victor's estate to settle his debt. We found some things he hadn't been able to fence before he died in his forge. We do think that is unrelated to the murders."

"That's an awfully convenient coincidence. I would think a desperate need for money would be a much more powerful motive than a broken engagement that was decades old."

Mains shrugged. The gesture was beginning to annoy me.

"Do you think it's fair that you seem to know everything about me, my family, my job, my landlady, and I know very little about you?" I blurted out, much to my own horror.

"Do you see that as a problem?"

"Not a problem, but a disadvantage."

Mains grinned. "What do you want to know?"

That was a scary question, and I didn't know how to answer it.

The waitress came and set our bills on the table. Before I could reach for my check, Mains palmed it. He grinned at my look of dismay. "You go. I've got these."

Rather than argue, I left.

When I got back to the library, Derek was shelving reference books. Bobby was behind the reference desk. "Your super fan has been waiting with bated breath for your return."

I slid into my seat. "I'm sure it's not that bad."

Bobby tapped his pencil's eraser to the tip of my nose. "He's telling everyone you solved his mother's murder. You're quite a campus celebrity."

I groaned.

When Bobby left, Derek came over to the desk. "I can't thank you enough for everything."

"Derek, that's not necessary."

"It is." His eyes gleamed.

I decided my best option was to change the subject. "Are you taking any time off from school? I'm sure your professors would understand, considering the circumstances."

"No, I'd much rather be here."

"I'm worried about you, Derek. Are you taking time to grieve?"

"You're worried about me?" He asked as if it was the best news he'd ever heard.

Well, that backfired, I thought.

Lasha called Derek to the checkout desk. I watched them as she spoke to him before sending him off with a full book cart. Who was I to say Derek wasn't grieving? Just because he wasn't curled up in a ball crying his eyes out didn't mean the pain was any less for him. And how did I know I wouldn't react that way when faced with the same amount of loss? It was wrong for anyone to judge another's grief. It was wrong for me to judge Derek's, and maybe he was crying his eyes out at night, and the rest was all a façade.

Chapter Thirty-Three

To give myself peace of mind, I needed to talk to the other two beaders, Beth and Jendy. After that, I promised myself I would stay away from the case. Mains was the cop. He knew what he was doing, after all. Or so I hoped.

Jendy and Beth were not members of the co-op, so I wouldn't be able to find them that way. Luckily, I remembered the large packet of vendor information that Carmen had given me at the start of the festival. Inside there was a listing of the crafters participating, including their phone numbers. The packet was upstairs in my office. I ran up to the third floor to retrieve it.

Bobby was in the office, working on a lesson plan. "Well, hello there, Sherlock. Erin told me all the details about your run-in with the campus newspaper. All in all, this whole thing has the makings of an excellent story." He tapped his chin with his pen.

Like I was a painter outside of the library, Bobby was a budding romance writer. He'd recently signed his first book contract and now walked around the library with his chest puffed out like a proud hunter who'd felled a lion. I was proud of Bobby, too, and of myself, since I was always his first reader and grammar corrector. Bobby's grammar is atrocious.

I winced as he brought up Erin. This was the perfect time to talk to him about her. I didn't look forward to it. I closed our office door.

Bobby laughed. "You don't have to tell me everything now.

Wait until your shift at the reference desk is over."

"This isn't about that, and the reference desk can wait."

Bobby closed his laptop and folded his hands on top of it.

"It's about Erin."

Bobby made a face and reopened his computer.

"You need to stop socializing with her outside of the library. People are beginning to talk."

"People? Which people?" he snorted.

"That student reporter Erin told you about made a snide comment to Erin about it today." I paused. "She even threatened to write about it in the paper. You could lose your job, and worse, you would have a hard time finding another job at any college with that type of reputation."

"We are just hanging out."

I clenched my jaw. "That's not how Erin sees it. I've seen how she looks at you."

He snapped his laptop closed. "Is it similar to the way Derek looks at you?"

I felt like I had been punched in the gut. "That's different."

"Is it?"

"Yes, it is, I'm not encouraging him. Bobby, Erin is head over heels for you, and you're making it worse."

"So agreeing to solve his mother's murder isn't encouraging him. It sure looks like it to me, but what do I know?"

I sighed. "Promise me you will be careful."

He opened his computer again. "Sure. Now I think you'd better get back to the desk."

Behind the reference desk again, I had a sick feeling in my stomach while I consulted the crafter list. I hated fighting with Bobby, but it seemed like we argued more often these days, ever since his last romance had ended in disaster, a disaster I'd played a large role in.

I was in luck; Beth was the owner of a gift shop downtown.

At four, I left the library and went directly to the Pumpkin Hutch. The store was on a side street but in view of the square. It sold antiques and collectibles. I had been inside once before, many years ago. The front door said the shop closed at four. The door was unlocked, and I stepped inside.

A jack-o'-lantern-shaped bell rang when I entered the store. All the displays were built around the upcoming holidays, Halloween, Thanksgiving, and Christmas. The store was empty, and I stopped and inspected a basket of hand-knit pumpkins, imagining what Templeton would do to them if he got his paws on those bright orange balls of yarn. Near the register, there was a large permanent display of the three beaders' jewelry. I noticed some of Celeste's designs among them. Loose beads and clasps were also for sale if shoppers preferred to create their own pieces.

"I don't want to talk about this anymore," a voice rose in anger. It sounded like Beth, and she was in the back of the store. Behind the cash register was a doorway.

"We have to talk about this. We have to help her." The second voice was Jendy's, I was certain.

"I'm doing what I can."

"It's not enough."

"It has to be." There was a pause. "Did you lock the shop up?"

I hurried back to the front door and opened it as if I had just come in, pulling it hard so that the pumpkin bell rang loudly.

Jendy stepped into the room. "I'm sorry, we closed at four." She blinked when she saw me. "What are you doing here?"

Beth appeared behind her.

I thought quickly. "I wondered how Celeste is doing. I know a good lawyer she might want to talk to. His name is Lewis Clive. He's been a huge help to my family for years. There might be a conflict because he works for the Lepcheck estate, but he's a good lawyer and could refer Celeste to someone."

"Celeste already has a lawyer, but thank you for your concern. Like Jendy said, the store is closed. If you'd like to come back tomorrow to buy something, we will be open at nine." Beth opened the cash register's drawer and started counting dollar bills.

"How is Celeste doing?" I asked, ignoring the dismissal.

"Fine. She's fine. It's all a misunderstanding. She'll be home very soon."

Jendy rolled her eyes but didn't say anything.

"Believe me, I know how tough this can be. I'm happy to help you any way I can."

Beth's eyes narrowed. "I think you have done enough damage. Celeste doesn't need your help and neither do we."

Fine, I thought. I offered help. I came and appeased my conscience. Mains can take it from here.

I could have been wrong, but I thought Jendy looked reluctant to see me go.

Chapter Thirty-Four

The next day, I decided to pay my favorite lawyer a visit during my lunch break. Lew was no longer taking my phone calls.

When I got to Lew's office, his secretary was at the front desk. She was about forty, wore glasses, and had her red hair pulled back in a severe chignon. She was also new. Lew had trouble keeping secretaries. He blamed it on the cigarette smoke, which permeated his office, but I think his barking of orders was the more likely reason. "May I help you?"

"I'm here to see Lew. Is he available?"

"Name?"

I gave her my name, and she picked up her phone. "Mr. Clive, there is an India Hayes here to see you."

I heard Lew through the receiver. "Tell her I'm out." His tone was gruff.

The secretary reddened. "He's unavailable at the moment. Can I make an appointment for you?"

"Is he with a client?"

"Umm . . . no."

I appreciated her honesty.

"I'll go on back then. It will only take a minute."

"You can't—"

The hallway was short, and I was already at Lew's open door before she could finish the sentence.

"I thought I told Myrna to tell you I was out," Lew said when I stepped into his office. He was sitting behind his barebones desk with a half-eaten hoagie sandwich sitting on the blotter. He had mayonnaise on his red beard. I pointed to his chin, and he wiped his face with a paper napkin.

"I don't think Myrna's a very good liar," I said.

"She won't be much of a lawyer then. Cripes, maybe I should fire her."

"No, keep her. I like her."

"You would," he grumbled.

The phone rang, and Lew picked it up. "No, no, Myrna, it's nothing to worry about. I'll talk to Miss Hayes and send her on her way very shortly." He glowered at me and hung up.

"You've heard about Jerry Ross's death, I assume." I sat on the sofa under the window.

"I have, and the police told me too about Jerry' sticky-finger policy when it came to Victor's antiques. You were the one who figured that out?"

"Who told you it was me?"

"Detective Mains."

I felt a rush of pleasure. Mains certainly didn't have to give me the credit, but I relished the fact that he had. "Were you able to get the coins and antiques back?"

"A lot of them. Jerry hid some in the storeroom behind his forge. Probably knew Tess would run across them if he hid them at home. As for the rest of the stuff, who knows if we will ever see them again? We've put out bulletins to the coin traders and antiques dealers to be on the lookout for the items which have already been sold. Not that I expect to get them back. He probably sold them over the Internet. They could be in another continent by now, much less in the county."

"Mains said he did it to pay off some debt."

"He had some pretty major loans called in because of the economy. He used the loans to keep his blacksmithing business afloat and didn't have the money to pay them." Lew patted his pocket for his packet of cigarettes.

"I thought he was doing well. He said he had a big commission."

"He did, and that would have helped but not paid off the loans completely. The blacksmithing jobs were just too few and far between for him."

"Did he have any heirs?"

Lew shrugged.

I pursed my lips together in thought.

"If that's all," Lew said, gesturing to his hoagie.

"I want a dog update."

"There has to be someone else who can take that dog. All I have gotten from you is grief since I handed the pooch over."

"Let's just say, Mom's not pleased with how attached Dad is getting to Zach. Wouldn't you prefer I come here and talk to you about it rather than the reverend?"

"I see your point, but like I've said to you countless times already, I'm stuck legally. The dog can't be put in a kennel for more than four hours at a time."

"That seems like an awfully specific rule for Victor to insist on beyond the grave. Can you do that in a will?"

"It's not part of the will, it's part of the trust. Let me give you a legal lesson."

"I'm all ears."

Lew stopped just short of rolling his eyes. "Before Victor died, he set up a pet trust for Zach. The trust would take effect after his death. A trust doesn't go through probate. Even with that said, the will was only in probate court for three months, even though Samuel Lepcheck took issue with it."

"If Lepcheck contested the will, how could it go through so quickly?"

"The judge was an old golfing buddy of Victor's. He pushed it through. I didn't have to do much of anything."

"Nice to have friends with power."

Lew nodded. "With a trust, the creator of the trust—in this case, Victor—can give specific instructions detailing the care of his pet. It can be something as simple as allotting a set amount of money for the caregiver to spend at his or her discretion, or as specific as to the number of walks the dog must have during a week. If the instructions are part of the trust, they have to be carried out for the caregiver to receive their funds from the trust to care for the animal." He sighed. "Another issue with the trust Victor created was that Tess Ross was made both Zach's caregiver and trustee. Usually, someone would make the pet's caregiver and the trustee of the pet's trust a different person. This is to avoid any potential abuse."

"Did you advise him not to do that?"

Lew squinted at me. "Of course I did. But Victor wasn't one to listen after he made his mind up on what he wanted to do. Also, usually someone will not put all of their money and possessions in a trust to sustain a pet for the rest of its life. I advised Victor not to do that as well, but he insisted in putting everything in a trust to the dog. There is no way two million dollars could be spent on a dog's care."

"I don't know. Look at all those Hollywood socialites buying their puppies designer outfits and jewels."

Lew gave me a look. "If Tess had lived, she would have received all the remainder of the trust because she was named the sole beneficiary."

"To use however she pleased? She didn't have a list of instructions she had to follow as the beneficiary?"

"Beneficiaries don't work that way. Only trustees do. After Zach's death, the money would no longer be in a trust."

I thought for a minute. "No other beneficiaries were named?"

He shook his head. "Because no one was named as a secondary beneficiary, all the heirs have a chance to make a grab for the money."

"Who are the potential heirs?"

"Tess's siblings, Debra and Sam, and her son, Derek, to some extent.

"Ultimately, it sounds to me like Victor wanted Tess to have the money. If that was the case, why didn't he leave some of it to her right off?"

"I don't know, and any time I would question him about it, which admittedly wasn't often, he wouldn't answer. Victor wasn't the easiest man in the world to get along with, and he was adamant this was what he wanted to do with this money."

"Was he crazy? Senile? Loony tunes?"

He pulled at his red beard. "I get what you mean. And no, I got the sense Victor, even in his advanced age, knew exactly what he was doing. He was doing what he wanted to do, and nobody, but nobody, was going to be able to change his mind."

I thought for a minute. "So what are you telling me about Zach?"

"You might have a house guest for a long while."

I grimaced. "My parents might, you mean." I stood. "I need to get back to work."

Lew picked up his hoagie. "This isn't the last I'm going to hear from you about this dog, is it?"

"Nope," I said and showed myself out, giving nervous Myrna a finger wave as I passed her desk.

On the way back to the library, I called my dad. "Do you mind keeping Zach for a little while longer?"

"Why? Is something wrong?"

"No more than usual. Lew's having hard time finding a kennel for Zach."

"It's no trouble at all to keep him here until everything is settled."

I heard a woofed agreement in the background. Dad laughed.

"We were just at the farmers' market picking up a few things for dinner before your mother gets home from church."

I suspected Mom wouldn't agree with Zach's living arrangements, but I took Dad's word for it. "Can you tell Mom for me? About Zach?"

"Sure, but she's not going to like it." There was a smile in his voice.

With Zach's housing settled for the time being, I entered the library determined to put Tess and Jerry's murders behind me. The police had a very good suspect in jail. Celeste had means, motive, and opportunity. No wonder Mains arrested her. If I was so confident Mains and his cronies had the right person in lockup, why did I have to keep repeating it to myself? And why couldn't I get Celeste's face out of my head?

Chapter Thirty-Five

For the next two days, I did what I promised myself: I put Tess, Jerry, Celeste, and the murders behind me. The only reminders were the news coverage in the local section of the Akron newspaper and the grateful look on Derek's face when I arrived at the library each day.

The following Thursday was Halloween. Lasha was pro-holidays and encouraged (i.e., threatened) the library staff to participate. On Halloween, a costume was a requirement. Lasha felt it made us more relatable to the students. I thought it made us larger targets for ridicule, but what did I know?

As I walked across campus to the library, I noticed many of the students were in costume. Superheroes, witches, mummies, zombies, and sexy cats were all present and accounted for.

When I stepped into our office, Bobby was already at his desk. He was wearing a designer suit and his hair was slicked back. "Are you supposed to be a waiter?"

His eyes narrowed. "For your information, I'm an international spy." He looked me up and down. "I'd hoped you'd be more creative this year."

"What's wrong with my costume?" I looked down at my gypsy outfit of a gaudy wrapped skirt, peasant blouse, bangles, and beaded necklace, all of which I'd found in my mother's closet. I completed the look with red lips and a scarf tied around my head. This was my fourth consecutive year of wearing it. Sadly, I gave the clothes back to mother every year because the pieces were staples in her wardrobe. Not as an everyday ensemble. At least I didn't think so.

"You could have worn the frontier girl number Carmen gave you."

"I hope to never see that dress again. And how is an international spy creative? All you did is put on a suit."

"Did you even see what I did to my hair? It took a lot of product to get this effect."

I rolled my eyes, but I felt relieved Bobby was joking with me after the heated Erin conversation.

"I'm glad you stopped up here before I have to go down to the reference desk."

"Because?" I arched an eyebrow. It seemed to me Bobby was on the cusp of asking for a favor, which usually involved me picking up one or more of his library tours.

"It's about Erin. I just want you to know you're right. I talked to her." He grimaced. "She misunderstood our friendship. I won't be spending time with her outside of the library anymore."

I winced. Erin was a good kid, and I would be sad to see her go when she graduated in the spring. I didn't want her hurt, but in this case, it was unavoidable. "Was she upset?"

"She called me some words I didn't know. I need to brush up on my insults."

"I'm sorry, Bobby. Do you want me to talk to her?"

He shook his head. "Let her cool off for a few days. She'll get over it soon enough. At least, I hope so. I feel responsible."

"You are."

"Gee, thanks." He paused. "Talking to Erin was something I needed to do. I just didn't know it. Thanks for telling me to do it."

My jaw dropped. A Bobby thank you was so rare. Before I could say anything, he stood.

"I need to get downstairs," he said as he left the office.

Bobby was downstairs at the reference desk, which meant I had the office to myself for most of the morning. I was updating the library's website when there was a knock on the opened door. I looked up, half-expecting to find Bobby there to retract this gratitude, but instead found Jendy. Her purple hair stood on end, and she wore a miniskirt with leggings under her black leather jacket. The outfit was a long cry from the mobcap and gingham dress she'd worn during the festival.

"Can I come in?"

I nodded. She sat in Bobby's desk chair and picked up the paperback romance Bobby had left on his desk. It had a picture of a burly shirtless man and a voluptuous woman staring off into the distance. She made a face. "The lady you work with reads these?"

"It's a guy, and yeah, he does. You met him at the festival. Remember Bobby?"

Jendy curled her lip and shrugged. "Whatever works for you, I guess."

Looks like I nipped that infatuation in the bud, I thought happily.

"Nice outfit."

I thanked her even though I wasn't sure her comment was meant to be a compliment.

Silence fell on the room. "Jendy, did you have something to talk to me about?"

"I know O.M. Blocken."

I felt myself go still. O.M. was the sister of my friend who was murdered last summer. It was a summer I'd tried to forget.

"She's a few years younger than me, still in high school." She made a face again. "But she's cool. We have mutual friends. Anyway, I told her about what happened with Celeste, and your name came up. She said I should talk to you, that you could help Celeste."

"I don't know what I can do for Celeste now."

"You came into Beth's store a couple of days ago and offered help then."

I sighed.

"I know she didn't do it. Celeste wouldn't hurt anyone."

"She still cared about Jerry, and Tess was in the way."

"Tess and Jerry were married for three years. Wouldn't you think she'd have done something before now if she was so upset about it?"

She had a point.

"Do you have any proof she's innocent? Does she have an alibi for either night?"

Jendy drooped. "You sound like the stupid lawyer Beth found. If she had an alibi, do you think she'd be under arrest?"

"Is she still in jail?"

"No, she's out on bail now. You should go talk to her. She's at her house."

"How do you know she'll talk to me?"

"I'll go with you."

"Why do you think I will help you?"

"Because O.M. said you would."

Her tone was matter-of-fact, and she was right. "What's her address?" I asked.

Jendy told me, and we agreed to meet at five-thirty outside Celeste's house.

After work, I stopped at home to change out of my gypsy outfit and into my version of suburban chic—a hoodie and jeans—instead of driving directly to see Celeste. Even with the stop, I beat Jendy there. I parked on the curb in front of Celeste's home. The house was a small Cape Cod with bright blue shutters. From the awning, a mobile of glass beads tinkled in the cool October breeze. Up and down the street, porch lights flickered on to tell the trick-or-treaters which houses had candy. The beggars would be hitting the neighborhood at six and would continue until eight.

Across the street a mother lined up her three children, all in their Halloween best for the obligatory photographs. An engine wheezed down the street. I looked behind me and saw Jendy ride up on a motorized scooter. "Sorry I'm late," she said. "I had to kick-start my ride."

I could see why. The vintage scooter looked as if it could fall to pieces with the slightest impact.

Jendy led the way up the walk. She rang the doorbell, but when there was no answer, she produced a key from her pocket. "Beth had one and gave it to me when I said I'd check on Celeste after work." We stepped inside. The house was dark. A nightlight was the only lighting in the small living room. The blinds were closed and shades were pulled over them for good measure. When my eyes adjusted, I made out the sofa and a lumpy form on it.

Jendy stepped into the room and turned on a table lamp. The form, someone, I assumed Celeste, moved under a blue fuzzy blanket. "Celeste, it's Jendy, and I brought India with me."

Celeste peeked out from behind her blanket. Her dark blue eyes were red and puffy. A half-empty tissue box and a mountain of used tissues sat beside her on the sofa. She sniffed. "Why?"

Jendy sat on an ottoman, and I perched on a flowered armchair that matched the sofa.

"Because she can help you. She can find out who really committed those murders."

I stiffened. Jendy was making promises I might not be able to keep.

Celeste blinked. "How? She's a librarian."

Jendy told her how I'd helped find the murderer of O.M.'s sister last summer. It was the first time I'd heard the story from someone else's mouth but that didn't make it any less painful to remember.

Celeste pulled the blanket securely under chin. "I don't know how that will help me."

"I don't know how it can either, Celeste, truly, but Jendy asked me to come here and I have," I said.

She lowered the blanket a half inch.

"Who do you think killed Tess and Jerry?" I asked.

"I don't know. I don't know why anyone would kill either of them, especially Jerry."

"You can't think of anyone."

"I knew Jerry was angry with Tess's family over her uncle's will."

"Did Jerry talk to you about the will?" I asked, a little surprised. I'd gotten the impression from the outburst between Celeste and Jerry a few days ago that most conversations between the two were one-sided.

She shook her head. "They were in the co-op one day and arguing about it. My studio's not far from Tess's in the barn."

"Do you remember what they said?"

"Tess was saying she wanted to give away part of the money. I didn't know until later she meant to give a portion of the money to the co-op. Jerry was trying to convince her not to."

"Did she say why she wanted to give the money away?"

Celeste reached for a fresh tissue and blew her nose. "Tess said she didn't know why Victor left her in charge of the trust and felt she had to do something good with the money."

Jendy whistled. "She was given two million dollars just for the heck of it. I wouldn't mind having an uncle like that. The only uncle I have has a beer belly and runs a bait shop."

"Did you overhear anything else?" I asked.

"Tess said she was searching her uncle's things to see if she could find out. I think she felt bad that her brother and sister were essentially written out of the will. That or she felt bad that they were giving her such a hard time about it. Maybe if she knew Victor's reasons for the decision, she'd feel better about it and her brother and sister would, too."

Knowing Lepcheck, I doubted that.

"Did she ever find anything?"

Celeste shrugged. "That was the last I heard of it."

Jendy leaned forward. "Do you think that's why she was killed?"

"I don't know," I said.

I stayed for a few minutes longer before making my excuses. Jendy stayed behind to microwave Celeste a cup of soup. I was surprised nineteen-year-old Jendy would spend Halloween night in with Celeste instead of out with her friends. She was what Ina called "a good egg."

As I pulled into my driveway, Templeton's black figure sat in my kitchen window for the whole street to see, as if he knew this was his night to shine. Ina was on the white resin chair on her front porch. A large plastic bowl of candy sat on her lap. Theodore, my brother's cat and Ina's ward, sat at her feet. He wore a pirate hat and a black patch over his left eye. He didn't move and his other eye was closed, so I assumed he was sleeping as a form of self-preservation. At least Ina hadn't put a peg leg on the poor creature as her original plan included.

Chapter Thirty-Six

After the quick stop at home to grab my own bowl of candy, I drove to my sister's house. Carmen and Chip lived in a Dutch colonial house just three blocks away from me. As it would be Poppy and Lilly's first Halloween, Carmen invited the family over to see the girls and Nicholas in their costumes.

My dad's van was in the driveway when I pulled in. Nicholas was on the front porch. He wore a policeman's uniform.

"Hello, Officer Tuchelli," I said.

He giggled and patted the holstered toy gun on his hip. "Daddy's taking me trick-or-treating."

"That sounds fun."

He nodded. "We are going to where the rich people live so we can get the king-size bars." He held a finger to his mouth. "Shh, Mom's not supposed to know. She thinks we are staying in our neighborhood."

"Your secret's safe with me." I stepped into the house.

Nicholas skirted around my legs and pulled his gun on his grandmother. "Stick 'em up!"

"Carmen, how can you a let a child have a gun?" Mom asked. My mother was a black cat for the holiday. She had a black nose and white whiskers painted on her face and a headband of cat ears on her head.

"First of all, it's a toy, and second of all, his father gave it to him." Carmen scowled at her husband as she adjusted the girls' costumes. Chip, in fireman garb, slunk out of the room. He was a pretty smart guy.

I paused to take in the twins' adorableness. Poppy was dressed as a peapod, and Lilly was dressed as a carrot. I also noted Zach was dozing on Carmen's hearth as if he belonged there. He was even in costume in the form of a superhero cape.

Nicholas saw me looking at the girls. "Peas and carrots. Mom said it's cute. I don't get it."

"Not much to get," I said. "But it's most definitely cute. You're cute, too."

"Eww. Policemen can't be cute!"

"Oh, yes, they can." I tickled him.

He chortled. "Don't make me throw you into the big house!"

Carmen arched an eyebrow at our mother. "I wonder where he'd have learned that phrase."

Dad, who was dressed as a farmer in bib overalls, a red bandana around his throat, and blacked out teeth, reached over the arm of the couch to wiggle Lilly's ear. She smiled. "Please, let's not fight." He picked Lilly up and deposited her on his lap. Rolling the wheelchair a little closer, he plucked Poppy from the couch and plopped her down beside her sister.

Nicholas left the room. Maybe he and Chip were going to work on a map of the best houses to hit in Stripling.

Mom looked around frantically. "Where's the camera? Aren't they darling?" She found her digital camera and started clicking pictures of Dad and the girls.

Carmen turned to me. "Where's your costume? I told you to wear a costume."

Carmen was dressed in an adult-sized onesie. Her bobbed hair was separated into two pigtails, and a dusting of freckles was drawn on her face with eyebrow pencil.

"Really? You expected me to wear a costume after forcing me to wear that awful dress to the festival?"

"Don't complain. It wasn't that bad."

"It was. Trust me."

"You only wore it one day anyway." Carmen pursed her lips. "I'm just glad it's over. The whole thing nearly fell apart."

"Are you saying you won't be chairing the Founders' Festival next year?" I hoped I didn't sound too happy at the prospect. However, if Carmen wasn't involved in the festival, I couldn't be coerced into running the face-painting booth. My hands still smarted from cramps after painting tiny figures on children's cheeks in the cold.

"I never said that. I can tell you it won't be on Martin's campus. What a disaster." She looked thoughtful. "In fact, next year I will chair it, and it will be on the square. That's a more centralized location anyway, and it will attract people to downtown."

"The parking will be a nightmare," Mom said.

Carmen scowled at her.

"Better wait until it's closer to the time to make a decision like that," I said.

Carmen looked dubious. In her mind, it was always *why put off planning for tomorrow that which could be done today?* "I already have plans on how to improve it. Not just the change of location. Other things, too."

"All the crafters making it out alive would help," I said.

Carmen grimaced.

"We're off," Chip said. The front door slammed.

"Did you take an extra jacket? Chip! You forgot the flashlight." She hurried after her husband and son with a flashlight, jacket, and extra pillow case clutched in her hands.

Mom handed me the camera. "Take our picture." She squatted by Dad's chair, and I snapped pictures.

"How's the bell tower crusade going?" I asked between clicks.

"Minor setback," Dad said. "We will get it right yet."

"That's right," Mom agreed. "We have a plan."

"You're not going to chain yourself to anything, are you?" I handed Mom the camera.

"Not at present."

I decided not to worry about it at the moment.

Dad bounced the girls on his knees.

The front door slammed opened. "India, bring the candy. The beggars are starting to arrive," Carmen called.

I grabbed the bowl of candy and headed to the porch. I handed Carmen the bowl and sat on one of the white rockers. Carmen dropped a chocolate bar into the waiting hand of a little mouse.

After a witch and a gymnast came to claim their own pieces of candy, Carmen turned to me. "Does Ricky really think Celeste killed Tess and Jerry?"

I nodded. "The scene was pretty convincing."

Carmen's drawn-on freckles quivered. "You think he's wrong." It was a statement, not a question.

"I'm not sure," I admitted.

"Ricky can be bullheaded. I remember that about him. It's one of the reasons we fought so much."

Her mention of Mains caused me to remember another Halloween when Carmen was in high school, and I was still in grade school. There had been a dance on the square that Halloween. It was the only Halloween dance I can remember. Mains came to pick Carmen up for the dance. He'd already been her on-and-off-again boyfriend for two years, and he was a common fixture in the house. Carmen had worn a yellow dress, and Mains a white shirt and dress pants. I was in my construction worker costume, ready to start my beggar's night rounds, bent on scoring as many king-sized chocolate candy bars as I could.

Carmen twirled her yellow skirt for Mains when he arrived in his dad's minivan to pick her up. He'd whistled appreciatively. They hadn't noticed me there on the other side of the garage waiting for my friend Olivia to come so we could hit the streets. They whispered and laughed together before leaving. Their rapport with each other—when they weren't in the middle of a fight—was a central part of my childhood. I didn't know how I could think of Mains as anything other than my sister's ex-boyfriend. He'd been that for far too many years. I shook my head to clear out the Halloween cobwebs. This memory and the countless others like it were the reasons I held Mains at an arm's length.

Carmen sighed. "I don't believe Celeste did it, either. I know she and Jerry were engaged a long time ago, but if she was so upset about it, why didn't she kill Tess back then? It doesn't make sense to wait so long. A jealous ex-fiancée commits a crime of passion in the heat of the moment."

"Look at you, Miss Detective," I said.

Carmen grimaced.

I silently agreed with her assessment. So if Celeste didn't kill Tess and Jerry, who did and why?

Mom and Dad came out, each carrying a granddaughter, and without a word exchanged, Carmen and I agreed to drop our conversation.

On Carmen's front porch, surrounded by my family and as the hobbits, ballerinas, and firemen came to claim their goodies, I thought of Celeste alone in her home with that pile of tissues. This could be her last Halloween at home for a very long time.

Chapter Thirty-Seven

The Halloween decorations that were spooky and whimsical on Halloween night looked garish and cheap in the light of November first, All Saints Day. Even Templeton didn't seem to bask in his black catness as much. Not that he found himself any less handsome. He licked his paws and smoothed down his ruff.

I planned to paint all morning, as it was my day off. I was far behind on a landscape I'd hoped to enter into a statewide contest. If I won or even placed, I would have my name in newspapers all over Ohio. The exposure would be great. Instead, I decided to drop in on Debra Wagtail.

Outside, remnants of frost clung to the lawn and the cheerful faces of the leprechauns. Despite the chill in the air, Ina sipped her daily mug of Irish cream coffee on the front porch. It wouldn't be long before the snow would fly. I wondered if we would get yet another white Thanksgiving. "Where are you off to this morning?" she asked.

It was hopeless to keep anything a secret from Ina, so I told her.

"Debra's? Why?"

"I want to hear her opinion on Victor's will."

She clapped her hands. "Hot dog! I knew it all ended too easily. You're going to reopen the case!"

"I'm just going to ask a few questions, and I can't reopen a case. I'm not a cop, remember?"

"Pshaw! Let me grab my purse."

Debra lived in a condominium. Hers was one of several dozen ranch-style condominiums clustered around a clubhouse and swimming pool. The pool was closed, but a smattering of silver-haired retirees played an early morning round of bocce. Big pots of orange and burgundy mums sat under Debra's windows, and bird feeders hung from a large maple tree in the front yard. No surprise there.

Ina rang the doorbell. A minute later Debra opened the door. She invited us in as if she'd been expecting us.

Even knowing Debra's affinity for her feathered friends did not prepare me for the inside of her home. Birds. Birds everywhere. Not live birds, but ceramic birds, wooden birds, beaded birds, glass birds, metal birds. Birds on tables, birds on chairs, birds on the floor, birds hanging from the ceiling. I'd seen kitschy collections before, but nothing of this caliber.

"Have a seat." Debra directed us to the kitchen table, which had a finch-patterned tablecloth. I glanced over at Ina, who chose a seat closest to the wall and farthest away from me, to gauge her reaction to the birds. Ina seemed to take the chirpy decor in stride. But then again, this was from a woman who decked out her apartment in Viva Ireland style. Green was the color of choice for everything in Ina's world. I mused whether or not this was an older-woman trait. One day would I suddenly become the frog lady? It began small with a ribbit ringtone, and *bam,* I wake up at seventy with an amphibian infestation. I shivered and vowed to change my ringtone back to the ice cream truck song, no matter how much it annoyed Bobby. Perhaps, that was part of its enduring charm.

"Are you cold?" Debra asked.

"No, I'm fine," I answered quickly.

"I'll make us some tea, and I have muffins. One of my neighbors made them for me." She held out a plate of banana muffins to me, and then made the same offer to Ina. We each took one, and Debra put the kettle on the stove before she sat down in between Ina and me.

"Where's your husband?" Ina asked.

"My husband's at work. He's retiring at the end of the year."

"That's exciting," I said.

She nodded. "Yes and no. He's a good man, but he doesn't have many hobbies. He's bound to be underfoot. I married him for better or worse, but not for lunch."

I laughed, and Ina grinned.

"Maybe you can interest him in your birding."

Debra laughed. "Oh, no, I've given up trying to do that." The teakettle whistled, and Debra hurried to the stove. "Something tells me you aren't here to talk about my husband's retirement or birding."

"India thinks they've arrested the wrong person for Tess's murder." Ina took a large bite of muffin after her announcement.

Good thing Ina wisely sat out of reach because I could have kicked her just then.

Debra put a teapot in the middle of the table and rejoined us. "Is that true? I thought you were the one who caught her."

More like stumbled upon her, I thought. "Her friends don't think she's the one."

Debra looked dubious. "Don't friends always think that of someone they care about?"

"They were pretty convincing." I glanced at Ina, who gave me her little impish smile. "Ina was mistaken. I don't necessarily think the police arrested the wrong person. Celeste may turn out to be the killer, but I'm not sure."

"I don't know about you, but I want to be sure. I don't want the wrong person to go to prison."

"So you'll help?" Ina asked.

"I don't know how I can. I don't know Tess's friends well. I don't even know all of their names."

"What if this isn't related to her friends? What if it goes back to Victor and his money?" I asked.

"Oh, that again. I thought the police ruled it out."

"We are trying every angle," Ina said.

Debra poured the tea. "Fine. I'll do what I can to help."

I swallowed a bite of muffin. "Why do you think Victor left his money to Tess? Were they close?"

"Not at all. In fact, Tess might have been the most distant from Victor out of all of us. She was too caught up in her artist world to pay much attention to Victor."

"Were there any restrictions to the trust aside from Zach's care?"

"Not that I know of. I believe Tess could do whatever she wanted with the money after Zach's death."

"I heard Tess planned to use some of the money to help the co-op."

"I wouldn't know that. You might want to ask David Berring."

"You know David?" I asked, surprised because she had mentioned a few minutes before that she didn't know any of Tess's friends.

"Before he and Tess opened the co-op, he was my uncle's executive assistant. I believe that's how he and Tess met."

I blinked. "When was that?"

"Oh, my, I don't know. I think he worked for Uncle Victor until eight or ten years ago. After he quit, my uncle didn't hire a new executive assistant. He said there wasn't anyone he could trust like David."

"So he was upset when David resigned."

Debra ran her finger around the rim of her mug. "No, I wouldn't say that. Anxious was more like it. I think he was worried about handling his affairs on his own. Although by that time, he was just a figurehead in the company." She looked thoughtful. "He made a big donation to the co-op to help Tess and David get it off the ground. They had another business partner, too, a woman, but I can't remember her name."

"It was Celeste, the woman charged with the murder."

Debra's eyes widened. "Really. Oh, my."

Ina leaned forward. "What kind of donation did Victor make?"

"He bought the property for them. I remember because Sam was livid about it. He said it was a huge waste of our inheritance, not knowing of course that we wouldn't be getting a dime in the end."

I could imagine the scene. I'd witnessed Provost Lepcheck lose his temper in one too many faculty meetings. It wasn't pretty.

"Did Victor usually support local arts?" I asked.

"No, not before this. I guess he was just supporting Tess and David."

"Did he support the causes you and your brother cared about? Your birds and Lepcheck's Martin?"

"No, he didn't," she murmured. "Sam tried to convince Uncle to leave some of the money to Martin in his will, but as you know, that didn't happen. Sam was furious." She reddened. "Not that I think he had anything to do with either murder."

"Of course not," Ina said soothingly.

Ina and I finished our tea and muffins and left.

"Where to now?" Ina asked when we were back in my car.

"Victor's house."

"Are we going to break and enter?" Ina had a gleam in her eye.

"No, but I'm going to call in a favor."

"You're no fun," Ina muttered. "When will I get a chance to try my lock picks? They just arrived in the mail yesterday."

Chapter Thirty-Eight

Lew met us outside Victor's home. The house was a centennial gray Victorian home, which looked like it was better suited for an estate in Vermont than a small town in Ohio. Two massive oak trees dominated the front yard. Their leaves covered the lawn and shrubbery like a brown paper blanket.

Lew was staring at the leaves with his hands on his hips when Ina and I pulled into the brick driveway.

Ina shuffled her feet through the leaves. "You should get someone over here to rake these up. The neighbors are going to start to complain, especially on the account that his house is so close to the square. You don't want the garden club on your behind."

He reached into his jacket for his ever-present pack of cigarettes.

"Thanks for letting us in, Lew," I said.

He shrugged. "I owed you. How's the dog doing?"

"Fine. Dad's taken a shine to him. I'm thinking about getting him a pet when this is all settled."

Lew grinned. "I'd gladly turn Zach over to him, but I can't, since the dog's a millionaire." He blew out a puff of smoke. "So why exactly do you need to get in here?"

"I thought it would help me feel more at ease about Celeste's arrest."

He arched an eyebrow.

"Aren't you curious as to why Victor left his money and dog

to Tess? From what I've gathered, she and Victor weren't particularly close."

"I don't need to know why my clients do things, especially if they settle their bills with me on time, and Victor always did." He walked to the front door. "But if you want to go on a wild goose chase to find out, be my guest. If you find anything, it might help me settle up his estate in the end."

The front door opened into a small foyer with a stone-tiled floor. Ina wove between Lew and me and hurried into the house. "I've always wanted to visit this house. It's one of the oldest in Stripling. Juliet is going be green with envy when I tell her." She disappeared down the hall.

A second later, there was a crash.

"It's okay. It was just a vase. Not an antique or anything," Ina called from deep in the house.

Lew gave me a look before stalking off in the direction of Ina's voice. I went in search of Victor's home office. In the library I found a large desk. By the papers piled there, I suspected that's where Victor did most of his business after he sold his company, Summit Polymer. There were two large file drawers on either side of the desk. They were unlocked. The left-hand-side drawers were files that referred to Victor's business. I gave them a cursory look, but since I knew next to nothing about chemical engineering, I didn't glean much from that drawer. The drawer on the right side was more promising. They looked like Victor's personal files.

Deep in the house, a cell phone rang. A minute later Lew stepped into the room. "That was Sam Lepcheck's lawyer. I have to go for an emergency meeting about the trust. Hopefully, everything can be settled today."

"That would be a relief. Zach's a great dog, but I will be happy to turn him back over to his family."

Lew tossed me a set of keys, and I caught them in midair.

"Lock up before you leave. You can drop those at my office later today."

"Sure."

Lew looked around. "Where's your pal?"

I shrugged.

"Don't let her break anything else, okay?"

"I'll try."

I opened the filing cabinet. Bills, tax returns . . . police reports? I removed this last folder. There was only one document inside, and it was dated ten years before. It was the police report from the hit-and-run that killed Derek's father. The document was depressingly short. After reading it, I rocked back in the leather desk chair. I knew families could get police reports if they requested them. They were part of the public record after all—but why did Victor have a copy? Did Tess even know he had a copy of the report?

Seth Welch was hit by a car when he was walking home from his CPA office on the town square. It was tax season, and he was heading home later than normal, so it was already after dark when he left the office. He was crossing at a crosswalk when he was hit. He died instantly. The police on the scene reported the streetlight near the accident had been out, and Welch had been wearing a dark suit, which might have contributed to the driver of the car not seeing him. There were no tire marks on the road that would give an indication the driver had tried to stop before hitting Welch. The driver was never caught. The rookie cop, who filed the report, was none other than Officer Richmond Mains.

There was a crash from the floor above me.

"I'm okay," was Ina's cry.

I put the report back where I found it and followed the direction of Ina's voice.

I walked up the mahogany staircase, trailing my hand up the

railing. I disturbed a thick layer of dust lingering there. The second floor was lined with closed mahogany doors. At the end of the hall, a door was cracked open, and I could hear Ina muttering to herself. "Why would a man have such a breakable trinket?"

I found her in what must have been Victor's bedroom. A king-sized four-post bed dominated the center and two large black dressers flanked the walls. Despite the open drapes, the room was dim with dark carpet and wallpaper. A heavy-looking chandelier hung low from the ceiling at the foot of the bed. There was no sign of the medical trappings that I knew must have been there in his final illness. I tried to imagine Debra there, caring for her elderly uncle. It was easy for me to imagine Debra bustling throughout the room with a sure sufficiency.

Ina crouched on the floor to pick up bits of ceramics. Somewhere she'd found a dustpan and small brush, and she brushed the sad remains of the trinket into the pan.

"What was that?" I asked.

Ina looked up. "Just a little elephant. Pink even. I wonder why Victor would have such a girly knick-knack."

I sighed and knelt down to help Ina pick up the tiny pieces. "You're telling Lew, not me."

"It was an accident. This has been a bust. I haven't found anything good at all. What about you?"

"I'm not sure." I sat on the edge of Victor's bed, still thinking about the file I'd found. I opened the door to the nightstand beside the bed. Inside I found the normal items that are found in such a drawer: medicine bottles, pens, pencils, bits of this and that. I edged these items around in the drawer with my fingers and took hold of the edge of a photograph. I pulled it out of the drawer. It was wrinkled and worn, as if it had been handled many times before. It was a couple standing in front of a small house with their child. The couple was white, and the child was Asian. I immediately realized the child was Derek, and the parents were Tess and her first husband, Seth. In the photo, Derek couldn't have been more than eight, and he grinned at the camera. Behind him, Tess and Seth smiled benignly, happily at the photographer. I realized it was the same photograph that had appeared in the *Stripling Dispatch* article about the hit and run. Who knew, ten years later, Derek would be the only one left?

Why would Victor Lepcheck have a photograph of the Welch family? I wondered. Of course, Tess was his relative, but so were Debra and Martin's provost. Their pictures weren't in the drawer. I checked.

There was a clatter as Ina unceremoniously dumped the shattered elephant into a small wastebasket in the corner of the room. "What do you have there?" Ina asked.

"I don't know," I said honestly. "But I think it's important."

Chapter Thirty-Nine

Not even the chance to catch a killer could keep Ina from one of her weekly Irish-American Club meetings. The club was having a potluck lunch at noon at my mother's church, so Ina and I headed back home.

If I asked Mains about Welch's death, he would know I was still meddling in his case, and I would rather not get a lecture. My next best option was to talk to David Berring. Since he was Victor's executive assistant at the time, perhaps he would know why Victor had a copy of the police report or why he left Tess the dog and money.

After eating a peanut butter sandwich over my sink, I left for the co-op.

It was the first time I had been to the co-op in the daytime, and the pines lining the drive, which had looked so sinister at night, looked like Christmas tree stand-ins in the daylight. The small lot in the back only held a few cars, all of which had seen better days. Being an artist was not glamorous.

The large barn door was closed, so I entered through the smaller side door. The sound of power tools immediately accosted my ears. Ansel Levi was sipping from a bottle of soda when I walked in. He asked if he could be of any help, so I told him that I wanted to speak to David.

"He's in his stall, making paper. He won't mind. Do you know the way?"

I nodded.

David lifted a soaking wet piece of blue and white paper out of a large plastic tub. He smiled at me, but didn't say anything until he hung the piece with a clothespin on a line next to five other identical pieces. He dried his large hand on a tea towel. "What brings you here?"

"I was wondering if you had a minute to talk."

"Sure. I'm at a good stopping place anyway." He unlatched the stall door that came up to his waist. "Let's go outside."

The air outside was cool, and I reached into my pocket for a thin pair of cotton gloves.

David apparently was made of stronger stuff because he was without a coat. There was a small patio behind the barn that overlooked the parking lot and the back portion of the property, including Jerry's forge, which had crime scene tape encircling it.

"What can I do for you?"

"I've just had an interesting conversation with Debra, Tess's sister."

"Oh?"

"And she told me you used to work for her uncle."

His forehead smoothed. "Yes, I was Victor Lepcheck's executive assistant for fifteen years. It was my day job while I was building my art career. Many artists have other jobs. You yourself said you work for the college."

"Since you worked so closely with Victor, maybe you know why he wrote his will the way he did."

"I worked for Victor, but he did not confide in me that way."

"You don't even have a guess?"

"No."

"Do you think it was because he knew Tess would give some of the money to the co-op?"

"If that is what he wanted, why didn't he bequest some of

the money to the co-op in the first place? I can tell you he did not."

He had a good point.

"But Victor bought this land for the co-op?"

"He was a generous man."

"Debra gave me the impression the donation was out of character."

"Debra might not have known her uncle as well as she thinks she did."

"She cared for him in his illness."

He shrugged. "Sickness changes a person. Most likely, she spent time with a different man than I worked for."

"I learned Victor had a police report of the hit-and-run that killed Tess's first husband."

He started. "How'd you hear that?"

It was my turn to shrug. "Why do you think he'd have a copy and keep it for all this time?"

"How should I know? I didn't even know he had a copy."

"But you were working for him at the time of the accident."

He gritted his teeth. "Yes. I really don't know where you're planning to go with these questions."

Truthfully, I didn't either. It seemed as if I was getting nowhere. Realistically, the only one who knew why Victor did those things was Victor himself, and he wasn't available to ask.

He put his hand on my shoulder. It was heavy. "I can see you love a mystery, but the truth is there is no real mystery here." He shook his head sadly. "It's hard for me to imagine Celeste doing what she did, but I have to accept it." He removed his hand. "Now, let's talk about something much more pleasant. I've looked at your website and some of your pieces, and I think there might be a place for you in the co-op."

"Really?" I was pleased and surprised.

"Really. You have a good eye, and I think you would be a

great addition. We need some young blood in our group, and you'll be our first painter."

"I'm flattered."

"It's not a done deal of course. The co-op members have to vote, and it has to be unanimous."

"Makes sense."

"The co-op is meeting here tonight at nine. I'd like you to come and see what we are all about."

Even though I was interested in joining the co-op, or at least seeing how it could help my painting career, I had no desire to visit the place at night so close to my gruesome discovery earlier in the week. Then I remembered my out. The school board meeting was that evening, and my parents were planning on being there to make the case for saving the bell tower. They'd asked me to join them. At the time, I'd said I couldn't make it. They would be happy, thrilled even, if I changed my mind. I told David about the bell tower and the school board meeting.

He nodded. "Oh, right. The school board meeting is tonight. It completely slipped my mind. I'll be there, too. I'm presenting a new arts program for the district using co-op space."

"Really? That sounds like a wonderful plan. The arts have been cut a lot since I was in a kid."

David touched his Santa-like beard and smiled. "We do what we can here for the community. Since you're here, let me show you around. I know you got to see a bit of the co-op at Tess's party, but I want you to have a clearer picture of what we do before joining."

I agreed and followed him in back inside the barn.

CHAPTER FORTY

After getting home from the co-op, I reluctantly called Mains.

"Hi. How's it going?" he asked. I heard a smile in his voice and told myself not to be happy about it. My stomach did an involuntary little flip. Traitor.

I cut to the chase. "What can you tell me about the hit-and-run that killed Seth Welch ten years ago?"

"Seth Welch?"

"Yes, he's Derek's dad, Tess's first husband."

"I know who he is." His tone was guarded.

"Do you remember the case? You were the reporting officer on the scene."

"Yes, I remember the case." The smile was no longer in his voice. "I'm not even going to ask how you know I was the officer on the case."

"I'll gladly you tell you. I found the police report at Victor Lepcheck's house."

"And what were you doing there?"

I bit my lip. "Helping Lew."

"This is about Tess's case, isn't it? That's what you are really after."

"The two cases might be connected."

"That's a stretch even for you." There was a pause, and it sounded like Mains was talking to someone else. "India, I'm going to have to let you go." He rang off.

A second later, my cell rang. I looked at the screen hoping it was Mains calling me back and hating myself for that hope. It was a number I didn't recognize.

"India, I need to talk to you," Derek said, with the sound of tears in his voice.

"Is something wrong?" I asked.

"I found something, and I think it's important, but I'm not sure."

"Important for what?"

"It's about my dad."

I blinked. "Where are you?"

"I'm at mom's house."

"Where's that?"

He gave me the address. "Can you come?"

I chewed on my lip. With how Derek felt about me, it probably was a really bad idea to meet him alone. "I'll be there in twenty minutes."

Tess and Jerry's house was in a small subdivision on the outskirts of town. There was a nice large park nearby, and it was the perfect neighborhood to raise a family. To me, the community seemed too suburban for Tess and Jerry's artistic sensibilities.

Derek waited for me in the drive.

"What did you find?"

"Come inside, and I'll show you."

We sat at the kitchen table. "What is it?" I asked.

"Let me tell you. I decided to take your advice and get off campus, but the only place I could think to come was here. I asked Uncle Sam if I could crash at his place, but he said no, and I didn't want to go to Aunt Debra's. She would fuss over me the entire time, and I didn't want that. I wanted to be alone."

"That's understandable."

"So I came back here, and I couldn't sit still. Everything reminds me of Mom." He closed his eyes for a second. "I thought it might help if I looked through some of her things, so I went up to her room. I opened the drawer to her nightstand at random, just thinking about her, you know. I didn't really have a plan. I wasn't looking for anything. But I found something."

"What did you find?"

He reached into his back pocket and pulled out an ivory stationary envelope. "It's a letter to my mom from my great uncle Victor."

"What does it say?"

"You can read it."

Dear Tess,

How I wish I had the strength to give you this letter in my lifetime. How I wish I wasn't a coward. But I am. Even though I'll be gone when you read this, it doesn't make it any easier to write.

I am the reason you no longer have your beloved husband Seth. It was late, and I shouldn't have been driving. The doctor advised me not to drive at night because of my poor eyesight. But I was stubborn and didn't listen. You don't know how many nights I lie awake at night wishing I heeded the doctor's advice. I was driving back from a meeting with my shareholders in Akron. I told them I had a buyer for the company and planned to sell. It was an emotional meeting for all, and I was upset. Summit Polymer was my entire life, but I knew I couldn't care for the company as I once had. I saw an out, an out that would make me a lot of money, and I took it.

The shareholders were not pleased with the announcement. The company I was selling to was located in North Carolina, and my local shareholders knew they would lose what little control they had.

It was dark and late as I drove home, and I decided to come home through backstreets. I was no longer confident driving on the highways. As I came around the square, I thought I was home free. I didn't see Seth crossing the street. It was so dark. I felt the bump when I hit him. I stumbled out of the car and saw him lying there. I cannot express the horror that washed over me at that moment. He was dead. There was nothing I could do to save him, and I knew it was Seth, which made it so much worse.

I know I should have called the police then and confessed and received the punishment I so justly deserved. But I was selfish. I knew my deal to sell Summit Polymer would fall through with the bad press this would create. I would lose my money, the company, everything.

I swear to you, Tess, if he had still been alive, I would have called for help. I would have, but since he was gone, I'm so ashamed to say I went home and used my money to make it go away.

I have thought of that night every minute of every day for the rest of my life. The pain was especially acute whenever I saw you or your son Derek. All I can say is that I am truly, truly sorry. I know that isn't enough.

I take a risk in telling you this even after my own demise. Someone will want this to remain a secret, but now that I am gone you deserve to know the truth. I hope the money I have left in your care will provide for you and for your son.

My deepest regrets,
Victor H. Lepcheck

I set the letter on the table between us. Derek watched me. I didn't say anything but picked up my phone to call Mains. This time I called his cell number. "I have the answer to the question I asked you."

"What are you talking about?"

"Can you get away for a little bit? I have something very important to show you about Seth Welch's murder."

"I—where are you?"

I told him. Mains must have been nearby because he was at the Ross-Welch home within five minutes. He came into the kitchen. "What's this about?"

I pointed to the letter in the middle of the table. Mains sat down and used a pen to pull the letter toward him. Anxiously, Derek and I watched Mains read the letter. Finally, he looked up. "I'm glad this solves your father's case."

"What about Tess and Jerry's death?" I asked.

"This doesn't change anything for Celeste, if that's what you are getting at."

"But the letter says someone won't want her to know this. Maybe Tess took it upon herself to find out who that person was and was killed for it?"

Mains arched an eyebrow at me. He slipped the letter into a clear evidence bag. "If it makes you feel better, I'll have this checked for fingerprints. Did you both touch it?"

We nodded guiltily. He put the bag in his inside jacket pocket. "I'll take it to the station right now." He stood. "India, can I talk to you a minute outside?"

I walked Mains to his car. "I want you to cut this out." His tone was fierce.

"Don't you think Derek has a right to know what happened to both of his parents?"

"Of course I do." He ran a hand through his thick dark hair. "Don't you realize you're making yourself a target? Two people." He showed me two fingers for emphasis. "Two people have been murdered in the last week. If you're right and the killer is still out there, you're in some serious danger."

"What do you want me to do? Nothing?"

"I want you to go home, lock yourself in, and let me do my job."

"Can't tonight. I'm going to the school board meeting. The bell tower issue is on the agenda, you know."

"Fine. Just promise me you will stay with your parents the whole time." He laughed. "No one's going to get to you with Reverend Hayes in the way."

I grinned. "Nope."

Mains looked at me, and I felt my chest tighten. "I don't want you to get hurt." He kissed me on the cheek before jumping into the sedan and driving away with lights flashing.

I touched my cheek before going back inside the house, not knowing how I felt.

I returned to the house, relieved to find Derek in the kitchen. I hoped that meant he hadn't seen the exchange between Mains and me.

"I know Celeste isn't the one who killed my mom. It's the person Uncle Victor mentioned in this letter." His eyes gleamed with tears.

"Derek, don't get any ideas. Whoever it is could be dangerous," I said, essentially repeating the same warning Mains had given me.

"They killed my mom." His voice quavered.

Professional distance be darned. I pulled the weeping child into a hug.

Chapter Forty-One

The school board meeting started at six. I didn't tell my parents I'd be there in case I changed my mind. After considering Mains's warning, I felt I would be safer with some people around. I was half-tempted to invite Ina along but thought better of it. I didn't want her to jump on the bell tower bandwagon. If she did, I would have no peace from that particular issue.

The administrative office for the school board was located inside the high school, and so the meeting would be held in the high school auditorium. Even though I had been there many times since I graduated, it always felt a little off to return to school. Instinctively, I parked in the same space I had used when I was a student there.

By the time I walked into the auditorium, the meeting was already in full swing. A high school student, who looked like she'd rather be just about anywhere else on the planet, took a break from texting to hand me the evening's agenda. The board was still in the middle of item number one: a new arts program for fourth through eighth graders.

David stood at the podium on the floor presenting the program to the board. "We at the co-op know the school system is having trouble providing arts education for the students, so we open our doors for any interested students who would like to take free after-school art instruction. This plan would be especially successful if these students could apply their time at the co-op toward class credit. We can't let the arts die out in our community for lack of money."

There was cheer from the crowd, and I found myself clapping. It was an excellent plan and would give the school system an out on the expense of an art program. The program had already been cut by two-thirds since I was in school. I shivered to think what kind of art education my nephew and nieces would receive by the time they were old enough to join the co-op's program.

The dour-faced president of the school board didn't look nearly as enthused. "Thank you, Mr. Berring, we will take it under consideration."

If that's the kind of reaction David's free arts education plan received from the school board, my parents and their bell tower crusade were doomed. I spotted them in the last row on the first section of the seats. I hurried over to them. As always, the row was full of their band of faithful groupies: church members and middle-aged leftists. "I'm so glad you decided to come," Dad whispered hoarsely as I knelt by his chair.

Mom looked down at me. She reached into her expansive bag and pulled out an enormous stack of pro-bell tower pamphlets. She thrust them at me. "Hand these out at the end of the meeting. Make sure you're at the main exit that leads to the parking lot. You will catch most of them. We need as many of these people on our side as we can get."

I took the papers without a word and consulted the evening's agenda. The bell tower issue was the very last item. Perhaps the school board was hoping there wouldn't be enough time for that particular item. They should know better, after having wrangled with my parents once before.

I was surprised when I read my mother's pamphlet. It wasn't about saving the tower; it was about a concert that would be held on the square next month to raise money to restore the aging building. It seemed like Mom was jumping the gun to plan such an event. From past experience, I wondered what she had hidden up her sleeve for tonight.

I found a seat in another section and listened to the next presenter talk about new computers for elementary school. His monotone voice lulled me into a bored daze. It was nearing eight and the close of the meeting. The board president raised her gavel. "I believe that's all we have time for tonight. Is there a motion for adjournment?"

"I—" A member of the audience began but was cut off my mother. Her preacher voice could overpower a foghorn.

Mom stood. "I move that we continue the meeting to address the important issue of the bell tower."

The president narrowed her eyes. "There are only ten minutes left in the meeting."

"This won't take long." She made her way down the aisle with the same confidence she displayed when she approached her pulpit on Sunday morning.

The president scowled but gestured for her to come forward.

"The bell tower is part of Stripling's legacy. I have documents here that declare the tower a state historic landmark, making it illegal for you tear it down."

The president bristled. "How can you do that without the board's consent?"

"I don't need the school board's consent, only the support of the city council, which the Save the Bell committee obtained yesterday. The city council was very pleased with the idea of saving another historic building in town. You know how much they hate to lose any bit of our Western Reserve heritage."

The president looked like she was ready to spit. "This is on school property."

"Of course, but your school property is paid for by tax levies, and so essentially you work for the town."

The board couldn't argue with that. Several of the members

began whispering to each other.

Mom put her hand to her cheek as if she were thinking. "One more thing I learned, Madam President; the demo company that believes we should destroy the tower is owned by your brother-in-law."

"I don't see what that has to with anything. His company is the one the city uses on a regular basis."

"Yes, but did you get a second or even third opinion about the stability of the structure?"

"I don't know why that would be necessary."

"I should think it is in any case when the school system is contemplating a large and expensive project. However, in this case it would be even more necessary, considering your close relationship to the company's owner."

The president's face was beet red. "What are you suggesting?"

Mom's shoulders shrugged. "I'm not suggesting anything." She reached in a large tote bag she had at her side and pulled out a thick sheaf of paper. "Here are four statements from four different local contractors, none of whom have any relation to the school board or any members of the Save the Bell committee, who have inspected the tower and declare it is structurally sound." She placed the stack of papers on the table. "You can keep those. I have my own copies."

The president went from red to white.

Mom turned to the audience. "Even though the structure's sound, it will take time to raise the funds to restore the tower to its former glory. Out of concern for our children's safety, I recommend the tower be locked and closed to the public until the necessary funds can be raised. Let's put it to a vote."

The ayes had it.

Mom checked her watch. "Excellent, we are three minutes early. I move to adjourn." Yet another commanding performance delivered by my mother. The school board never stood a chance.

She quickly received a second, and the president's gavel hit the table. I wondered if there would be a dent.

Chapter Forty-Two

As the last person walked across the parking lot with a pro-bell tower concert flyer in hand, I stacked the rest of the pamphlets on the edge of a windowsill. Dad rolled up. "India, I think we're in trouble."

I looked around. There was no one in the hall. "Trouble? Why? Where's Mom? Did she get herself arrested? I'm not in the mood to bail her out of the Justice Center."

"It's worse than that."

Something worse than my pastor-mother being arrested and thrown into the city jail? There's the Hayes family perspective for you.

"Where's Mom?"

"She got a ride with some of the bell tower team. They are going to meet at the church to plan the next move." He looked down. "I just feel so awful about this."

"What is it?" I was starting to worry.

"It's Zach. I can't find him."

"He was here at the school board meeting?"

"Not here per se. He was out in the courtyard. I had tied him with his leash to one of the benches there. He's gone. His leash is gone, too. He must have untied himself somehow. I don't know how he did it. I tied those knots extra tight. He must have worked for a magician in a former life."

"Dad! I can't believe you did that."

Dad's forehead wrinkled. "I'm sorry."

"We have to look for him."

"Darn this chair," Dad said. "I'm useless."

Dad rarely complained about his wheelchair, so I knew he really felt upset about losing Zach.

"Don't worry, Dad. I'll find him. He probably wandered off. And you're not useless. You can stay here in case Zach comes back to the school."

David stepped up. I hadn't realized he was still in the high school "I can help you look," he said.

"No, that's okay," I said quickly. "I'm sure it won't take me long to find him."

Dad beamed. "Great idea. India would love your help."

"I—"

"It's settled then," David interrupted. "We'd better start looking before it gets much later."

David and I walked across the parking lot to the courtyard where high school students could take their lunches outside in nice weather. In northern Ohio, nice weather during the school year is all of a couple months long. There was a dim security light in the courtyard, providing us a full view of the place. Zach wasn't there. I peered behind the bushes and called the dog's name.

David stood off to the side and occasionally called as well.

I glanced at him. "I'm going to look over by the stadium. There are a lot of little places to hide there, and Zach might have been attracted by the smell of discarded popcorn from last weekend's game. You might want to start around the front of the school." I started off at a fast walk.

I heard David's heavy footsteps behind me. Quickly, he was at my side. "I'll go with you."

"I think this would be more effective if we split up," I said, not breaking my pace.

Before David could respond, I heard an unmistakable bark. I

broke into a run in that direction. The barking led us to the foot of the bell tower. I turned the doorknob. It was unlocked. "He's in there," I said in disbelief. I peered into the inky black inside of the tower and saw nothing. "Zach! Zach! Come on boy. Come here!" I continued calling for a few more minutes.

Zach's barks were becoming increasingly hysterical, but he didn't appear.

I looked up. The barks and howls were coming from above. "Oh, crap."

"Looks like he's at the top," David said.

"Crap. Crap. Crap," I said. "Zach! Zach! Here, boy!"

Nothing but frenzied barking from above.

"I don't think he's coming down," David said. "Maybe we need to go up after him."

"Double crap!"

"It will be fine. Didn't your mother report that four contractors found the building sound?"

"I don't think they inspected the building in the middle of the night."

I looked inside again. There was very little light coming from the windows at the top, certainly not enough to climb the treacherous stairs by. A small penlight hung from my keychain. I clicked it on. It gave us all of two inches of light.

"You've got to be kidding me," I muttered.

"If you want to stay down here, I can go up," David offered.

"No, no, I'll go. Zach's my responsibility."

"Let's both go then."

"Fine. You go first."

David and I shuffled to the foot of the stairs. He stepped on the first step, and it creaked under his weight.

I grimaced. "I'll wait until you get to the first landing before I start up."

A minute later, David's shadow paused. "I'm at the first landing."

"Okay." Under my breath, I added, "Here we go."

I held my breath the entire walk up the staircase. My tiny penlight provided little comfort. David reached the top quickly. "You're almost there," he said encouragingly. "You won't believe this when you see it."

"Is Zach up there?"

"Yes."

"Is he okay?"

"He's fine."

I heard a deep growl, and I quickened my pace.

I reached the top. With the open windows, there was enough light around the bell to see pretty clearly. It was a cold, clear night with a half moon hanging low in the sky.

Zach's leash was tied in knots around the railing. Whoever had done it had spent a lot of time making sure the dog couldn't get loose. "Poor baby," I cooed. The dog nuzzled my hand. I looked at David. "Who would do this? I hope he's not hurt." The long leash was also wrapped around his neck several times. I put two fingers between the leash and his neck. It was tied loosely there, but I worried that he'd choke himself if he moved too much and tightened the leash.

"He looks okay. Probably some kids thought it would be a funny joke," David said.

"Well, it's not. You wouldn't happen to have a pocket knife on you? It's going to take forever to untie these knots."

"No, sorry."

I stood and reached into my jeans pocket or my phone. "I'd better call Dad, so he won't worry." I hit the number five on my cell, which speed-dialed my dad. The line began to ring, and Dad picked up.

"Dad—"

David bumped into me and the cell flew out of my hand and over the rail. We heard it crash on the cement floor below with a sickening smash. I stared at him in shock.

Chapter Forty-Three

I looked over the railing. It was pitch black, but I most likely didn't want to see the sad remains of my cell scattered on the cement.

David stood beside me, looking down. "I'm so sorry."

I moved away from him back to the tethered dog. "It's okay." I hid my face and started working on the knots.

David circled me. The knots were tight, and I wasn't making any headway on them. Damn my short fingernails. Lasha's dragon claws were better suited for this type of canine rescue.

"You're a very bright girl, India. I'm sure you know that."

I didn't respond and concentrated on the knots.

"You just wouldn't let Victor go."

I looked up for the briefest moment at David, and involuntarily cowered at his massive size. A chill ran down my back. Zach must have felt it, too, because he shivered. "Victor?"

"Yes, Victor. This is his dog after all."

I doubled my efforts on the knots, but my speed made me clumsy. I took a deep breath and ordered myself to calm down and concentrate on the knots. The letter came to mind.

"I can't wait for you to figure this out. I need to take care of it now," David said.

I felt cold because I'd already figured it out. David was the killer. He'd murdered Tess, and Jerry, too, to keep Victor's secret safe.

"I don't know what you're talking about."

"You'll never get them untied without a knife. I made sure the knots were extra, extra tight when I tied them."

I froze. Zach growled low and deep in his throat. I scratched behind one of his ears and stood slowly. "Why would you murder Tess to cover up a crime Victor committed?"

"I wasn't covering up his crime. I knew what Victor had done, and it was only a matter of time before she learned of my own indiscretions. Stupid woman. Just like you."

I swallowed. My throat was dry like ash, funeral ash.

David leaned against the silent bell. "She was just like you, you know. She was looking for trouble. She said she found a letter from her uncle, a confession of sorts, and she wanted to know more of what happened. She said she wanted to know everything, so she could tell her son and he could know the truth about what happened to his father. She came to me because she thought I would know, because I was his assistant. I knew everything about his life, and she was right.

"You see, after dear old Victor killed, accidentally of course, his niece's husband, he asked me to take care of it. I went back to the scene to make sure there was no damning evidence there. I got the car fixed. I made the whole mishap go away."

"You must have thought a lot of your boss." I desperately scanned the area for a weapon, but all I saw were pigeon feathers, mouse droppings, and cobwebs, none of which would be much help to me. "That was a big risk you were taking, covering it up for him."

"Yes, it was a risk, but I didn't take it for Victor." He walked calmly to the other side of the room, giving me a clear escape route down the stairs. He knew I wouldn't leave Zach trapped there with him, and he was rubbing my face in it.

There was a skittering sound from down below, and I jumped. Zach began to whine. He felt my body tense. David peered over the edge. "Long way down. I imagine there are some pretty huge rats in this old place. It's just like your parents to want to save some worthless relic, isn't it?"

"We were talking about Victor, not my parents."

"You're right. You see, after covering up the accident, I owned Victor. I owned him and his millions."

"You blackmailed him."

"How else was I going to open my own artist co-op? It had always been my dream. I could be an artist full-time and dedicate myself to my craft. You, yourself, said you have that same wish."

"I wouldn't reach it the way you did."

"Then you never will, my dear. The art world is not kind. Very few can make the jump from avocation to vocation." He wrinkled his nose. "And I've seen your paintings. Your odds aren't good for making the leap." He sighed. "I even threw the old man a bone by asking his widowed niece to become one of the founding members of the co-op. I liked to keep her close to remind him I could tell her the truth at any time."

"If you told her, the money would run out."

"How true, but it was a gamble Old Vic wasn't willing to take."

"What about Jerry? Did he know? Is that why you killed him?"

David snorted. "Jerry didn't know anything, but I was afraid Tess's murder wasn't going to stick to him like I hoped. Celeste turned out to be a better person to frame."

"You killed Jerry to frame Celeste for both murders?" I felt my eye begin to twitch.

He shrugged.

A scrape-scrape came from below. Zach leaned against my leg. I placed a comforting hand on the top of his head. I thought I saw a light. My mind is playing tricks on me, I thought. It's just the moon's reflection off the bell.

"So what now?" I asked.

"You're going to have a little accident. You'll be a hero though. I will tell them you fell trying to save the two-million-dollar dog."

I imagined how awful my parents would feel, especially my father, since he felt responsible for Zach going missing. Unheeded, I thought of Mains and his warning, of the fact I might never get a chance to figure out how I felt about him, of the fact I was no longer afraid to think about how I felt about him. "I don't think so," I said.

"This isn't a choice, my dear." He started walking toward me. I stayed close to Zach. The big curly dog bared his teeth.

"Go ahead and bite him," I told the dog.

David paused only for a millisecond. "If he bites me, he's the next one over the side."

Bang, bang, bang. Footsteps rushed up the stairs. A form flew across the room and catapulted itself onto David's back.

My mouth dropped open. It was Derek.

David was knocked down in surprise, and the two rolled on the floor. David quickly had the advantage and pinned Derek in place. I rushed David from behind and kicked him hard just south of the border. He yowled.

Zach barked wildly. I helped Derek to his feet. He had a black eye and a bloody nose, a matching set to the ones he'd gotten from the dorm fight.

David stood and leaned on the railing. "You . . ." He held himself up, gasping for breath.

Derek wiped the blood from his nose, which only smeared it across his cheek.

"Derek, do you have a cell phone?" I asked.

He didn't hear me.

"You killed my mother."

David was panting.

"Derek! Derek, give me your cell phone. I'll call for help, and we'll be fine."

I was torn between working on the knots that tethered Zach and getting Derek out of there. I patted the dog's head. I had to hope David wouldn't do anything to him. I had to get Derek out of there.

Derek was crying, and I couldn't make out what he was saying.

David groaned and stumbled to his feet with murder in his eyes.

I grabbed Derek's arm and pulled him toward the stairs. "Be careful," I warned as I pulled him behind me. I held the penlight out in front of me like a sword, but all it illuminated was my hand. We made it to the first landing when I heard heavy footsteps on the stairs above.

"You bitch!" David's steps hit the stairs with force. He was coming down at a run. I pulled on Derek's arm and increased our pace but was afraid to break out in a run.

From the landing above a cry rang out followed by a thud, thud, thud. I pulled Derek to the side of the stairwell and flattened us both against the rough brick wall. A moment later, I felt David brush past us as he tumbled down the stairs.

We stood there for a minute. I clutched Derek's arm. I wouldn't be surprised if he found a bruise there later.

"Stay here," I whispered. I inched down the steps with my weak penlight to lead me. I found David sprawled at the bottom of the stairs. His neck was bent at a sharp angle. He was most certainly dead.

I don't know how long I stood there with my penlight trained on David's blank face. Derek placed a hand on my arm. I hadn't even heard him come down the steps.

"What are you doing here?" I whispered.

"I was at the library and told Bobby I needed to talk to you. Bobby said he thought you were here tonight for the school board meeting. By the time I got here the meeting was over, but I met this guy in a wheelchair who said he was your dad and that you and David were looking for Zach. I heard barking and came to the tower. You and David were already there."

My throat felt scratchy. "The bell tower might not be as safe as my parents think."

Zach howled agreement from above.

I sent Derek outside to find my father, and we cut Zach free with Dad's pocket knife. The dog, Derek, Dad, and I sat outside of the tower waiting for the police to arrive. They didn't take long. With sirens blaring, lights flashing, they took over the high school parking lot.

Mains was the first one out of the car. He jogged over and stopped short when our eyes met. His expression was a mixture of relief and frustration. "I told you to leave it alone."

Dad was fondling Zach's ear. The dog was half in his lap and looked as if he never wanted to leave. "You should know by now that a Hayes never does what he or she is told."

Mains's eyes softened. "I'm learning."

Epilogue

The Saturday before Thanksgiving, my family and I were all at the New Day Artists Cooperative's holiday craft show, held in the co-op barn. With the recent deaths, the question had arisen whether or not the show would go on as planned. However, when Celeste was cleared of any wrongdoing, she turned her grief into action and took over the organization with abandon. Without Celeste's leadership, the co-op would have degenerated into disarray quickly, as Ansel, AnnaMarie, and Carrington were too shocked to do much of anything. Within a week, Celeste was unanimously voted in as their president.

Celeste claimed that the co-op might have a place for me after all, and I told her I'd think about it. I knew I needed some distance from my recent experience with the co-op and its members. I did, however, take the free vendor table she offered me to sell my paintings at the craft show.

My parents, Carmen, and her family were milling around my booth, Mom making what she thought were helpful suggestions. "Honey, your paintings can be so provincial. Why don't you try something more daring?"

"The people who come to these shows don't want daring. They want landscapes and portraits of kittens."

Nicholas sat in my chair behind the booth. "I love landscapes."

Chip laughed. "Maybe we should enroll him in art classes here."

"That's a great idea," I said.

Nicholas was thoughtful. "Ina said she could give me art lessons."

Carmen looked aghast, but the rest of the adults laughed. The twins giggled, even though I'm guessing they didn't get the joke.

"Nice show," Mains said from behind me. Because of the laughter, I hadn't noticed him approach. He was wearing an olive green sweater. His changeable hazel eyes reflected the color.

I smiled. "I'm glad you could come."

Carmen's eyes widened.

Dad reached up and smacked Mains on the elbow. "I didn't know you were into the arts."

"I'm starting to get more interested."

I felt myself blush. I bent my head and rearranged a few of my paintings.

"That's good. That's good," Dad said.

While Mains was engaged in a conversation with our father, Carmen mouthed, "What's going on?"

I shrugged as if I had no idea what she was talking about.

"I hope Zach is doing okay," Dad said. His tone was wistful.

Zach was in his new home with Debra. She, Lepcheck, and their lawyers finally came to an agreement. Debra would receive the dog and the trust, but the money would be divided evenly between the two siblings after Zach passed on.

"I checked on him last week," I remarked. "He's doing great and is a big hit at Debra's condo complex. I hear he's a fixture on the bocce court."

Dad sighed. "That's nice."

Mom crossed her arms. "Don't even tell me you want to get a dog. Do you think I have time to take care of dog with everything else?"

"I'd be the one taking care of it." He pouted. "And what do you mean by everything else?"

"The church. The kids. The bell tower. You know very well we are nowhere near our financial goal for the tower."

"I don't see how a dog would hurt the bell tower. Why, he could be the bell tower mascot! Dogs are very good at that sort of thing. My dog would be the perfect mascot. Don't you think so, Rick?" Dad asked.

"Absolutely." Mains grinned at me, and I felt my chest tighten just a little.

Mom tried to scowl, but her face cracked into a smile. Nicholas giggled. Dad didn't know that she was already planning to give him a dog. Mom, Nicholas, and I had visited Hands and Paws the day before, and agreed that Trufflehunter was the perfect pooch to bring home. Mom had already signed the adoption papers, and Truffie would be coming home in a week's time.

Dad cocked his head, reminding me of Zach. "Are you up to something, Lana?"

Nicholas giggled even harder. This made the twins start up again. Their chuckling sounded like high-pitched hoots of baby owls.

Chip put an arm around his son. "We're going to take a look around," he said. He bent close to his son's ear. "Before you spill the beans."

"Why don't you all go exploring while I finish putting out my paintings?" I asked. "I need to concentrate."

"Are you implying we are distracting?" Mom asked.

"I'm not implying it. I'm saying it." I said this with a smile before I ducked under my table to grab a few more kitten paintings.

"Hello?" I heard a tentative voice ask while my head was under the table.

Carmen gasped.

My heart flipped in my chest. I knew that voice. I yanked my head out from under the table, and it painfully connected with the edge of the table in my haste to stand up. The paintings on the table toppled over from the impact.

Mains stepped over to me. "Are you okay?"

I said nothing, just rubbed the back of my head. No one else in my family seemed to notice my clumsiness.

They were all staring at Mark. Tears pricked my eyes. Numbly, I felt Mains squeeze my wrist.

Mark looked nervous, but my once rail-thin brother had filled out. His chest was broader, and he had a full growth of beard. There was no mistake; it was Mark.

"Ina told me you all were here."

My mom hurried toward him, arms outstretched.

Mark looked behind him. "Come on, honey, I want you to meet everyone."

Mom pulled up short as if she had hit some invisible wall.

Honey?

Then I noticed a short Latina with lovely black hair and broad shoulders standing behind my brother.

"Everyone," Mark announced. "I'd like you to meet my wife."

To my right, I heard Carmen's yelp and my father's choked sob.

Wife?

My legs tingled as all the blood in my body rushed to my head. Mains stood behind me, and I felt his hands on my back steadying me. I was glad he was there.

ABOUT THE AUTHOR

Amanda Flower, the author of the Agatha Award–nominated *Maid of Murder,* the first in the India Hayes Mystery Series, is an academic librarian for a small college in northeastern Ohio. When she is not at the library or writing her next mystery, she is an avid traveler, aspiring to visit as much of the globe as she can. Recent trips have taken her to Jordan and Great Britain. She lives and writes near Akron with her family and two mischievous cats, one of whom looks suspiciously like Theodore from her series. Visit her online at www.amandaflower.com.